Meant to
Live

by

DustOn Dueitt

To Mom and Yuengling,
without you two, I couldn't have done it

Acknowledgements

Cover photo by Darlena Parnell

Photoshop-y things by Britton Hall

Behold this ruin, 'Twas a skull
Once of ethereal spirit full.
This narrow cell was Life's retreat,
This space was Thought's mysterious seat.
What beauteous visions filled this spot,
What dreams of pleasure long forgot?
Nor hope, nor joy, nor love, nor fear,
Have left one trace on record here.
Beneath this mouldering canopy,
Once shone the bright and busy eye:
But start not at the dismal void--
If social love that eye employed.
If with no lawless fire it gleamed,
But through the dews of kindness beamed;
That eye shall be forever bright,
When stars and sun are sunk at night.
Within this hollow cavern hung,
The ready, swift, and tuneful tongue;
If Falsehood's honey it disdained,
And when it could not praise be chained.
If bold in Virtue's cause it spoke,
Yet gentle concord never broke--
This silent tongue shall plead for thee,
When Time unveils Eternity
                    -Anonymous

The mood was somber. The assembly gathered was heartbroken at the laying to rest of their own Jackson Hughes. As his Uncle William explained in the eulogy, he was a charming kid. He was a talented kid. He was funny, handsome, smart, and athletic. He was the only member of the soccer team to ever be even in the running for valedictorian. None of this mattered to the aneurysm, though. It took Jackson as easily as it would have taken an elderly woman sitting quietly in her recliner.

Sunlight streamed through the elaborate stained glass of St. Ignatius Church. The midday sun kept it warm with shades of red, gold, blue, and green, betraying the month of December. William tried his best to wipe away tears while making it seem as though he was only blotting his forehead. He could choke down the lump in his throat to give his favorite nephew the sendoff he believed he deserved; but he could not deny the tears. Just as the sun illuminated random parts of the church, so too did it reflect off the streaks on his face. With a steady voice and a proud stance, he concluded his speech about Jackson. Aside from prayer, which would never stop regardless, the only thing left to do was to take Jackson's body to the Hughes family crypt in the Virginia Street Cemetery.

"I can't believe he's really gone." Jon said what all of them were thinking. While he was the largest of the pallbearers, he was also the one with the tenderest heart. Tears streamed down his face and collected at the base of his chiseled jaw as he gave the nod for everyone to hoist their friend's coffin from the foot of the altar of St. Ignatius. The young men lifted their teammate and beloved friend and began making their way from the church to the hearse.

Jon Williams, Ryan Francis, and Paul Smith were on one side. Chad Boyd, Mike Foster, and Brandon McNeal were on the other. All friends, all teammates, the six of them were all devastated at the loss of Jackson. They were all dressed in their school uniforms, even their friend in the coffin. Gold-buttoned blazers with black and orange striped ties weren't the traditional all-black attire for a requiem Mass, but Mrs. Hughes wanted them to be as she had remembered seeing them, not in the color that fate had forced upon her life.

Family members wept as the boys carried Jackson past them all down the aisle. His sister, Anna, consoled his girlfriend, Meggie Paulez, who seemed to be taking it almost as bad as Jackson's parents. After loading the coffin into the hearse, the boys each made their way to their respective rides to the cemetery.

The procession was long. Well over half of the McGill-Toolen Catholic High School student body was in attendance at the funeral, and most of them followed to Virginia St. A few traffic cops had to be called in to keep things orderly. After about half an hour, the procession made its way to the cemetery grounds.

The rest was just a formality. People had said their "goodbyes" and "I love you's" to him. All that was left was to place his remains with those of his family that had gone on before him. Father Hayes, the parish's oldest priest and long-time friend to the Hughes family said a prayer. Once it was done, Jackson's pallbearers proceeded almost immediately to Meggie.

"So where do we go from here?" asked Ryan. The red-haired, freckle-faced teenager inquired to the group. He wasn't trying to sound deep, only genuinely wondering what they were supposed to do next. He was not expecting any philosophy.

"I don't know, bud," said Mike. "I guess we try to get on with our lives. I think Jackson would have wanted it that way. Don't forget him, but don't forget to live *for* him either, ya know? What about you Meggie, what are you going to do, now?"

The mournful little Hispanic girl tried her best to talk without blubbering indecipherable syllables. It was no use. She lowered her head, and the parts of her face she couldn't cover with her hands were shielded from view by her wavy black hair.

"Give her a break," Anna snapped at the boys. In his life, Anna was always protective of her younger brother. Now it seemed as though she had transferred that maternal instinct to his grief-stricken girlfriend. "Let's all just be here for one another. We're all going to go through some rough patches at different times because of this. We all loved Jackson; Meggie just doesn't want to have to think about it right now."

Big Jon raised a big, hairy hand and placed it

on Meggie's shoulder. The oaf was hardly aware of his body's strength and obtrusiveness, so much so that, with the force which his hand found Meggie, it jostled her. She was a little surprised, but looked up to see Jon's bright blue eyes glazed over with tears similar to hers. She grabbed his hand and leaned her head on it. "He was my best friend, Meggie. I don't want to think about it either."

She responded in a weakened and cracked voice. "Thanks, Jon. I know you know how I feel."

Everyone gathered around Meggie and formed a big huddle. The classmates and Anna all embraced one another. For a few moments, no one said anything. No one moved. And no one knew which fond memory of Jackson the other people in the group were having, but they all knew that each meant something special and different to all of them.

Mrs. Hughes walked over to join the others. She moved her black veil aside to reveal her timeless face. She was still a beautiful woman, even with puffy, red eyes and tear stains streaking her face. The cold December wind whipped her graying brown hair behind her and gave her a chill as it found the wet lines on her cheeks.

"I want to thank you boys for doing this. It means a lot to me, and I'm sure it means a lot to Jackson."

All the boys each gave a response equivalent to "No problem, Mrs. Hughes," and then she took turns hugging each of them.

"Later tonight, we're going over to Callaghan's if y'all are interested. We've rented the entire place. It was Jackson's favorite place to eat. It would only be right if y'all all came." Mrs. Hughes began to tear up again as she reminded herself that she had to start talking about her beloved son in past tense.

"Yes, ma'am, we'll be there," Jon said. His eyes too began to well up with tears as he was thinking about all the times he had shared lunches with his friend there.

***

Later that night at Callaghan's, the mood was a little lighter. The mourners of Jackson that were invited to the Irish pub seemed solemn, but they also looked very ready to eat, drink, and be merry again. Their beloved Jackson Hughes had been dead for a total of four days. For many at the pub, it would be their first attempts at going on with their lives and trying to, themselves, live again. All of Jackson's friends were underage, but Anna had been sneaking them booze all night. Their spirits were raised some as a result.

"Okay," Jon said as he began to address the rest of the table, "favorite memory of Jackson. Foster, go!"

Mike Foster looked off for a moment to collect his thoughts and formulate a response. His long neck craned over his shoulder at a seemingly unnatural length and angle. After a few seconds, he cleared his throat to begin. "I think it would definitely have to be when J-dog's mom let us all go down to their beach house in Dauphin Island for spring break. He was so wasted by the time we got down there, he couldn't tell us where the damn thing was." The whole table erupted in laughter. "We spent the first night sleeping on the public beach."

"And we couldn't call Mrs. Hughes, 'cuz we knew she'd flip out and think he had alcohol poisoning or something," Brandon said. He had been pretty quiet since Jackson's death. But the fond memory of his friend put a smile on the little dark haired kid's face.

Anna took a sip of her wine, and then said, "That boy never could hold his alcohol."

Jon chose to take his turn telling a Jackson story. "Alright, alright. My favorite memory of him's gotta be the red card incident."

Everyone at the table knew exactly what Jon was talking about, as indicated by their laughs. "This kid from Murphy, Gary, something, was playing dirty the whole damn game, scratching, pushing, kicking- a lot of it should've gotten him kicked out. Anyway, Jackson told Coach Tolbert and the referee to watch out for it, 'cuz he was getting sick of it. Nothing ever got done about it. It was getting bad enough that a lot of people in the crowd started noticing it. But the guy was a master of not getting caught by the referee.

"Coach tried to calm Jackson down and tell him to shake it off, 'cuz, 'Good players can overcome bad officiating,' he said. But by halftime, even Coach was yelling at the ref telling him to open his eyes."

"Finally, Jax had had enough. When we took the field again after halftime, the whistle blew to start, and Jackson walked right over to Gary and knocked him out cold with one punch. The ref definitely saw it and came running over with his whistle blowing and his red card ready. But it didn't matter any to Jackson. He knew he was gonna get ejected. He walked off the field and took off his jersey. The ref didn't know what to do. He was just standing there holding his little red card like, 'Who do I give this to?'"

Even Meggie couldn't help but laugh about the incident as Jon retold it. "He didn't even get in trouble from the coach, the school, or nothing."

"That's because everyone watching that game knew that Gary kid was a douche," said Chad. Everyone laughed in agreement of his statement.

Jon was tipsy, so he was able to talk more openly about his deceased friend, so long as it forwarded the conversation. So he said, "It just was so *not* Jax to do something like that. He wasn't a fighter at all. Didn't have a fighting bone in his body."

It was strange how every one of his family and friends knew the same seventeen-year-old. Typically people, especially teenagers, choose to paint different versions of themselves depending on the others around them. Clearly Jackson was not one of those typical people. They all knew the same Jackson Hughes: smart, funny, nice, lovable, slow to anger, even slower to act on said anger.

The rest of the night went swimmingly. Jackson's family and friends carried on like they would have at any other party. Onlookers might have mistaken the festivities for a Christmas party. In between rounds of drinks and various foods to snack on, his loved ones would take turns telling stories about him. On the surface, everyone seemed jovial, but just beneath everyone's surface rested the same cold, hard truth. And everyone gathered around in his honor at Callaghan's knew it when they looked at anyone else's face that was in attendance.

Jackson was dead. Dead. And gone.

2

Thoughts had been flooding his head for what seemed like an eternity. He wasn't sure, though. None of his other senses seemed to be working; so he assumed his concept of time had been affected as well. It was as though he was dreaming, but the canvas upon which dreams are painted was blank, its void only filled by memories that *he* painted upon it henceforth. Was this a dream he could control? If it was a dream, it seemed as if he had been sleeping for entirely too long, or at least lying down too long. For the time being, he reckoned he was awake somewhere in the dark. He also reckoned that he would get up and find some light. But his body was not obeying his mind's commands. Then he thought of his body. It was a strange thing. He felt, for sure, that his body was still there, but he did not have any evidence to indicate that. He could not look down and see it. He could not feel whatever bed he was lying on. He could not even feel his own weight and warmth. He felt nothing. He could sense nothing… except the thoughts. It was all he had.

Thoughts of his family came first. His mother, father, and sister had to be worried about him if he had been sleeping (or whatever he had been doing) for even half as long as he thought he had. Thought. There it was again. Was he in some strange nightmare brought on by reading Descartes too late at night? "I think, therefore I am... though I don't know when or where." No. It couldn't be. He was awake. He just knew it. But how could his gut feeling that he was awake prove it to his logically thinking self? Without any sensory stimulation, he could never get both sides of his brain to believe it.

Then he began to mentally rummage through stimuli. The way his mother's "I'm going out tonight" perfume smelled. The layout of his bedroom. If he was in his bed, there was a lamp just to the left of him on the nightstand, if only he could get his left arm to obey him and turn it on. Instead the darkness persisted as he resumed rummaging.

The way an ice cream cone tasted came to mind. How it made the hand that was holding it grow cold. Then he thought for a moment that that might be what he was feeling all over right now. It wasn't like jumping into cold water, because then your insides retain warmth that you can feel. He thought that maybe he was experiencing a different kind of cold, more like holding the ice cream, a kind of cold that permeates every inch of you and freezes the soul to a point that you can't even shiver. Again he had no way to prove this to himself. Any feelings of cold he might think that he had could be explained away by the fact that he talked his mind into experiencing such a stimulus. But it still "felt" like what he was "feeling."

He scoured his memories once more for more stimuli. What did my friends look like? Jon was a hairy mountain of a guy. The rest of them were about the right size for soccer. They all had skinny to medium upper bodies with strong, muscular lower bodies that felt like they were carved out of wood. Not, Jon though. He looked more like a defensive lineman. Meggie always used to say he got in the wrong "football" line back in the day. She always laughed at that joke she made up herself. Then he thought of her laugh. Her sweet and wonderful laugh. Then he thought of her other sounds. Her voice, her screams at a horror movie, her singing as a cantor at Mass, even her crying was beautiful. He remembered them all. Then he swore he heard something. Really *heard* something. A stimulus outside of the ones he relived and re-experienced in his own head. He strained with all that his thinking self was to *hear* it again.

He was right. He had heard something. The voice of a girl! She sounded to him as though he was listening from underwater, or maybe she was in another room. That's it! She was outside his room. What was she saying, though? He focused all his sensory perception on trying to make out what she might possibly be trying to say.

"I told you I wasn't asleep," he said to his naysaying, logical self.

"It could be your subconscious making you actually dream. I mean, how else could I be talking to you? Or maybe she's trying to wake you up, huh? Have you *thought* about that?"

He didn't like the way logical side had said "thought." It was as if he said it with a certain amount of disdain, like thought, Descartes' proof of existence was more of a curse than a blessing. Without the senses, whether they are misleading or not, what was the point of being able to think?

"Shut up." He resolved to ignore the logical devil's advocate that was his reason. He listened intently as humanly possible. Though it was faint, he recognized the voice!

"Meggie!" He thought he said.

"Nope, just me." Logical self was all but mocking him. "Why don't you just try and listen to what your 'dream' is trying to tell you instead of interrupting."

If he could feel anything, it would have definitely been his body seething with heat from adrenaline at logical self's anger-invoking comment. Instead he obliged. It took all the concentration he could muster to be able to focus enough to hear what his girlfriend was saying.

"Well, it's day . . . 176, baby." There was an audible pause in her sentence. And before she continued, there was a long silence. He thought that he might have heard her crying.

After the silence, or intermission to weep, Meggie continued. "We came here today because not only did we graduate today, but it would have been your birthday."

"Would have been?" He thought, what the Hell was going on? Had he really been sleeping so long that he missed graduation? Was he in a coma or something? Were they all gathered around his hospital bed, hoping that all their support and happiness would somehow bring him back to them? And who the Hell were "they" anyway? Whoever they were, he had to figure out a way for them to know that he might still be in that coma, but he was conscious. He was awake. He was going to make it. He had pulled through. As he racked his brain trying to figure out just how to

12

move a finger or open just one eye, Meggie continued talking to him.

"I got into Auburn. I will be going there in the fall. Chad made a joke about it, too. He said since you won't be going to Alabama in the fall, I won't have as far to drive to see you. He said he didn't mean to be mean, but it still made... me... cry." Another silence came. He was sure it was a pause for her to cry this time.

Then he began to find out who "they" might be. His friends. His teammates. Chad Boyd was the next one to speak.

"Hey, J-dog, I really didn't mean to upset her with that comment, you know that right?"

"I know," he said mentally.

"They still can't hear you..." That damned logical self was mocking him again.

"Anyway, bro," Chad continued, "me and Foster are going to Auburn too, so we got Meggie's back. We'll take care of her. I hope wherever you are, you always know that we got your back too."

He thought about Chad and Foster escorting Meggie around Auburn, making sure she was safe. Chad, with his long, silky, straight, blond hair, made Jackson giggle mentally. Foster would look almost like he was strutting around with two girls. It was then that he heard his friend's voice rumble into his ears. It was as muffled as the previous two, but Foster had a very deep voice. It seemed louder, if maybe harder to understand, like hearing another car's stereo whose bass is turned all the way up.

"Hey, bud. Ryan and Paul didn't come today. They went straight over to Brandon's grad party to help him set up. He's not here either. Just me, Chad,

Jon, and Meggie. About what Chad said, though: we will be there to make sure nothing happens to Meggie. She's become one of us since you've been gone. None of us try to replace you, like we even could. For a little guy, you left some pretty big shoes to fill." Foster chuckled once. Had any of the others done it, he might not have heard it, but given Foster's timbre, it was quite audible.

I'm not little, he thought. I'm just average, Foster, you tall, lanky bastard. And I can bench press more than you. Hell, I probably weigh more than you. His letting them know that he was awake was a matter of defending his manhood now. I'll show Foster when I get up and get my hands around his skinny neck, he thought.

What came next was a long, long pause. Had they begun talking too low for him to hear? Was he drifting back into the sensory void he was in before? He hoped not. While they were talking about him in some weird future-past-perfect-participle tense he didn't understand, and they were speaking at a volume that made him border on frustration, it was still better than returning to the nothing from whence he had come.

"Why hasn't Jon spoken yet, damn it?" asked logical self. What was this? An occurrence that was off-putting to calm, witty, collected left-brain?

"Maybe he's not in this dream." It was his turn to mock the logical self.

"You still don't get it, do you?" The pause continued for a little while longer, until he finally heard Jon's familiar voice. It was a relief and a comfort to hear his best friend again.

"Hey, Jax. Sorry I waited until Chad and

14

Foster left. Meggie knows how bad I can get when I talk about you, but I don't like to let the other guys see me like that.

"I don't know why Foster felt the need to lie to you. It seems fucking absurd. Brandon *is* throwing a graduation party that he had to go and get ready for. But Ryan and Paul aren't here because they had to help B set up. They didn't come because they said they have already let you go. They don't see it as helpful or healthy: us coming here and basically talking to our selves to help us with closure. Whatever, though, right. People deal with loss in different ways. And I think the fact that they are both going to Spring Hill next year helps. If they ever want to come see you, they will be able to, unlike the others leaving Mobile to go to college. But Hell, I'm going to South. I'll still be around. I don't care, though. I'll be here whenever I can to come by and see you."

Another pause came. This one was filled with horrible sobbing sounds. Jon was crying. He was crying the kind of cry you never want to hear. When a guy that big and burly wails, it is nearly scary. Jackson could almost picture how silly his friend must have looked, like a Spartan in a bear costume, weeping. Jon regained his composure and continued.

"Sorry, bro, I didn't mean to sound like a little girl just then. Anyway, man, I just wanted you to know that we miss you a lot. You were my best friend. It's just not fair, god damn it! I should've been first! I know you would've been able to deal without me, but this sucks without you."

"What the Hell is happening? I'm right here, big guy. Stop acting like I'm gone. Just have a little faith. I'll come back." In his head he was screaming it.

He wanted his best friend to know he was there. He could hear him.

"Your level of denial is almost as impressive as your ability to think at all." Logical self was starting to get annoying.

"Baby," Meggie was talking to him again. Could he have felt or moved his ears, they would have just perked up.

"Living without you is the hardest thing I have ever done. I want to hate you for it. But I can't. I love you. I will always love you. I know you would want me to move on and be happy. So that's what I will try to do. Just know that whatever happiness I find, it can never compare to the happiness I could've had with you. Goodbye, my love."

"'Live without you'? What the Hell is going on? I'm still here, Meggie. Guys, I'm still here, y'all! I'm not gone. I'm awake. I will find a way to come out of this coma, or whatever I'm in, so we can all be happy again.

"Ha!" Logical self actually laughed. "Just accept it, and it will be easier."

"Shut up! This is not a dream. This is not a dream. I am awake. I am awake. I just have to get up. Get up. Get up, Jackson... Get up, god damn it! Get up. You're not dreaming. You can get up."

Logical self finally conceded. "You're right. You can get up... probably. And this is *not* a dream . . . It is a nightmare."

3

Meggie walked into her dorm room. Her roommate, some goth girl named Emily Ross, sighed in relief, as if Meggie returning somehow alleviated some torture device from her body.

"Thank God you're here!"

"What?"

"Your speakers have been making the 'bloop' IM sound every two minutes for half an hour. I was about ready to puncture my eardrums for solace."

Meggie rolled her eyes. "Why didn't you just turn the speakers down?"

Emily guffawed. "No way, I don't want a PMS'ing roommate in my face because I 'touched her shit.'" She even did air quotes.

Meggie squinted her eyes and made a raspberry with her mouth. "Well, that was last week anyway, so ha."

"Whatever, just make it stop." Emily went back to reorganizing her collection of morose poetry books.

Meggie sat down in front of her computer screen. After looking at the time stamps on the instant messages, sure enough, Jon had sent a "Hello," "ya there?" or a "MEGGIE" at least once every two minutes for the past thirty minutes. She scrolled down to the bottom and finally typed in a response to let the oaf know she was no longer "afk."

How wuz ur date?

Jon's, or midfieldmenace22's, font choice was quite indicative of himself. It was big, noticeable, and awkward looking against anything else near it.

It was ok. Somebody mustve told him about Jackson tho. He said 'I don't think ur a black widow' right at the dinner table. Like that's supposed to make it less awkward.

Meggie's, chicachicaboom's, choice of font revealed less of her persona. She had just stuck with the default font, and she liked the way italics looked.

Do u think it mighta been Chad or foster???

No, I know they said theyd protect me, and they do make sure im safe but I don't think they would sabotage a date to do it. I'm thinking it was one of the other mcgill girls that is a freshman- probably mad at me cuz a frat guy asked me out and I didn't even have to join a stupid sorority :)

Jon took a little while to respond. He liked keeping up with Meggie, but he hated it when she talked about other guys. Somewhere in his head she and Jackson were still together. They were still together when Jackson died. Technically, they never broke up. That was nonsense, though, wasn't it? Jon suppressed these thoughts at least for a moment to be there for his living, breathing friend, the one he still might be able to help. He would just make friendly, smalltalk and not make any mention of Jackson, no matter how badly he wanted to. Fortunately, he wouldn't have to bring him up.

So what else is new? U Been to many parties in the trailer parks up there at auburn lol

No silly head :P unlike most college kids, schoolwork takes up a lot of my time LMAO! Bein up here without the whole group together makes me miss home. And I really miss Jackson.

      Wow, a totally unwarranted subject change back to his dead friend. Before Jackson's untimely death, Jon and Meggie didn't talk much unless they had to. But now, they had something real in common. Since Jackson died, the two of them, though separated by more than a few miles, were closer than ever.

      Lately, Meggie had tried to avoid bringing up the subject of Jackson dying when they talked. She was at least making an attempt to move on. It had always been Jon that brought up the sore topic. This time it was Meggie that brought it up. This came as a relief to Jon. He jumped at the opportunity to talk about his friend.

I miss him a lot too I visit his grave at least once a week. I know that whatever part of him that we loved and that made him him is gone but somehow bein

19

outside that crypt makes me feel like hes somehow with me again.

Meggie was equally disturbed and amused when Jon wrote long messages to her. The content of his monologues usually made her pretty uncomfortable, but the thought of the Neanderthal of a guy on the other end, banging at a keyboard one letter at a time to compose such a long message, always gave her a mental giggle and a grin.

I know what you mean. The last time I was there was right before I moved into my dorm, at the end of summer. When I'm home, we'll go together and put some fresh flowers in there for him.

I would like that... when will you be home?

Umm h/o ill check brb

K

After a small wait, chicachicaboom responded with message that was most pleasing to midfieldmenace22.

My last final is on the 4th

Jon didn't know if she caught the significance, but he did. December 4th was the day Jackson died. He soon found out that she, too, remembered.

If it's a late final and we end up not bein able to go

on that day, well def go on the 8th

She remembered, he thought. The 4th was his death, and the 8th was his funeral. She remembered. He was glad to know he wasn't the only person preoccupied with deathdays and whatnot. He suddenly felt like a healthier person, mentally.

Sounds gr8. anywho im gonna go do not internet things, ok TCNBBT

Then he signed off.

Ok then, but grrrr to u for using abbreviations that not everyone knows! I may but one day someone might get the wrong idea lol j/k bye bye.

Then she signed off. Emily heard the door-slamming sound Meggie's messenger made whenever she signed out of her account, so she knew it was okay to talk to her again.

"I have a question, Miss Paulez."

"Umm, ok." Meggie gave a quizzical look to the skinny, ghostly-white girl as Emily's tone and use of her last name made her wary. It was like she was on trial or something.

Emily's tone changed back to normal, though the question wasn't what Meggie was hoping to have to answer. Emily brushed back her jet-black hair and asked, "Why do some people call you Black Widow?"

Son of a bitch, Meggie thought to herself. This nickname I got only in my senior year has followed me to college. She swallowed a lump that was starting to form in the top of her throat and decided to address the issue head-on and get it out of the way.

"I had a serious boyfriend of three-and-a-half years, and he died unexpectedly and suddenly, last year, our senior year."

The look on Emily's face was priceless. It was a cross between sympathy and something that looked as though she had just discovered that her roommate was descended from Sylvia Plath's secret lovechild. "Oh. I'm sorry."

"It's okay. I still miss him a lot. But I've accepted his death and I believe that he would want me to move on and be happy, so that's what I'm trying to do." Meggie only halfway believed the words herself as she said them. But she did sound convincing. And strong.

"So is that what your little IM buddy is for? Helping you move on?" Emily couldn't have been more incorrect. Meggie felt it appropriate to let her know.

"Actually, that was his best friend, Jon. We were just hammering out the details for when I go home for Christmas after finals. We're gonna go to the cemetery and visit Jackson."

Emily's interest was piqued. The little morbid freshman began to prod for more information. "Where is he buried?"

"He's in his family's vault in Mobile."

"Oh, so he's in a crypt and not in the ground? Sounds like my kind of man."

Meggie sighed and gave a smile at the little joke. "Well he was definitely my kind of man."

"If you don't mind me asking, how did he die?"

Meggie's mind rushed back to that fateful day.

He and his other friends were in Jackson's den playing video games after school, when he complained of a headache. She walked in as the pain was too much for him to continue playing. She remembered vividly him placing the controller down as she gently massaged the side of his head that was hurting him. He said he wanted to go lie down. She had no idea that would be the last time anyone would see him alive.

"There was a hemorrhage in his brain while he was sleeping."

"Oh my God, that sucks." Emily sounded genuinely sympathetic. "Well at least he didn't have any pain."

Meggie gave a half smile. "Yeah, I thought the same thing." She also thought that Jackson had left all the pain behind for his friends and family to deal with. She wasn't angry about it, just confused about why it had to happen the way it did.

Death seemed to be a topic of interest for Emily. She was a stereotypical goth girl through and through. Meggie thought that if the conversation went on any longer, this would be the most she had ever said to her roommate in one sitting.

"Is this still a touchy subject for you, Meg? I won't keep bringing it up if you don't wanna talk about it."

Meggie choked back her emotions and cleared her throat. Now was as good a time as any to open up about the whole thing. "No, it's fine. Talking about it actually helps me deal with the whole thing." She hoped like Hell that Emily wouldn't be able to tell that she had just uttered an obvious lie.

Whether she didn't notice or, out of respect for Meggie's courage to open up about the situation, she overlooked the little falsehood. She continued with her inquiry. "Okay. So, how long has he been gone?"

"It will be a year on the 4th. That's when I'm supposed to go with Jon to the cemetery. I may wait until the 8th, though. I have a final on the 4th and I'll get home later. And I don't wanna be roamin' around a graveyard at night."

Emily let out a little chuckle. "Don't knock it 'til you try it." It made Meggie laugh a little too. "I can understand that, though, but why the 8th? Couldn't you just go the next morning?"

"The 8th was the day of his funeral."

"Oh, okay."

"After the funeral, we went out to eat and drink with his family."

"An old Irish wake, huh?"

"Yeah. It was actually at a pub too. Eating good food and getting drunk with the friends and family you still got is not a bad idea after losing someone."

"Yeah, the Irish got it right on that one." The two shared a laugh. "Well, I notice that you don't have any pictures of him anywhere."

"Oh I have pictures of him. They're just not hanging up. Can you imagine what would happen if it got out I had pictures of my dead boyfriend hanging up all over my wall. I can just hear 'em now: 'who wants to be the next lucky guy to get a picture on the Black Widow's wall of fame?'"

Emily burst into uncontrollable laughter. After a few moments she was able to regain her composure. "I'm sorry, that's just hilarious. Do you have any pictures of him here with you?"

"Yeah. I do." Before Emily could ask to see

them, Meggie had begun reaching under her bed to pull out a gray metal box.

When she opened it, right on top was a picture of Jackson's senior portrait he had taken the summer after junior year. He was so beautiful, she thought. His short, brown hair. His deep green eyes. He smiled at her from the picture with a mischievous little crooked half-smile, almost like he knew a secret. She was reminded of how much he had looked like his mother. Meggie handed the picture to Emily.

"Wow. He's gorgeous."

"Yeah. No need to remind me."

Emily sat on her bed with a very contemplative look as Meggie saw her from across the room. Meggie asked, "What is it?"

"I don't know how to ask you this-"

Meggie scoffed. "Well just ask it then! Jeez, you already got me blabbing on about everything else."

"Would it be alright if I came with you to his family vault?"

Meggie was very surprised by the question. "Um, sure, I guess. But why would you want to?"

"Are you kidding me? I love cemeteries. They're so peaceful and somber. And if Jackson is in a family crypt that means it's a really cool cemetery, hopefully with a bunch of old stuff to look at. I get done with finals on the 4th too. Mom is expecting me back in Birmingham after, but I can just tell her one of them got pushed back a few days and go stay with you in Mobile a little while."

"Well- okay then."

If Meggie thought she was creeped out by her goth roommate before, she knew she was definitely creeped out now.

4

Jackson had been coming to terms with his "nightmare" for a while now. Other than the periodic visit from his old friend, Jon, he really had nothing to look forward to, except think about it. I am dead, he thought. But I can't be. I'm still here. How did I "die?" How the Hell did I get here? Something must have gone wrong with my soul for me to still be around in any form. Maybe I didn't cross over. Maybe this is what Hell *really* is, being visited by old familiar voices from somewhere on the other side of the darkness.

"You'll figure it out." The damned logic still popped in from time to time.

"What, that I'm in Hell? I think I'm slowly accepting that fact. I'm just left alone in the dark with my thoughts. Sometimes I'll hear things that my thoughts didn't produce. Traces of life somewhere off in the distance. Things that I'll never get to interact with again. Yes, I'm slowly learning this Hell."

But what did I do to deserve Hell? He wondered. Did I do something wrong and not even realize it? Who or what did I hurt without remorse?

"What if you aren't in Hell?" the logic asked quizzically.

"Oh, what, and I'm in Heaven! Believe me, if this is what Heaven is like, I may rather go to Hell!" There was no way this could be Heaven.

"Since your mere 'existence' right now defies most logic and beliefs, perhaps you could consider a many number of possibilities. But maybe you should think about the most probable."

"Would you just shut the Hell up about possible and probable? I never thought I'd be spending eternity in Hell, most of all, arguing with myself." Jackson could have sworn that he felt a cold chill all of a sudden, but before he could fixate his mind on the sensation, it had passed.

He was ready to accept that he was in Hell, for what he had no idea. But at least it helped him understand why he would occasionally hear the voices of his friends and family weeping just outside the dark, why they said they missed him, why they said they hoped he was in a better place. Well he wasn't in a better place! Sorry, Mom and Dad, he thought, your little boy didn't go to Heaven! I'd love to be able to at least tell you that so you could move on. But I guess this one-sided communication is part of Hell's package deal.

"I got a question: why did my inner voice get split into me and a sarcastic jerk?" Jackson tried to remember how anger made his insides feel. How when he got mad, his heart would race; and adrenaline would rush all over his body like a surge of heat. If he could feel anything, this is what he would be feeling for that other voice inside his head.

"I don't think you were split in two. I've always been here. The calm, collected, rational side. I think that this recent turn of events has proven without a doubt that I don't always have to be here, though. That's why I think it appears to you that I am something else entirely. It's easier for you to accept that you have a logically thinking person inside your head than it is for you to even consider what might really be going on right now. Quite ironic really."

"Now I know that I'm in Hell. The only company I have is a jackass!"

"Oh, would you come off that 'Hell' talk and listen?"

"Listen to what? You! I don't think-"

"Shh!" The logical one cut him off.

"I can't believe you talked me into this." He heard Meggie's sweet voice. She continued. "It's dark, it's raining, and it's freezing cold!"

Cold, he thought.

"Don't blame me, I could've waited, it was Dead-y Dead Girl that just had to come out tonight." Jon's tone seemed to display an amount of resentment.

"Oh, come on now. This could be fun, plus I'm helping you both overcome your irrational fear y'all have."

A new voice. A *brand* new voice. A voice Jackson had never heard in his life. Who could it be? He thought, have my best friend and my beloved sought help to brave the depths of Hell to save my soul?

"Stop with those foolish thoughts! Pay attention. This time they might actually say something to get you up to speed." This time he could remember fully the feelings of anger. He felt like he was experiencing them again.

"Well, Jackson. It's been a year, and I'm still

talking to you like you're still here, filling you in on Life." Meggie's voice seemed a little harder for him to hear than usual. It was the rain she had spoken of drowning her out. He listened as hard as he could to hear every word she spoke with her soft, sweet voice.

As she went on about her first semester in college, Jackson began to think about what he was hearing. The world had gone by without him. The only updates he received were when the ones he loved prayed and said things to him. But what about this new voice? How could he hear her?

"Again, stop with the stupid thoughts. I must say that I will be relieved when you finally realize the situation." Now it seemed to Jackson that the logical voice in his head was growing a little perturbed. He tried to clear his mind and focus only on the words being said to him.

"Hey, bud. Tired of hearing from me yet?" Jon asked. No, Jackson thought. "Anyway, I thought I'd keep it short and sweet so it doesn't get any scarier out here, and we don't catch a cold." The cold again. Was Jackson feeling it again? He didn't think about it. He just wanted to listen.

"So, uh, miss you. Love you. Good night. Come on, ya'll let's get out of here."

"Not yet, what about me?" the strange girl's voice asked.

"Oh, come on Emily," Jon snapped, "You didn't even know him. It would be disrespectful." So the new voice's name was Emily. Let her speak, Jon, Jackson thought. Let her speak.

"Just let her speak," Meggie said. Jackson was pleased to know that she and he were still on the same page.

"Hey, Jackson," Emily began, "I didn't know you while you were alive, but I've seen pictures of you. Meggie showed me. You were cute. She said you were sweet. I would have to agree with the good things I've heard about you since I was able to talk these two into coming to a graveyard in the middle of the night."

"Oh my fucking God! I'm in a cemetery! I'm still in my body! But-"

"Shut up!" the logical self seemed to shout into Jackson's ears.

"Anyway, dude, it was nice to finally 'meet' you." Emily faced the vault door and did the air quotes as if Jackson could see her doing it. "Hope you like your new residence. It looks pretty awesome on the outside. Maybe one day I'll be able to talk your family into letting me see the inside. It's kind of my thing. Check ya later."

"Awesome, Emily. Can we go now?" asked Jon.

"No! Don't go! I'm right here! I can hear you guys. I'm alive. Don't go."

"Alive? Don't get ahead of yourself. I wouldn't say you're exactly alive." Logic already knew something.

Jackson tried with all his might to scream out for help. He was certain he felt the cold air this time, and it was momentarily interrupted by the feeling of waves of adrenaline. He felt almost alive again.

"MEGGIE! JON! EMILY! ANYONE, PLEASE! I'm alive!" But his voice he used to cry out was still only in his head. Over the sound of the rain falling, he could hear them walking away.

Now Jackson thought to himself that he had found a fate worse than Hell. He was buried alive. But

31

surely he had to have died. He could not have been buried for a year and survived this long.

"Now you're getting it."

"I've come back from the dead."

"Man, I thought you'd never figure that one out." Was the logical voice in his head even his? Or was it some higher being trying to coach him through this process. Either way, he had discovered the truth. Now what to do with it?

"How do I get out of here? I was fine when I thought I was in Hell. But if I'm in my body and still on Earth, I definitely don't want to spend any more time than I have to in a coffin."

"Well," the logical voice said, "you got your presence of mind back. You got your hearing back, and some of your feeling. It's just a matter of time and a matter of your will until the rest returns."

So I did this? He thought. I refused to die, or *stay* dead, rather. Now I've just got to will my body to get up and out this cemetery.

"There you go! Just be grateful your parents didn't have you cremated."

5

Ever since the visit down to Mobile to visit, Meggie and Emily seemed to be getting along much better. They no longer merely coexisted in a little dorm room, making sure to stay out of each other's way. They were actually becoming friends. Meggie had found out that Emily was majoring in English because she wanted to be a writer; and Emily found out that Meggie had no idea of what to do with her life. Her parents said "go to college at Auburn," and Meggie had said "okay." Meggie discovered Emily was a complete chatterbox once you got past her broody exterior. Emily discovered Meggie was nice enough to just listen to all of her chatterbox nonsense. Regardless of the differences in their life-plans, or conversation techniques, the two seemed to finally be getting along. It only took one visit to a cemetery in the middle of a freezing cold, rainy night.

"So, I've decided I am going to put up a picture of Jackson." Meggie breathed out and began to mentally brace herself for whatever Emily was about to say about it. She looked at her roommate who was sitting up in her bed and reading. She didn't give any sign that she had even heard Meggie's statement.

"'Kay." She didn't even raise her head from the book she was reading. The brevity of her response surprised Meggie. She was never brief about anything! There had to be a reason.

"That's all you have to say? No questions about what might have changed my mind or anything?"

Emily sighed, put her bookmark in place, and closed the book. She looked up and faced Meggie. "Well, I look at it like this: who are your friends at school? Me, Chad, and Foster, right? Chad and Foster are directly connected to you because you dated Jackson. And we became friends because I felt the need to ask you about your dead boyfriend- Jackson. Frankly, it would be an insult to him if you didn't have a picture or two of him hanging around. He's responsible for all your friends!" Emily gave a chuckle as she had cracked herself up.

"Oh, shut up, you."

"But seriously, what did make you change your mind?"

Meggie cleared her throat as she tried to think about the best way to form her explanation. "I just think it's something I need to live with, and anyone that might get involved with me needs to live with too."

"Good for you, girl, but you're not worried about that whole Black Widow thing anymore?"

"Nope." She crossed her arms and turned her nose up as though the people that might judge her were in the room with her. "If there is anyone who can't deal with it, then I'm sure they won't be able to deal with me."

Emily gave her roommate a big smile, put one

hand on her hip and waved her other in front of her as she snapped her fingers. "You go girl." The girls exchanged laughs.

Emily went back to her book she was reading, and Meggie began reaching underneath her bed for her metal box o' memories. She grabbed it and placed it on her bed, remaining knelt on the floor as she opened it. She said she had decided to put up a picture of Jackson, but her body language was full of reservation. She stayed kneeling by the bed almost as if- if she were to chicken out at the last minute, she could quickly shove the gray box back under the bed. But she didn't. She lifted the box and placed it on the bed.

Meggie took very deliberate breaths as she opened the box. She hadn't opened it since Emily had asked to see a picture of him. She knew his smiling face was waiting for her right on the other side of that metal lid. Just as she was about to open the box, Chad and Foster opened the door to their dorm and came barging in.

"What up?" Foster asked. The tall, slender guy dove onto Meggie's bed and propped himself up on his elbow to face her.

Chad was much more considerate than Foster. He closed the door quietly behind them and remained standing next to it. "I told him to knock, Meg," he said apologetically.

"That's okay, guys," Emily interjected, not even giving time for Meggie to respond. It was to be expected. Emily had been taken with Chad's piercing gray eyes and long, straight, silky blond hair since she had laid eyes on him. Meggie had heard her roommate talk about the boy at length since they had become friends.

"Thanks." Chad then took Emily's chair at her computer desk, turned it around to face the action, and took a seat. The little goth girl gave a little grin, but made sure that Chad didn't see it.

Meggie finally answered Foster. "Not too much, 'what up' with you?"

"Oh nothing, me and Chad just came by to let you know that we're throwing a party tonight."

"What's new? Y'all always throw parties."

Foster looked as though he were insulted. "No we do not!"

"Whatever, Foster," Meggie said. "What's the awesome occasion this time? Is it National wear a t-shirt day or something?"

Chad laughed at Meggie's joke from across the room, but composed himself enough to explain. "No, Meg, Brandon's in town."

Oh my God, Meggie thought. Brandon was the only one of her friends she hadn't seen since graduation. He signed up for the Marines their senior year and left for boot camp right afterward. He was home a little while after he got done with basic training, but she had been in Auburn getting ready for school.

"Brandon's the marine, right?" Emily asked.

"Yeah." The other three answered her in unison.

Emily offered her own opinion of the new marine. "He's probably a douchebag then. I'm sure he'll show up in his dress blues and expect to get free drinks and all the ladies."

Foster guffawed, but the other two just shook their heads, thinking Emily was probably right.

"I can't say I really blame him. Shit, if I was

getting deployed to Iraq in a month, I would be trying to get drunk and hook up as much as I could." Foster was trying to defend his friend from the goth girl attacker.

"Well, whatever, I haven't seen him in forever. I don't care if he acts like an ass because he's about to leave. I just wanna see him." Meggie thought about all the guys. *All* of them had been there for her when she lost Jackson. She didn't care if one of them went off and became a jarhead. He still mattered to her.

"Yeah, dude, his little brother told me he's gotten huge since he's been gone," Chad said. He was trying to ease the tension of the whole Brandon situation. Whether she let it go, or didn't come back with a smart-ass comment because it was Chad saying something, Emily just sat on her bed and said nothing.

"Well, what time is he supposed to be here?" asked Meggie.

"Some time tonight. He landed in Mobile earlier this morning and is supposed to drive up after he eats with his parents. Just come over to mine and Chad's later on. Both of y'all. It'll be fun."

"Okay. Will do." Meggie looked over at Emily, who was looking back at her smiling. She was clearly happy to have been invited to tag along.

Chad and Foster got up to leave. Foster just waved and headed down the hallway. Before Chad left he apologized for his roommate being raised in a barn, politely went behind him, and made sure to close the door.

There was a little silence in the room before either of the girls spoke. True to form, it was the chatterbox, Emily, that ended it.

"So, what was up with that? They never invite me to parties and stuff."

"I don't know, maybe they just want you to meet Brandon."

"A marine? No, thanks. I'll pass."

Meggie seemed disappointed. "So you're not coming with me?"

"I didn't say that. I just don't care one way or the other if I meet this marine or not."

Meggie giggled at her roommate. "You're going because of Chad, ain't you?"

The ivory skin on Emily's cheeks became a bright red. "Is it that obvious?"

"Only to me. And maybe Chad! Ha ha. Don't worry. Foster's too dense to notice anything, so he won't rag you about it. And Chad's too nice of a guy to do anything that would embarrass you."

"Thanks. Good to know."

"So you're going with me then?"

"Hell yes."

***

By the time Meggie and Emily got to the party, it was already going strong. Several cars were parked outside of the duplex Chad and Mike's parents rented for them. Because their next door neighbors usually attended their parties, they never had to worry about noise complaints. And as a result, their parties were deemed epic by anyone who attended them. Meggie had been invited many times, but never went to any of them, choosing rather to visit the boys when she knew there wasn't a party.

"Looks like it's hoppin' in there," Emily joked.

"Yeah, sounds like it is, too. Those boys have

been throwing down like this since high school."

The muffled rap music they heard outside blared into their ears as soon as Meggie opened their front door. In their living room was a ping-pong table with the net gone. The party-goers were enjoying a classic college pastime: beer pong. One of the two girls on the side nearest the front door sank a ball in one of the red plastic cups on the other side. As the crowd cheered, Foster chugged the beer that was inside the cup she rang, and Emily questioned Meggie about his teammate.

"Is that who I think it is?"

"Yep. That's Brandon."

Brandon looked over and saw Meggie. His dark brown eyes grew wide and lit up as he gave her a huge smile, He screamed her name, "Meggie!!" He gave his spot on Foster's team to someone else, and ran over to her and gave her a big hug.

In his hugging he had lifted her off the ground. When he finally let her back down, he said, "Well, how the Hell are you?"

"I'm fine. How have you been?" She asked a leading question and let him talk as she evaluated him.

He was going on about the Marines, basic training, and other general stuff she could ignore without letting him know. She was much more impressed with how he had filled out. He was barely half an inch taller than her, but his little brother had been right. He had put on a lot of muscle. Even his forearms rippled as he used his hands to talk. She noticed he had the numbers "0331" tattooed on his right one. And he didn't wear his uniform like Emily had predicted. He had on a t-shirt, blue jeans, and an old McGill Soccer cap. Except for his tattoo and him being in great shape, he was just the same old Brandon.

She interrupted him when it seemed she was going to actually have to pay attention to him. "What's this, little man? Huh?" she asked as she poked him on his forearm, pointing to the tattoo.

"Oh, that? That's my specialty. Oh-Three-Thirty-one, machine gunner. All the gunners in my company that are getting deployed got 'em."

"Cool. So when do you have to leave?"

"In July. I'm only home for a few more days, but I'm taking a couple weeks leave right before I have to deploy."

That made Meggie happy. "Well we'll be out of school then. We'll have to hang out."

"Hell, yeah, we will." Brandon looked over at Emily. "So who's your friend, here?"

Before Meggie could introduce her, Emily interjected. "I'm Emily, her roommate. So far, you're not a typical marine douchebag, but I'm watching you."

"Ha Ha Ha. Well I understand if you feel that way. I hope I pass all your tests. Come on y'all, let's go see what Chad's up to in the back yard." Brandon motioned with his hand, and the girls followed him through the sliding glass doors at the back of the living room.

When Brandon closed the door behind them, the loud music gave their ears a break. It must have been good, thick glass. It muted the noise from inside pretty well.

They found Chad leaned up against the wall that was the outside of their utility room. He had one of the red plastic cups in his hand.

Meggie walked up to him and remarked. "I thought you didn't drink anymore?"

"I don't, Meg," Chad raised his glass and jiggled it. "This is water."

"Loser." Meggie laughed.

"Well, we do drink," said Emily, "where's the damn booze?"

Chad pointed to an industrial size garbage can in the middle of the yard. "The keg's over there. Foster encourages the beer 'cause his liquor cabinet goes too fast on big parties."

Brandon quickly volunteered. "I'll go get y'all some. Be right back." He walked off toward the keg to get the girls drinks.

"Well, he looks good coming and going. He seems nice so far. What's his problem?" Emily asked.

Meggie answered her question with another. "Are you just determined to hate anyone in the military?"

"No. Just marines."

Chad spoke up to defend his friend. "Well, you don't have to hate all marines as long as Brandon's one. He was one of us in high school. He's still one of us. He just has to keep his hair cut." He laughed as he flipped his long hair behind him.

Emily shrugged. "Well damn, Meg, all the guys seem just great. Where the Hell did y'all find Foster, though?"

Chad was so caught off guard, and laughed so hard, he spewed a little water from his cup onto Meggie. She didn't mind. She was laughing pretty hard too.

"I'm glad that *is* water, boy," Meggie said as she wiped off some water from her arm.

Brandon rejoined them with a cup for the girls and one for himself. "What's so funny over here?"

"Oh nothing. Emily's just commenting on how Foster's the weakest link out of all us McGill guys."

"So you met all of us, huh, Em?" Brandon asked her.

"Well I go to school with two of them, and I met Ryan, Paul, and Jon when I went to Mobile with Meg. Jon's awesome, by the way, but I don't know if he likes me too much. And now I've met you. I'm not saying he's a bad guy. He's a lot of fun, but all you guys are just so nice and stuff. He's just in his own little world and doesn't care about anything. So unless Jackson was a complete tool, I gotta say Foster's the odd man out."

"Well, he wasn't," Brandon said as he pulled off his cap and used its bill to scratch his head. He was clearly bothered by Emily's bringing up Jackson.

6

He could feel his weight pressing against the base of his coffin. The sensations weren't exactly like they normally were when he was lying down. He felt lighter, almost as if he were floating in water. But he definitely felt gravity working on his body and holding him in place.

He could feel the clothes his family had chosen for him to be buried in. They too felt strange to him, like they weren't made of cotton, linen, or any other typical clothing material. He didn't think his loved ones would have laid him to rest in paper bags. Obviously his sense of touch wasn't working quite as well as the one that had started this whole thing: his hearing.

His hearing had become unnaturally sharp. He had gotten to where he could hear other families visiting other graves in the cemetery. He wasn't sure exactly from how far away he could hear them without being able to see, but he guessed that he could hear very well by being able to make them out at all.

He heard old widows visit there lost husbands. He overheard parents point out the marker to their children where their deceased siblings lay. He had heard an entire funeral procession for some lady with cancer, and the man she left behind weeping at her grave site long after the rest of the attendants had gone away. He heard so many of the people that came to visit their lost loved ones.

Then he thought about all the people that had visited him. His mom, his dad, his sister, his friends, they had all visited him. He had heard them all. His hearing Jon visit him over and over, going on about how he missed him; his hearing Meggie weep and how she was counting the days; if he could only get out of this prison and tell them that he had heard them all.

Then he thought about who hadn't visited him and how he missed them. He hadn't heard any of his grandparents outside. His favorite uncle, William, hadn't shown up, either. He always had a weird way of dealing with death, so Jackson didn't really hold that against him.

He thought about his friends he hadn't heard from: Ryan, Paul, and Brandon. Jon said Ryan and Paul had dealt with his death and moved on. But what about Brandon? He tried to think about what he might have done to make Brandon not at least come by or anything. Then he reminded himself of what Jon said. People deal with grief in their own way. He thought about how he dealt with his own death. He hadn't. He refused to let it happen. And now he was lying in his family's vault tormented by the thoughts and remnants of life that were happening without him. I guess Brandon's not visiting a graveyard is a good way to make sure you keep living, he thought. Then it became clear to him. The only way for people to know that I'm still alive is to get out of this place!

As he thought and thought with all his might,

44

he tried as best he could to move at all. He remembered how it felt lying on the weight bench, and pushing the bar up. He imagined that raising his own coffin lid would be a lot like that. For the first time since he had regained consciousness in his dead body, he heard a sound that came from within the coffin. It was the sound of his sleeves rustling against the side of whatever he was wearing. He moved! For the first time in he wasn't sure how long, he had moved. He wasn't sure how much he had moved, but he had done it. He could feel his arms as they moved, but the sensation was like moving an appendage that had fallen asleep. He knew he had moved it, but that was it. It was enough, though. As he thought about moving again, his task was reinforced by his beginning to believe that all this was possible. This made it easier.

He managed to bring one of his hands to his face. He could almost feel his face. It felt like he was feeling his face while wearing thick gloves, and his face felt like a rubber mask to his hand. But he could tell it was *his* hand touching *his* face. With every move and sensation he made and felt, subsequent moving became easier and easier. He began to turn his head from side to side. He wiggled his toes. He felt almost alive again. Now he had to get out of this box!

Just then he jerked and lay completely still. He heard something off in the distance that surprised him. His friends had finally come. Ryan and Paul were in the cemetery. They were a ways away from him, but they were walking around in his general area.

"What the Hell are we doin' here, man?" Ryan asked. He sounded like a little kid throwing a tantrum. "We finally get a chance to hang out, and we go to a damned graveyard."

"Shut up!" Paul snapped. "I told you I had to come here."

Finally, Jackson thought. Paul had to come visit me. He couldn't stand it any longer. His hopes that his friend had to come say his goodbyes were quickly defeated.

"Hughes family vault is over there, dog." Jackson could just picture his red-haired friend pointing toward his grave site. He could imagine himself asking him, "isn't that bad luck?"

"I know where Jackson is. I don't care."

Jackson knew that in his undeath, he still had a heart, because Paul had just broken it. He thought about being embalmed and how they remove all the organs, but he could feel the pain of Paul's words in the pit of his stomach.

What did he *have* to come for? If not for him, had Paul lost someone in his family that was buried near him? He could almost feel his friend as he heard their steps grow closer to him. They stopped at what seemed to him as right outside his family's vault door.

There was a brief pause that was interrupted after a while by Paul. "Maybe I do care."

"Aw, come on, man. This is really depressing. I miss him too, but coming here's not going to bring him back. It's just gonna bring back old memories and make us sad all over again." Ryan did miss him, Jackson thought. Not coming here really was his way of dealing with it.

Just then Jackson heard the creak of the hinges on the heavy vault door. They were coming in! The only people that ever came in were his parents and the cemetery's groundskeeper to sweep the leaves that came through the barred window in the vault door. Jackson thought about trying to make as much noise as he could to get their attention, but thought it best not to startle them. He lay perfectly still.

"So this is where you are, Jackson? It's like I can feel you. It's like I know that you can hear me." Paul's words sent a chill up Jackson's spine. He could hear him.

"Dude, you're starting to freak me out, Paul. Let's get the Hell outta here!" a panicked Ryan whined.

"I have to know, Ryan. I have to know."

He could hear Paul walk toward his coffin until he was close enough to feel the vibrations of his footsteps.

Jackson tried to think about the layout of the vault. There were markers at two different levels on top of one another on either side with an open walkway in the middle. He wondered exactly where he was. Then he remembered never seeing any coffins in his family's vault. His coffin was underneath an almost foot-thick stone slab.

All the memories and emotions heightened his sensory perception to the point of supernatural. He could feel Ryan's panicked breathing outside his coffin.

"I have to know," Paul whispered as he placed his hands on what Jackson knew to be the slab covering his coffin. He could feel intense vibrations and the sound of stone scratching against stone. He was trying to remove it! Paul was able to move it a couple of inches, then Jackson heard his friend Ryan scream.

"No!" he shouted as he ran toward Paul and

tackled him. The stone scratching stopped as Jackson heard the two boys hit the stone floor of the vault.

"Get off of me, damn it! I have to know!"

"Have to know what exactly, Paul? Yes, he's in there! Yes he's dead! And Yes! We should let him rest in peace!"

Jackson could hear his friend breathing hard with anger after he yelled at Paul. He didn't know whether to be happy because Ryan had such respect for him, or whether to be sad because he was so close to seeing his friends again.

"You're lucky the sun's out," Paul said.

"What is that? Some kind of threat, dude? You gonna wait until it's dark and come try some grave robbing? Just let it go, Paul. I know it sucks. He was my friend too, but pulling his body out of here ain't gonna bring our friend back! We just have to deal with it and move on."

It was almost as if Jackson could feel the tension between his two friends in the vault. One dead set on "having to know" and the other okay with just accepting the truth and getting on with Life.

After several seconds of what Jackson was sure was a staring contest, Paul relented. "Fine. Let's just get the fuck outta here."

He heard Ryan walk over to Paul and pat him on the back. "Thank you. Now, let's *please* get the fuck outta here."

"Yeah, let's roll," Paul said as the two walked out of the Hughes vault.

So close, damn it, Jackson thought. But what could he have said to his friends, really? "Hey, guys, I was wondering when someone would come bust me out of here. I been a zombie for a while now." He hadn't heard that mocking, logical voice inside his head in a while. He guessed he didn't really need it anymore. He was mocking himself at this point.

Then he remembered that Paul had moved the slab. If he had moved it enough, he could get his fingers on the outside and try to slide it off instead of having to push it up. He pushed up on his coffin lid and saw for the first time with his reborn eyes the light of the sun. Paul had slid the slab a good four inches, and the sun was positioned perfectly in the sky to come through the window at the top of the vault door. It was not a lot of light, but Jackson's sight quickly adjusted and sharpened to the acuity of his hearing. He was wearing his school uniform, and the liner in his coffin was a cream-colored satin. The lid was a dark wood with shiny, polished finish. Just seeing the real world again made him joyful. Knowing that he was no longer a prisoner of his own memories and thoughts made him happy. Reality set back in, though. He had to remind himself that he was dead to this world. He couldn't just get out of his coffin and walk around and rejoin the rest of the world. He did want to, however, get out of his coffin. Driven by thoughts and memories of strength he didn't know he had, Jackson raised his arms and stuck his fingers outside and pressed them against the slab that was holding him in. His angle didn't give him much leverage, but he pushed as hard as he could. Much to his surprise, the slab moved with relative ease. He slid it just enough to be able to slither out of the box. The less I move it, he thought, the less I'll have to move it back once I'm out. Jackson had felt drunk before, and all of his movements felt impaired as if he were intoxicated, minus the feelings of euphoria or giggles. Once he was on his feet, he turned around to face his "final resting place." Jackson put the slab back into place so his grave would look unmolested. When he was done, he turned toward the door to outside the crypt. He stopped himself, though, deciding it might be better if he left after nightfall.

Sunset seemed to last forever for Jackson. He wanted so badly to get out of the crypt and rejoin the world. But in what capacity? What was his place now? His presence would be, at best, awkward, and, at worst, horrifying. His sense of touch was still a bit off. If he moved around, or even crossed his arms, he had to look at his body to make sure it was doing the things his mind commanded it. All of this would take some serious getting used to for Jackson.

As he was finally able to free himself from his coffin, his thoughts became less self-loathing and depressing. So, out of nothing but sheer curiosity, he began to examine his pockets. What goodies might have been left on his person?

In his front pants pocket, there was a handful of pulverized notebook paper. *Mom must not have checked the pockets before she took my suit to the cleaners,* he thought. But in his jacket pocket were two neatly folded pieces of paper. He quickly pulled them out to examine them.

One was a letter from Meggie's kid sister, Maria. In 3rd grade handwriting it simply read:

DEAR JACKSON,
      WE WILL MISS YOU. I WILL ALWAYS REMEMBER YOU.

Jackson could feel his face move into the familiar position of a smile as he imagined the little girl writing this and placing it in his jacket. To think that he could have enough impact on someone who was not in his family made him happy.

The second one was something he felt he could actually use.

Dearest Jackson,

You will be sorely missed by anyone who ever knew you. You will always be in our thoughts and prayers. It was an honor and a pleasure to have known you these seventeen years. God was graceful enough for me to be blessed to have you as a member of the church. It is a great loss to the church, and the world, that you were called up so early. And, wherever you are, always know that I, personally, am always here for you, should you need anything in this life or the next.

Sincerely,
Fr. Gerald Hayes, S.J., O.L.

Father Hayes was always his favorite priest. Not only was he pastor of the church Jackson attended, but later in high school, he became his favorite teacher at McGill. Jackson always admired him, but he never realized that Father Hayes cared about him so much, too. He folded up the letter and placed it back in his jacket next to the one from Maria.

When nightfall finally came, Jackson was more than ready to step out. As he exited the vault, the love he had for the city came immediately back to him. He could hear so many cars off in the distance. Various birds and insects creating their symphonies of sounds. He remembered what it was like to breathe, and as he did, he found himself smelling the world again. It smelled like home.

His basking in the sensory overload was interrupted by a terrible feeling. He felt as if someone was watching, maybe following him. The sobering sensation was enough for him to set his sights and focus on the only place he might have a chance for help: Father Hayes' house.

"I sure hope he meant what he said." Jackson was barely out of the cemetery, but he stopped in his tracks. He had spoken audibly. His words had come out loud. He didn't even have to think about it. They just came out.

As he started walking again, the logical voice inside his head spoke up once more. "And *that's* why you don't need me anymore."

7

Jackson's feeling that he was being followed seem to come and go as he got closer to Father Hayes' house on Old Shell Rd. If he was truly being followed, it was as if his stalker was falling behind at points only to quickly catch up to him. He thought maybe he was just being paranoid at first, but then he decided to use his heightened sense of sound to his advantage.

He tried to walk as quietly as possible, which was difficult given his state. His head was still swimming, and he was still walking as if he were intoxicated. He had to concentrate harder on walking straight and softly than he had to on trying to hear a possible assailant. As he scoured his brain to find the focus he needed to accomplish the task at hand, it came in the form of a memory. Jackson suddenly likened his current debacle to trying to sneak past his parents' room after a night of drinking. He could feel and hear the skin on his face tighten into a smile as he thought about it. That was enough to focus. He was able to move forward as quietly and deliberately as a mouse.

Still he heard nothing, so he stood perfectly still. He was hidden well enough. The old oak trees along Old Shell Rd. grew up and over the street until they met right above it, forming a canopy that blocked even the brightest of street lights. It wasn't a particularly busy night for the road, so he was almost in complete darkness when there were no passing cars.

He was surprised at how well he could see in the dark. His eyes were remarkably better in death than they had been in life. When cars passed, though, they didn't blind him. They adapted to changes in light much quicker, too. As a matter of fact, all of his senses seemed to be much sharper now, except his sense of touch. Jackson wondered why it was lacking and why it felt like his whole body was asleep. If he was being followed, though, whatever it was had stopped as well. He finally brushed the whole thing off as paranoia and began walking again.

The feeling stayed with him almost the rest of the way. For some reason, though, as Father Hayes' home was in sight, the unsettling feeling vanished. Had he been breathing, he would've breathed a sigh of relief. His relief quickened his pace, and within moments he was on the priest's front porch.

Father Hayes was a Jesuit. He was employed by Spring Hill College, as both a minister and a professor. Because of that fact, his house was one of the Jesuit residences on the campus. It was a small, 19th century home with white, wooden siding and black shutters. The siding was amazingly bright to Jackson as it reflected the moonlight.

Hayes taught a few religion classes at McGill, too. He had taught not only Jackson and his sister, but also both of his parents. Hayes was a family friend who had been there for most of the Hughes' big family moments. Jackson wondered if it had been

Father Hayes that handled his funeral. Then he thought about his current situation, a dead kid trying to visit his old priest!

What the Hell am I doing? he thought. The absurdity of his circumstances made him wonder if he had made the right decision to leave the crypt. Father Hayes kept two rocking chairs on his porch, one on either side of his front door. Jackson walked over to one and sat down to think. All the concentrating, and now his doubts about it all, had made it harder for him to will his body to stand up steadily.

Sitting was easier. Gravity did most of the work for him. He leaned his head back and began to rock back and forth in the chair. What am I supposed to say? What am I supposed to expect him to say? His sarcastic, logical inner voice would be a welcome perspective about now, he thought.

He sat rocking and thinking for about three hours before he even came close to deciding whether or not to knock on the priest's door. He pulled out the letter and read it again. Father Hayes didn't have his porch light turned on, but the waxing moon proved to be more than enough light for Jackson's "new" eyes to make out all of the writing.

He mumbled the phrase "in this life or the next" a few times before he commanded his body to stand him up and knock on the door. As he stood facing the front door, he breathed in and let out a sigh of hope. His old habits hadn't died either.

"Here goes nuthin'." Jackson gave the door three heavy, loud knocks.

He hadn't meant to knock so loudly. He was still getting used to actively thinking about and concentrating on all of his actions. When he was alive, he just did them. He now had to think about anything he wanted to do before it would happen.

The loud knock was enough to get someone's attention inside. Jackson could first here the footsteps come toward the front door. The he heard a voice say "I'm coming." It was definitely Father Hayes. The hot wave of an adrenaline rush covered Jackson's body as the steps stopped sounding, and he heard the priest unlock and open the door.

Jackson saw that it was dark inside too. And the priest wasn't wearing his glasses. He saw Father Hayes squint his eyes as he moved his bald head from one position to the next. It was clear to Jackson that the old man couldn't quite make out his visitor.

"Can I help you, son?" he asked. Jackson didn't respond.
"Who are you, son? What is it?"

Jackson sighed another hopeful sigh and decided, if he had come this far, he would have to speak. "Yes, Father, I need your help."

Jackson could see in the man's face that he had instantly recognized the voice. A mix of fear, awe, happiness, and sadness came over Father Hayes' face. Jackson could see moonlight reflecting off of tears welling up in the priest's bottom eyelids.

"Please tell me that isn't you, Jackson." The man's voice was trembling and uneasy.

"Yes, sir. It is me."

"Oh my God, this is my fault. What have I done to you, Jackson?"

Jackson was taken aback by Father Hayes' response. His fault? Had he brought Jackson back from the dead? Did he say some old Catholic ritual at my funeral and bury him with some relic, guaranteeing my return to life? Father Hayes finally turned on a light inside and spoke again as Jackson tried to process such a possibility.

"I've never been a part of this before," he said slowly as he moved closer to Jackson to examine him. "There's only one way to know for sure. Come in, son."

Jackson was relieved to be invited in, even if he was considering that his reanimated state was because of his new host's doing. Regardless, he walked into the priest's house. Father Hayes closed the door behind the young man as he came in, never taking his eyes off him.

Jackson noticed that the priest made sure to keep a safe distance from him. Hayes pointed to a high-backed leather chair in his living room and gave a couple of grunts as he waved his finger. Jackson took his cue and made his way over to sit down.

"I will be right back, son. Please don't go anywhere," Father Hayes pleaded.

Where the fuck else would I go? Jackson wondered. He instead, just respectfully said, "Yes, Father." The priest hurried off to another room in his house.

After a few moments he returned to the living room.

"Okay, son, I've put something on my nightstand," said the priest. "Go into my room and bring it to me, please."

Jackson was completely confused. His face must have indicated as much.

"Just go get it for me, please."

"Um," Jackson stammered, "okay. Which room is your bedroom?"

57

"Only door on the left in the hall."

Jackson stood up and turned to head down the hall. He could hear everything in the house. His steps creaking the old hardwood floors. The humming of the electricity flowing through the wiring throughout. He could hear Father Hayes' labored breathing. He could hear the priest's accelerated heartbeat. The old man was nervous. He could feel the priest's eyes burning holes in his back as he entered the bedroom.

Hayes' room was simple. The only furniture in the room was a bed, a nightstand next to it with a reading lamp, and a dresser with a mirror on the opposite wall of the bed. Jackson could make everything out clearly enough, but then he realized he hadn't turned on the lights. He reached inside the door and flipped the switch. The room lit up.

He walked over to the nightstand and saw *two* things there, the priest's bible, and a rosary. Jackson wondered what kind of test this might be. Was he supposed to be inclined to grab one holy symbol over the other? If he brought Father the wrong one, would he undo the spell and re-kill him? Unsure Jackson just picked them both up and turned to leave the room. Before he did, though, he stood in front of the mirror.

This was the first time he had looked at himself since coming back from the dead. He could see how much the color had left his skin, because it was in contrast to the makeup the mortician had used to dress his face. He wiped most of it away with his coat's sleeve. He was completely intact, and only had a slight tinge of bluish gray to his skin. His lips looked a pale, purplish color. He ran his fingers through his hair. He thought it looked a little shaggy. But he kind of kept his hair like that anyway. At least they didn't

58

bury me with a bad haircut, he thought; I may be stuck with it for a while. It seemed to have lost a little of its color. No longer was it a rich, chocolate brown. It now resembled dirty dish water. As he examined himself, something was not quite right. He couldn't put his finger on it, but it was something. He moved closer to the mirror to get a better look.

Then he realized it. It was his eyes. They were as green, if not more, as they had been in life. With his eyes beaming so vividly out of their dead, lifeless sockets, he looked a little frightening even to himself.

"Having trouble, son?" Father Hayes shouted from the living room. Jackson jerked from the surprise and volume.

"Uh, no sir. I'll be right there." He put his vanity on hold as he walked back into the living room carrying the rosary and bible.

He held them in front of him as he said, "I didn't know which one you meant, so I got them both, Father." He handed them over.

Hayes' eyes grew wide and stayed on Jackson as he received them. "You're not a familiar. I don't believe it.

"A familiar?" asked Jackson. He thought hard about his response. His words came out slowly but clearly. "I'm Jackson Hughes, Father. I hope I'm familiar to you. I don't look that different, do I?"

"No, Jackson, I know who you are. But if you were just a familiar, then you wouldn't have been able to go into my room and bring me those things."

Jackson was completely confused. "What is a familiar?"

"A ghost, son. A ghost," Father Hayes said, his mouth never fully closing as he looked upon Jackson with wonder.

The thought that he was a ghost entered his head when he first started sensing the world again; but as time pressed on, and especially after he knew he was hearing all things from inside his coffin, Jackson *knew* he was alive and had to get back to the world he knew and loved.

The priest went on the further explain what he meant. "I sent you into my room for those things to see if I was right. While familiars can interact with the world of the living to some extent, they cannot go anywhere in death that they did not go in life. As far as I know, you never went into my room while you were alive…"

"No, sir. I didn't."

"Exactly! But you just went in there! You're not a familiar. It's really you, in the flesh. You've been reborn."

"Yes, Father, it's really me."

Father Hayes' demeanor relaxed. It seemed as though he were more afraid of a ghost than he was a zombie.

"I must ask, though, Jackson. Why me? Why did you come here instead of your house, or even a hospital for that matter?"

Jackson thought about telling him how he did think about going to those places. He thought about telling him he was certain he'd frighten his family into hysteria. He thought about being poked and prodded by countless doctors as they worked themselves into a frenzy trying to figure him out. Instead of trying to explain the whole thing, he simply pulled out the letter Hayes had written him and said, "You said you'd help me."

The old priest couldn't do anything but smile. "I guess I did, huh?"

Jackson spent the next few hours explaining his experiences to Father Hayes. He was surprised with his mental acuity and ability to recall every single detail. He told him about the inner voice driving him on, even if it was antagonistically. He talked about his heightened senses which led to him describing his unshakeable feeling of someone, or something, following him all the way to the priest's house. The priest would occasionally interrupt him and ask him to go into more depth about something, but for the most part, he just looked on and listened in amazement.

When he had finished telling Father Hayes about how bright his white house shone in the light of the moon, he said, "And then you let me in. And here I am."

"Yes, you are," the priest said. "You came back from the dead. You may have left it out, but, did the thought of final judgment frighten you? Is that what might have caused you to return?"

"I don't think I made it that far, Father." It was clear to Jackson that his priest was unaware the he had told him *everything* he could possibly remember.

"Well," Hayes continued, "you definitely seem yourself." He didn't seem to be telling Jackson everything he was thinking, like the old man was considering another possibility. A demon had possessed his corpse, perhaps. Because of the manner of his burial, in a crypt and not underground, it would be easy for a demonically reanimated Jackson to return and terrorize his loved ones.

"But I did say that I would help you. So I will." As Father Hayes spoke, the thought crossed Jackson's mind that the priest might begin performing an exorcism right there to be sure. But Father Hayes must have believed he had a way to either help him- if the boy he now saw really was Jackson returned- or to seek out and destroy the demon that had caused him to come out of his coffin. Jackson felt that the help Hayes was about to offer him was as just as much for the world of the living as it was for Jackson himself.

"Thank you, Father."

"There is someone I know that may be able to help you. His name is David Borbridge. He's a fellow Jesuit and a colleague of mine. He is better versed in these matters. If anyone can help you now, it would be him."

Jackson didn't like the idea of being pawned off to a complete stranger in his current state, but he wasn't really in a position to argue either. "Okay."

"Go to St. Joe's in the middle of campus and wait for him there. I will debrief him and send him that way shortly. You do remember how to get to the chapel, right?"

"Yes, sir." Jackson could remember going to St. Joseph's Chapel a few times for Mass. He tried to remember if he'd ever heard of a priest named Borbridge ever delivering the Mass.

"It's summertime. Most of the students are gone, so you shouldn't have to worry too much about bumping into anyone along the way."

Summertime! Jackson thought. That meant that all of his friends were back in town. Suddenly he didn't care as much at all about going to the church and waiting for some priest. He could only think about Meggie and all the other people he loved. He thought about Jon and the rest of the guys. He thought about his mom and his sister. Even in his current state, he couldn't help but long to see them. But that would have to wait until he at least got what help he could.

"Father Borbridge, right?" he asked.

"Yes. Just go wait in the chapel. I'll send him your way."

"Okay, Father." Jackson walked to the front door and opened it. Father Hayes followed behind him and made sure to close the door.

As Jackson walked away, he could feel the priest's gaze still upon him through one of the narrow windows that were on either side of the house's front door. The priest must have thought he was out of earshot, but even from a hundred yards away, Jackson clearly heard Father Hayes lock the door behind him.

The road that led up the hill to St. Joseph's was a lot like Old Shell Rd. Oak trees on either side blocked out most of the fluorescent light from the lights in the student parking lots. The well lit façade of the church slowly came into view as Jackson made his way up the steep incline.

That feeling was back. That terrible feeling that he was being pursued. But this time it felt hostile. Whatever it was, it was not only following him, but he felt like it wanted to catch him. Jackson accelerated his pace.

When he walked faster, the feeling grew stronger. He was getting close to the front doors of the church. The feeling was bearing down on him, so he decided to do something he hadn't done in a long time. With all the memories of Coach Tolbert's wind sprints, all the soccer games, and all the late nights running along the beaches of Dauphin Island with Meggie swirling in his head, Jackson commanded his undead body to flee to the sanctuary of the church. He began running.

It felt awkward, and his body wasn't quite in step with his mind, but he was running. He wasn't sure he was running as fast as he had in life. It would get him to the church faster than walking, though. It was the first time he had ever run and not felt and heard his blood pumping in his ears. It made the air he was cutting through seem that much more audible. None of this made the feeling go away, though.

He slowed to a jog when he was within feet of the church steps. He was back down to a walk when he was ready to step inside.

THUD!

Jackson felt something hit him from his right side. He could hear loud cracking sounds coming from inside him as it laid into him. He could only assume that those sounds were his ribs being cracked. The blow was powerful enough to lift him off the ground and send him flying. He landed about thirty feet away from the front of the church on some steps that were built into a hill and led down to the school's library. Upon landing he heard a similar cracking sound as his neck whipped and his head smacked the concrete. Feeling no pain but afraid to move, Jackson lay perfectly still. All he could feel was whatever had hit him slowly coming his way.

8

Foster's Blue Tahoe was cruising down Airport Boulevard in Mobile with the windows down. Chad was riding shotgun, while Jon, Meggie, and Ryan filled up the back seat. They were on their way to pick up Paul from his house. Though school had been out for a few weeks, this was the first time Meggie had gone out with the boys since they all got home. Foster usually sped everywhere he drove, but they seemed to be catching every single stoplight on the busy street.

"I thought you said Emily was gonna be in town, Meg." Chad sounded disappointed.

"She is," Meggie replied. "She's on her way, I promise. She just sent me a text that said she was on I-65."

"That's a really long road," Chad said dejectedly.

"Relax, dude. She'll be here. She'd probably be texting you instead of me if you'd have made a move at Auburn when you were seein' her every day." Foster had clearly embarrassed him. Chad's face turned a rosy shade of pink.

"Good to see some things don't change," Ryan said, trying to lighten the mood. "Chad's still not Mr.

Ladies' Man, and Foster, you're still an ass." The carpool shared a laugh.

"So what's new in Mob-town anyway?" Meggie asked as she looked back and forth between Jon and Ryan.

"Oh, not too much. Same ole city, we just go to college now." Jon wasn't much for information.

"Yeah, I mean some of the college parties are cool. But mostly we just go to class and stuff." Ryan wasn't much help, either.

"Well, y'all don't have football season like we do in Auburn!" Foster's excitement caused him to run a red light, but fortunately, no police noticed.

"Yeah that gave us a lot to do during the fall," Meggie said. "What do y'all do for fun nowadays?"

"Well me and Ryan go play disc golf on the weekends usually," Jon said as he pointed across Meggie at Ryan, clumsily clipping the tip of her nose as he drew his hand back.

Meggie rubbed her nose and asked, "What about Paul? What's he up to these days?"

"I dunno. Ask Ryan. He's the only one that ever really sees him anymore." Jon was obviously upset with Paul about it.

"Oh, so is there a big cross-town rivalry between South Alabama and Spring Hill?" Meggie asked jokingly.

"No," Ryan said. "Nothing like that. Me and Jon still hang out. Paul just got some new friends and doesn't really hang out with us much anymore. Hell, I'm surprised y'all got him to agree to come out tonight!"

Meggie smiled. "That's because I texted him and said I'd kick his butt if he didn't."

"Oooooohhhhh," Ryan drew out the syllable. "That's why. You better watch out, Meg. You wanna talk about a ladies' man? Paul's a pimp at Spring Hill."

"What?!" Chad, Foster, and Meggie exclaimed in unison. Jon remained silent, but looked a little surprised too.

Of all of their friends, Paul was the last any of them would've picked to be super successful with the opposite sex. Even Jon, the hairy, mountain of a teenager had more charm and charisma than he did. Paul was just awkward with girls.

"Oh yeah," Ryan went on. "The girls at Spring Hill can't get enough of him, Alex, and Ben."

"I'm guessing Alex and Ben are the 'new friends' you are talking about," Chad deduced.

"Are they in a fraternity or something?" Foster asked. "Frat dudes get stupid amounts of girls up at Auburn."

"No, he didn't join a fraternity. The girls just love them." Ryan said it as though he had accepted the fact a long time ago.

"Well I'll be the judge of that. He's still goofy, awkward-around-girls Paul in my head." Meggie was reluctant to believe college could've changed him that much.

Jon decided to change the subject. He was finally about to actually hang out with Paul for the first time since school started. He didn't want to think about it too much, or he'd just get mad at him all over again. He turned around and lifted the lid on the cooler that was in the back of the SUV.

"Who wants a beer?"

Meggie raised her hand. Ryan just turned around and grabbed one for himself. Foster said "me."

Chad looked at him as if he were crazy. "Dude, you're driving down Airport. Have you lost your mind?" Just then Foster pulled his vehicle to the side of the road and stopped.

"Fine, I won't drive. You will. Chinese fire drill!" Foster yelled as he opened his door and stepped out. Passers by were speeding by and honking their horns at him as he ran around to Chad's door on the passenger side. Chad just rolled his eyes, crawled into the driver's seat, and closed Foster's door before it got ripped off by oncoming traffic. Foster stepped in and Chad merged back into the cars driving down Airport Blvd.

"Now, Jon. Give me a damn beer," Foster said with a huge grin on his face.

Jon just shook his head and said "same old Foster" as he handed his friend a can of beer from the cooler.

They finally arrived at Paul's house. He lived with his parents in a house in a big subdivision. The teens lowered their beer cans as they pulled into his driveway. It wasn't necessary, though. They wouldn't have to go inside or even deal with parental units. Paul was waiting for them in his yard.

Meggie immediately noticed something different about him. He was walking differently. He had an air of confidence about him as he made his way to Foster's truck. He ran his fingers through his short, blond hair as he walked. He was almost strutting like all eyes were on him as he passed through the beam of the headlights. They might not have been, but Meggie's were for sure.

He walked up to Ryan's window and peered in,

locking his piercing hazel eyes with Meggie's for longer than simply a moment. Then he spoke. "Any room for me in there?"

"Oh I'm sure we can squeeze you in," Meggie chattered back. She twitched a little and wrinkled her forehead. Was she flirting with Paul?!

Paul gave her a big smile as he stared into her eyes for another moment. Then he laughed and said, "Well alright then, I'm coming in."

"Fuck that, dude, I'm not ridin' bitch!" Ryan proclaimed. "I'm not getting' all claustrophobic in the middle. I'm sittin' by the window." Ryan got out and held the door. He directed Paul into the Tahoe with his hand as if he were a chauffeur. Paul did a little curtsy, to mock him, and climbed in next to Meggie.

Ryan squeezed himself into the seat. They were now four-wide in a seat designed for three. "Think thin. Especially you, Jon."

"Oh, piss off!" the big guy said defensively. He might have said more, but grunted when he was cut short and further cramped when Ryan closed the door.

They had barely gotten back onto Airport Blvd. when Jon had had enough. "Alright, screw this! Meggie, get in somebody's lap."

Meggie laughed at him. She looked at Paul, and he shrugged his shoulders. She gave him a little smile and hopped onto his lap.

Paul put his hands on either side of her waist and readjusted her. His touching her made Meggie jump. "Jesus, Paul, your hands are freezing!"

"Yeah my bad. My mom keeps it cold as shit in that house. That's why I was outside when y'all pulled up."

"Oh, I was wondering about that." Meggie

turned around and looked at Paul. He was a *lot* cuter than she remembered. Confidence looked pretty good on him.

"So where the Hell are we goin', anyway?" Paul asked.

"Florida Bowl," Chad answered. "All-night bowling, biyatch!"

"Oh, sweet, so we'll just eat there? They have awesome French fries." Paul made a smacking sound with his mouth.

Aside from some singing along to a few songs, everyone was pretty quiet for the rest of the ride. Meggie had intended on asking him about Alex and Ben, and why he ditched Jon and Ryan. But she was comfortable just sitting in his lap. The rest of the guys were quiet because they were just glad to be hanging out with their friend again.

Florida Bowl was named such because it was located on Florida Street in midtown Mobile. The bowling alley's parking lot was packed. The nights with all-night bowling were by far the establishment's most profitable. When they finally found a parking spot, Chad, Meggie, and Paul got out.

"What are you guys doin'? Get out," Meggie commanded.

"We'll be in there in a minute, babe. We got some more beer to drink," Ryan said.

"Yeah, they both wear elevens, I wear a twelve." Foster took another gulp of beer and opened a new can as he continued. "Tell 'em we got seven, and get our shoes." He then went back to his beer.

"Sometimes I think my friends can't function unless they have alcohol in their system," Chad said and shook his head.

"I know what you mean, Chad. They're ridiculous." Meggie looked back at the Tahoe like a disappointed parent.

Paul scoffed at Meggie. "Who are you foolin', girl? I smelled a little on you in the backseat, too."

"Well, yes, I like a few every now and then. But I'm not as bad as *them*," she said as she pointed back toward Foster's SUV. "And what about you, Paul. I noticed you didn't reach into the cooler as soon as you got in. Don't tell me you're a teetotaler like Chad here."

"Heyyyy, now. Don't judge my lifestyle," Chad said with a grin.

"Nah, I'm not on the wagon or anything. I just don't see the need to drink *all* the time."

"Good. Me neither." Meggie was really liking this new Paul. Just then, her cell phone rang with the ringtone she had designated for Emily. She answered.

"Hey, girl. Where you at?"

"How the Hell do I get to this bowling alley? I'm on this abomination you people call 'Airport.'"

Meggie laughed. "Okay, well just stay on it until you see Florida Street, then turn left. You'll see the bowling alley."

"Never mind. Got it. See you in a second." Emily hung up without saying goodbye. She always did that.

"That was Emily, Chad," Meggie said, poking him in the side. "See, I told you she was coming. Let's wait for her. I think she just turned onto Florida."

After a few minutes, they saw Emily pull up in her car. She drove an old, black Dodge Dart. It fit her broody, goth persona perfectly. She spotted Foster's

SUV and parked right next to it.

She got out of her car and pulled out her phone, before she could dial Meggie's number again, she saw them waving at her from across the parking lot. She quickened her pace a little as she walked over and met them.

Meggie noticed that Emily had dressed up for the occasion. She was wearing a little jewelry, some rings and a necklace, and some make-up. The slight hint of blush and red lipstick went well with her pale skin and jet-black ponytail. She had even sprayed a little perfume on herself, Meggie noticed. Emily spoke the unspoken language of girls with a single glance to her friend. The glance asked, "How do I look?"

Meggie gave her a smile and tilted her head a little, which Emily knew meant, "You look great, now tell me what you think of Paul."

Emily hadn't made her mind up, apparently, because she chose to involve the boys and communicate with words. "What's up everybody? Y'all ready to get whipped?"

Paul raised an eyebrow. "Are you serious?"

"Hell, yes, I'm serious!"

He laughed. "Well brace yourself, because we're all pretty decent. We used to come here all the time in high school. I'm Paul, by the way."

"Yes, I've heard about you. I feel like I already know all of Meggie's Mobile friends. I'm Emily." Emily extended her hand. Paul shook it obligingly. "But seriously, I can bowl."

"A little friendly competition. I like it!" Chad tried to share some eye contact with Emily, but he shook his head and looked away as soon as she looked back.

The guys walked together a little ahead of the girls who had slowed down a bit to whisper.

"I saw that look Chad tried to give to you, girl," Meggie murmured, nudging Emily with her shoulder. "When are you two gonna quit messing around and just get together?"

"I don't know. But he's gonna have to make the first move. I don't do well with rejection. And besides, he's supposed to be the one to ask me."

Paul looked over his shoulder with a smile. He looked over to Chad and began his own whispering. Meggie couldn't hear them.

"Oh my God, Em, I think they heard us." She didn't know how they would have been able to, but it appeared that way. And her new- worried whisper- was much more audible. Just then Paul grabbed Chad by the arm and stopped walking right before they were about to open the door to the bowling alley.

"Chad, bro." Paul was speaking aloud. He wanted to make sure the girls were in on the conversation. "I know Ms. Emily here is Meggie's friend, but I'm pretty sure she came down here to see you."

Emily's and Chad's faces both flushed with embarrassment.

"Now," he went on, "Me and Meg are goin' inside to get the lane. You two sort this out." He grabbed Meggie's hand with one hand, and opened the door with the other. As the two entered the bowling alley he said "fill us in later" without ever turning around.

There was an awkward moment of silence as the two shuffled their feet and looked down at the ground. Finally Chad decided to speak.

"So did you-"

"Yes," Emily interrupted.

"So... Does that mean you want to-"

"Yes." She interrupted again.

"Okay, then." Chad smiled. "Well can I, uh, hug you or something?"

Emily burst out laughing and threw her arms around him. "Wow, you really are shy, aren't you? Don't worry, I was a little scared too. It's not how I wanted to have this conversation, but whatever."

The new couple decided to wait for the other three to finish drinking and go in as a group. It seemed to be the least awkward choice at the moment.

While Paul and Meggie waited in line to pay for the lane, they began to catch up.

"So what's with the new you, Paul?" Meggie asked.

"What do you mean? I'm still the same old me."

Meggie scoffed. "Yeah, right. You used to be awkward. Even around me! And now I think you just helped hook two of my friends up."

"Oh, that?" Paul gave a wide grin. Meggie returned the gesture. "That was nothin.' You're a terrible whisperer, and it looked like they both needed a shove in the direction they wanted to go in the first place."

"Uh, huh," Meggie raised an eyebrow in disbelief. "Well what about what Ryan told me about you? Say's you're a little flirty player over on the Hill. That's not same old Paul."

"Well how would you know? No one ever had a shot with you in high school."

Meggie thought of Jackson. She remembered how it was when he was around. No one else *did* have a shot. But that was over. Right now all she could think about was Paul. He was no longer one of her boyfriend's cute buddies. He was smooth, confident, sexy Paul.

Meggie didn't realize that her thinking about the new possibilities produced a lull in the conversation. But Paul did.

"Look, I didn't mean anything by that. You know I loved Jackson. He was my boy."

"No it's okay," Meggie replied. "It sucks, but there's nothing we can do about it now. I know he'd want me to be happy."

"Well," he asked, "are you?"

Meggie stared into his eyes and smiled. "Yeah, I think I might be."

There exchange of looks was interrupted by the old man behind them. "Hey, love birds? Move up." They hadn't noticed that it was their turn to pay.

Paul handled the transaction. He paid for the lane and everyone's shoes. He even got everyone's shoe size right. He gave Meggie hers and carried all the others over to their lane.

Meggie took her shoes off and slipped on the god-awful red and white bowling shoes. She finished lacing them up while she watched Paul enter everybody's names into the lane's computer. She hadn't looked at someone like this since Jackson.

Just then, the rest of the group showed up. They had already stopped at the racks and picked out the balls they wanted to bowl with. Jon, Ryan, and Foster were red-faced and had silly smiles on their faces. Their mission to get drunk had clearly been accomplished. Jon plopped down beside Meggie and put his big arm around her.

"I love you, Meg. I just wanted you to know that."

Meggie lifted his arm off her shoulder and smiled as she pat his hand. "Aww, I love you too, big guy. Is someone a little drunk?" Jon winked and held his thumb and index finger about an inch apart.

Paul passed out the shoes to everyone and waited for them to get them on their feet. "Okay, y'all, I got everybody set up. Emily, I put you first since you think you're so good."

Emily stood up slowly and self-assured. She didn't say anything. She simply walked up to the lane and threw her ball. Strike. Emily sat back down.

"Damn," Paul said as he scratched his head.

After six frames, it was clear that Emily was better than the rest of them by far. Ryan was terrible, and Foster got a warning from the Florida Lanes to stop tossing the bowling balls like shot put. Paul was the only person even close to her on the scoreboard. That's when it happened.

Ryan saw him come in. He rolled his eyes and mumbled, "Damn it."

Meggie and Jon heard him. They both leaned their heads to the side and mouthed "what?"

It was Paul's turn to bowl. Ryan leaned into the rest of the party that was seated and pointed toward the entrance. "It's Alex. Jesus, how does he always find Paul when he's not with them?" The others turned to see a tall kid with long brown hair. He had it pulled back into a loose ponytail. He was walking with the same confidence that Paul did,

Meggie thought.

"Uh, they're friends. Paul prolly told him where he was." Meggie was taking up for him.

"Yeah, I bet that's it," Chad said. He was trying to diffuse Ryan's apparent hostility toward Paul's new friend.

"Whatever." Ryan leaned back and crossed his arms. His face was now redder than his hair.

Paul finished bowling his spare and turned around smiling. Then he caught sight of Alex, who had stopped short of coming to their lane, but still faced them.

Paul's smile faded a little. He never took his eyes off of Alex, but told his friends, "Hang on just a second, guys. Lemme see what Alex wants. He looks serious." Paul walked over to him.

Paul's back was to them as he spoke with his other friend, but Meggie could see Alex's face. It had a definite look of concern on it.

"Twenty bucks says he ditches us," Ryan said. He still had his arms crossed and was intentionally looking in the opposite direction of Paul and Alex.

Shortly after that Paul turned to Meggie and the others. Alex kept his distance and just looked on from afar, but after they briefly exchanged words, Paul returned to the group.

"I'm really sorry, guys. But I gotta go."

Ryan chuckled sarcastically under his breath as Meggie asked, "What's wrong?"

"Alex's uncle is sick. He's gonna go and see him. I wouldn't go, but Alex is really close to him, and I think he needs someone."

"Whatever, dude." Ryan still wasn't convinced.

"No, that's sweet. He's your friend," Meggie

said. "If you wanna be there for him that's fine."

"Thanks for understanding," Paul said.

"Yeah it's cool." Foster didn't seem bothered one way or the other about the matter.

"As long you accept defeat," demanded Emily. "It's a forfeit. You lose."

Paul smiled. "Fine, as long as we have a rematch at some point."

"Deal."

Before he left, Paul leaned down and kissed Meggie, who was sitting down, on the cheek. "Good seeing you, Meg. We'll have to catch up some more later."

Meggie looked up at him when he leaned back up. He stared right back at her. "Yeah, I'd like that." Paul rejoined Alex and they left the bowling alley.

Ryan decided to turn his gaze back to his friends, now that Alex wouldn't have to be in his periphery. "Told you."

"Yeah, but did you see him?" Meggie asked. "Even if Alex wasn't telling the truth, Paul obviously believed him."

"I know that's what I'm worried about. He just believes and does whatever they say. Whatever. Fuck it. It's my turn." Ryan picked up his ball and walked over to attempt to bowl away his resentment toward his buddy's new "friends."

9

Jackson was afraid to move. He was afraid he might begin to feel the pain that was supposed to come with broken ribs and a fractured skull. He was afraid that he had cheated Death long enough, and it had finally come for him. Most of all, though, he was afraid that his attacker wasn't done with him.

As he lay motionless, he discovered that it wasn't a 'what' that had hit him, but a 'who.' Jackson could hear the person's footsteps echoing off the façade of the church. The sound grew closer and closer with each step. They were coming for him!

The attacker was about halfway to him when Jackson heard the sound of what he could tell was four girls. He could hear fast footsteps moving in the direction of the attacker. He only heard four different voices, but if there were more, he couldn't know for sure. Looking in the direction of their voices would've required turning his head. He was too afraid. For some reason, he believed he was safer the less he did anything. Am I really *playing* dead? He thought.

"Are you taking classes this summer?" one of the girls asked the attacker.

"Yes." The assailant was definitely a guy. "I am." Judging by his speech, Jackson's attacker clearly didn't feel like greeting and entertaining the girls' little chitchat. He was much more interested in pulverizing the zombie.

"That's awesome!" another girl exclaimed. "Well, we all are, too. We were headed to the coffee shop in the student center. What about you?"

"Oh, sweet. Me too. Let's go! They have the best biscotti. I just can't get enough of it." The guy's tone changed from perturbed and distracted to quite friendly. Asking the girls if they wanted to watch him pummel a corpse must not have been the best choice.

Jackson listened to them walk away from him. He could tell when his attacker turned his attention toward the girls. That dark, piercing feeling went away. That same feeling that he had when he was walking the entire way from the crypt to Father Hayes'. Jackson was convinced this guy that attacked him was the same person following him from the cemetery.

The sounds of their footsteps and voices as they talked grew fainter until he heard a door open and close. He gathered that they had made their way to the student center. It was time to get up.

His first movement was sitting up, just a little. He wanted to remain low to the ground for now. He wanted to make sure no one else was around before he got up to walk to the church again. He looked around. He didn't see anyone. Time to get up.

As he rose to his feet, he stumbled and nearly lost his balance completely. He had focused too long on remaining perfectly still that some of his body was apparently still trying to do it.

Jackson's side didn't feel any different to him. There was no pain. He reached to touch the back of his head where it bounced off the concrete. He ran his hand down a small crack at the point of impact; the crack appeared to be seeping.

It felt wet, thick, and kind of oily. Jackson panicked. His brain was the only thing he was sure that was actually working in his new life. The thought that his brains might now be leaking out of the back of his head frightened him. He wasn't ready to die again. Jackson wiped the purplish liquid on his pants and headed toward St. Joe's. He was going as fast as he could go, but with his second death permeating his every thought, he found it harder to make his body obey. As a result, he wasn't going as fast as he could have.

The doors were unlocked. As he walked in, he wondered if he might burst into flames or turn to dust for being some kind of unholy abomination. Neither happened. In the back on the church was a large marble basin filled with holy water. What could that do to a zombie? Whether or not he was worried about burning or evaporating, habit took over when the Catholic schoolboy was back in the chapel. He dipped two fingers in the basin and made the sign of the cross as he genuflected and took a seat in the last pew.

He almost immediately made the sign of the cross again and started to pray.

He prayed for his head. How it would heal or be okay, Jackson had no idea. But he wasn't in a position to pray for just the rational. He prayed for his family and friends. He prayed for Meggie, especially. He wanted more than anything for her to be safe and happy. He prayed for understanding of his new life. Just then he heard one of the front doors behind him creak open. He didn't turn around to look. When he didn't feel that piercing feeling of his attacker's stare burning into his back, though, Jackson quickly wrapped up his prayer and put his face into his hands. If it wasn't the priest he was waiting for, he didn't want to scare anyone else away from the church.

"Jackson?" asked a deep, booming, yet welcoming voice.

He turned around to face the voice, as he was now sure it was the Father Borbridge Hayes told him he would send. "Yes, Father Borbridge?"

He looked upon a giant of a man. He was well over six-and-a-half feet tall with a substantial frame. The priest had slicked back gray hair, that was more salt than pepper, and a bushy beard that was almost completely white. He wasn't wearing any priestly vestments. Instead, he wore a tan button-down, short sleeved shirt with matching slacks. It looked like a dress shirt, but it was extra long and had six pockets down the front. He was also wearing socks and sandals. He was the most oddly dressed priest Jackson had ever seen.

"Oh, my-" Father Borbridge cut himself off as he looked on the boy through his glasses with awestruck eyes.

"Thanks." Jackson wondered if anyone would ever look at him like a person again instead of a circus sideshow. Maybe that was too much to ask.

"Oh, I'm sorry. I didn't mean to be so rude. It's just that Gerald told me all about you, but I couldn't believe it. Seeing it for myself is just a new experience for me. You're the real thing."

"Yeah, I guess I am."

"Well, I have so much I would like to know. But that's not why we're here. Gerald sent me to you so I could help *you*. So, how can I help you? What would you like to know?"

Father Borbridge spoke fast and excitedly. He didn't sound or act like any old priest Jackson had ever met. He seemed more like a young, talkative man who hadn't been allowed to speak for a while.

Jackson wondered where to begin. "Everything! Why did this happen to me? *How* did this happen to me?" He thought about telling him about the attack, but decided to wait until he had answers to the more basic questions.

"Okay, Okay. It'll be alright. I will try to give you some answers." Jackson felt genuinely comforted by the priest's words.

"Yes, sir."

"Now- what is your most pressing question?"

"Why?" Jackson pleaded, "Why am I back from the dead?"

"Well that's simple," Father Borbridge said. "You simply refused to die. You exist by sheer will alone. Your love of life outweighs death."

Jackson tried to think of any other question that mattered. "Why did Father Hayes think me coming back was his fault?"

"Well, because he thought you were a familiar. That's why he tested you to see if you were."

"What does me being a zombie or a ghost have to do with it being his fault?" Jackson made sure to say "ghost" instead of "familiar." Zombies and ghosts just sounded better than "reborn" and "familiars."

Borbridge readjusted his glasses and cleared his throat. "Familiars- ghosts, are almost always suicide cases. Because of their disregard for the great gift of life, their punishment is to continue to roam the world of the living... being in it, but not being able to experience it anymore. He thought it was his fault because, familiars usually 'haunt' the people that led them to want to take their own lives in the first place."

"So, I'm guessing ghosts are more common than zombies."

"Oh, definitely yes. You are the first Reborn case I've ever seen personally. And after a year. That is simply astounding."

Jackson thought about other people that might have been reborn, others that might not have been as lucky as he. He thought about others that might be buried in the ground, trapped in coffins, but as alive again as he was now. They beat death but most likely had to willingly submit to it again just to avoid eternity in confined darkness. The idea of such torture horrified him.

He tried to put it out of his mind and went back to questioning the priest. "How is it that I'm not more, uh- um, dead looking?"

"You mean, how come it's been so long and you are still so well preserved?"

"Yeah." Borbridge had a way of putting Jackson's question so that it sounded a little better.

"Well morticians' embalming procedures and the fluids they use to preserve corpses get better and better all the time. But the main reason you are in such good shape considering is *you*."

"Me?" Jackson asked. He was confused.

Father Borbridge tried to better explain. "There aren't a lot of theories on this one. It's simple, though. It goes back to your will to live. People in your situation have taken the Lord's greatest gift, life, and refuse to yield it to anyone or anything. Your rate of healing is directly proportional to your will to persist on this world at all."

It did sound pretty simple to Jackson. I'm here because I willed it so, he thought. He rubbed the back of his head again. There was no more liquid than had been there before. He tried to feel around for the leaky spot that had cracked upon when he was attacked. No more leak. Whatever had closed it up, Jackson was relieved. I'll continue to be here as long as I have the will to carry on. Jackson wondered if he would have the willpower to do that. He also wondered what the point of sticking around would be.

"Well do I have any weaknesses?" Jackson was a little unnerved by any of the priest's knowledge about the undead and even more so by Borbridge's calmness in the face of a zombie!

Borbridge chuckled and said, "I'm sure you've already figured out your biggest one."

"Excuse me?"

"The living." Jackson gave him an acknowledging half-smile. "The Reborn aren't really allowed to just go right back into their loved ones' lives. Not only do you look like you do- uh-"

"Dead?" Jackson said. He had accepted it. He didn't mind if others said it.

The priest continued. "Yes, not only do you look dead, but you will never age. If you returned to the land of the living, not only would you watch others around you grow old and die, but they would also watch you stay the same. People don't really like immortal. It tends to make people jealous or angry. Maybe that's why Jesus left town shortly after he came back."

"What, Father?! Jesus?" The idea of Jesus Christ being a zombie was mildly humorous, but felt a tad blasphemous to Jackson as he heard it so matter-of-factly implied by a priest.

"Well, yes. I'm sure you know the story. I don't know of a better documented case of a Reborn. If Jesus wasn't a zombie, I don't know who could've been."

"Well at least I'm in good company." He wasn't completely comfortable with 'Night of the Living Jesus,' but it at least seemed plausible in his current condition. "Well, do I have any other weaknesses?"

"As far as we know, only consumption by fire or decapitation can destroy a Reborn that can heal at its fastest rate. A blazing-hot fire has the ability to burn faster than they can repair."

"'Kay. Fire bad. Got it. But what's with all this 'we' and 'theories' talk? Who is 'we?'"

"Ha ha ha." Borbridge laughed. "Why, the Catholic Church of course. There are certain orders in the church dedicated to research in such subjects."

"Well," Jackson said, "I'll worry about church conspiracies later. What should I do as a new zombie, Father?"

"For now, you should stay in the church. Down in the basement. Only priests and servers ever really go down there, and the priest is usually me. It's big enough that you can hide if someone besides me comes down there, too. And I want you to take this."

Father Borbridge reached into one of his many shirt pockets and pulled out a rosary made completely of silver. It felt heavy in Jackson's palm when he received it. "What's this for?"

"God will protect you, son. Dead people can pray too. Just wear it around your neck if you don't feel the need."

"Okay."

"Well, Jackson, I am going to get some sleep. It's one of those things you have to have when you're living. I will be back to check on you first thing tomorrow." Borbridge placed his hand on Jackson's shoulder. "Do you think you'll be alright?"

Jackson pulled the rosary over his head and straightened it. He held its cross as the beads lay across his chest like a necklace. "I'm already dead. What's the worst that could happen?"

10

Meggie had been mind-numbingly flipping through the channels on her family's living room TV ever since she and Emily returned from the bowling alley. She had to do something to keep herself entertained. Emily was completely consumed with her telephone, which had not ceased chirping repeatedly since she was out of Chad's sight.

"What could you two possibly have to talk that much about?" Meggie asked.

"Gimme a break, Meg. Me and Chad have been dancing around each other all year long. We got a lot of I-almost-said-something-then times to discuss."

"Whatever." Meggie smiled at her lovestruck friend as she arose from the sofa and made her way into the kitchen. "I'm getting some water from the fridge. You want anything?"

Emily never took her eyes off her phone as she typed her latest message to Chad and told Meggie "Yeah, sure" simultaneously.

Meggie walked into the kitchen. She could feel the change from warm, soft carpet to cool hardwood beneath her feet, even through her socks, as she entered. She was feeling sort of carefree and playful, so she did a very animated slide across to the double-door refrigerator. Meggie misjudged the force needed, and her shoulder knocked off a couple magnets and a picture. She couldn't help but giggle at her childish behavior and resulting mishap. Before picking up what had fallen, she went for what she came for and grabbed a bottled water from the fridge. But when she closed the refrigerator door, she gazed down and her heart sank. The magnets were irrelevant, but the picture stopped her in her tracks.

Staring straight up at her was Jackson. It was a picture of him and Meggie's little sister that had been taken during the Thanksgiving holidays, the last one before he passed away. As far as she could remember, it was also the last *picture* taken of him. She remembered the conversation she had had with her mother about keeping it on the refrigerator. As Meggie peered into the photo, he seemed to be looking right back at her. His green eyes pierced through the glossy photo and into the real world, landing upon Meggie. Immediately all those feelings, thoughts, and memories that Paul seemed to be capable of driving away came rushing back. She put the picture back on the fridge along with the magnets. No sliding exit. Just a sober walk.

Meggie's mood change must have been written on her. Emily took one look at her and asked, "Jesus, what happened in there? Did the refrigerator call you fat?"

Meggie forced a half-smile for her friend's little joke, but it was clear that it was insincere.

"What's wrong, Meg? Tell me."

Meggie crossed her arms and averted her gaze.

She was certain that Emily was getting sick of having to deal with the "bad days." As her roommate, Emily not only lent her ear and shoulder when it got bad, she also had the bad days thrust upon her when she didn't even volunteer.

"I know all that that you're doing right there," said Emily. "It's about Jackson, ain't it?" She didn't sound like she was sick of it at all. Her tone was that of a truly sympathetic friend.

"Yeah." Meggie looked at her friend, relieved Emily hadn't asked her to change the record.

"Well at least these past few times, you haven't broken down in tears the way you used to," Emily said optimistically. "That's an improvement, right."

"Oh, yes, definitely." Meggie paused for a moment to formulate her feelings into words. "I mean I know he's gone, and he's never coming back. But I know the feelings that I had for him were so real and so strong. Honestly, I saw his picture on our fridge just now, and I felt guilty for having a happy, carefree time tonight out with Paul and everybody."

Emily raised an eyebrow. She was a little more perceptive than the average co ed. "Notice how you just said that. You don't feel guilty because you had a good time with everyone tonight. You feel guilty because of what you felt or thought about *Paul* tonight."

Having it said out loud like that made it real for Meggie. That was the real reason for her guilt. She asked, "Is that bad?"

"No," said Emily, "I think a certain amount of guilt for having those kinds of feelings for somebody new is natural. I mean, you've told me how serious you and Jackson were. But I also don't think he would've wanted you to just be sad forever, either. You're not betraying his memory or anything by feeling for someone else."

"Yeah, but what if the situation were switched around, huh?" Meggie asked. "What if it had been me that died, and Jackson wanted to date one of my friends. What would that mean?"

"Well, from what I can tell," Emily smiled, "that would make him gay, because I honestly think I might be your first female friend."

Meggie was grateful for the levity, but quickly returned to the question at hand. "You know what I mean. I'm serious. I get that eventually I will have to move on, but my next move being into his friend's arms?! Is that cool?"

Emily shrugged. "It's really your call, Meg. But, try and look at it like this: Jackson would want you happy, right?"

"Right."

"And Paul was Jackson's friend, right?"

"Yeah. Duh."

"So if the real question is about disrespecting his memory, then this is the best thing to do. You can be happy, and Paul, if he also respects Jackson's memory, will treat you right."

After taking a little while to process her friend's advice, Meggie smiled a little and deflected with a rhetorical question. "How come you can give such good advice and still go a whole year without doing a single thing with your own situation with Chad?"

"Oh, don't you make this about me, skank," Emily said playfully as she bobbed her head back and forth. "I got my man." The two shared a laugh.

"Speaking of," said Meggie, "I haven't heard your phone go off in a few. Did he fall asleep on ya?"

"Nah, I told him I had to go as soon as I saw that look on your face. I could tell I was needed."

"Well, thanks a lot." Meggie paused for a bit. "Soooo... what do you think of Paul, anyway?"

"Ugh!" Emily exclaimed. "I knew you were gonna ask me that eventually. Just kidding."

"Well?"

"He's alright, I guess."

Meggie was surprised. Emily must not have seen the same Paul she had. "Alright" was insufficient. But then again, Meggie thought, her friend had not felt his strong hands toss her into his lap. She had not looked into his eyes. She had not felt his cool lips on her cheek.

"Just, alright?" Meggie asked.

"Yeah. Not for me, but you obviously dig him. And that's what matters, right?"

Meggie did not seem as reassured as she thought she would have been. Emily could tell.

"Put it this way, Meg: I do not object. Have fun."

Meggie figured that was as good a blessing as she was going to get from her friend, so she just said, "Thanks, Em."

"No problem. Can we please go to sleep now?" she asked.

"Sure."

The two girls made their way to Meggie's bedroom. Her king size bed was more than big enough for the two of them. Emily turned out the lights and, not bothering with pajamas, tucked herself in comfortably on one side. Meggie took a little time to get dressed for bed and changed into sleep clothes. Then she crawled into the other side of the bed. As Meggie was placing her cell phone on her nightstand, a fluorescent glow came from the other side of the bed. She turned over to see Emily texting "good night :)" to Chad.

"Oh, brother," Meggie said.

"Don't judge me, skank."

***

The next morning, Meggie awoke alone in her bed. The digital clock on her nightstand indicated it was almost noon. She didn't care where Emily had wandered off to, she was just grateful that she had let her sleep in.

After lying in the bed sleeplessly for about ten minutes, Meggie rose up and kicked her way out from underneath the bed's thick lavender comforter. Just then, she heard Emily and her sister, Maria, in the living room. She got up and joined them.

"Whoa, Sissy! Somebody put a bird nest on your head!" Maria, who was a miniature replica of Meggie, didn't waste any time laying into her big sister. Emily just burst out laughing.

"Laugh it up. You're next. Maria don't play favorites when it comes to insults."

"But she's sooo funny, dude! She's had me rollin' since I got up." Emily was still giggling

Meggie sighed. "Whatever. She's like that because she always hangs out with my friends. She don't like hanging out with people her own age."

"That's 'cuz they're lame." Maria's defense brought a laugh to both of the other girls.

"Oh, by the way, Meg," Emily said. "Check your phone. I think Paul sent you, like, four text messages."

Meggie smiled a little and began making her way back to her bedroom to retrieve her phone. Then she stopped and spun around and looked at an equally smiley Emily. "How do you know they're from Paul, huh?"

"What?" she asked, pretending she didn't hear.

"How do you know?"

"Huh?"

"Ugh! Never mind." As Meggie continued to her room, she could hear Emily yell a drawn out "Love youuuu!"

Just as Emily had said, Meggie had four texts from Paul. The first three were sent not too long after she and Emily had called it a night. She scrolled through them.

Sorry I had to bolt like that.

I'll have to catch back up with you later. Maybe tomorrow?

I hope ur not mad at me. I was just tryin to be there for a friend.

The last one, however, was sent pretty recently, almost right before she woke up.

Hey I feel real bad about ditchin yall last night.

Esp u. any way I can make it up to u?

Meggie hadn't had a guy come after her like this for a while. At least she hoped it meant he was coming after her. After all, they were friends all through high school, and Paul was one of Jackson's closest friends. Maybe she was reading too much into the texts. He might have sent all of the guys similar texts, apologizing for leaving on the first time they'd all gotten together in a while. But then again, he did say especially her. Her mind was racing back and forth between the words he wrote and the hypothetical intentions he might have had when he wrote them.

Still holding her phone, but unsure of what to text back to Paul, Meggie walked back into the living room to find Maria looking at someone through the open front door.

"Well don't just stand there like an idiot," she told the visitor, "you can come in."

Just then the light that shined through the open doorway was darkened by none other than Paul himself.

Paul scanned the room with his eyes until they landed on Meggie. Never looking away from her, he rustled the hair atop Maria's head as he passed by her. "Thanks, for lettin' me in, kid."

"Yeah, yeah," Maria said as she tried to readjust her hair.

"Hey there." Meggie said to Paul. She sounded weird even to herself. She didn't realize it, but the reason was because she was smiling so big that her syllables were coming out differently than they normally would have.

"Sorry I had to run out on y'all last night," Paul

said as he finally unlocked his gaze on Meggie and glanced at Emily too. "My friend really needed me."

"It's okay, Paul. You were just being a good friend. We're not your only friends." Meggie was so happy to see him that she was very ready to forgive last night's interruption. Emily was a little more skeptical.

"Look, dude, I know you got your new friends and all. But that's no reason to just ditch your old friends without even providing an explanation." Paul was sort of taken aback by Emily's words.

He quickly recovered and tried to change the subject. "I notice you're wearing the same clothes you had on last night. Did ya get that drunk?"

Emily was unaffected. "Nah, the only difference between sleep clothes and regular clothes is whether or not I'm dreaming. Good avoidance though, Paul."

Emily's demeanor towards him was still surprising to him. Apparently he had grown comfortable in his new confidence that made the ladies fawn after him. But this girl was seemingly immune to his new-found charm.

"Anyway," Paul cleared his throat. "I would like to, at least, try to make it up to you."

"How do you plan to do that?" Even Meggie noticed the flirty tone in her voice.

Before Paul could say anything, Maria stopped right beside him and said quizzically, "You're all different."

He looked down at her and back up at Meggie as he laughed nervously. "Can I take you to lunch?" he asked.

Meggie smiled at Paul, but then she looked

over at her friend for her blessing. Emily rolled her eyes and simply said, "You don't need my permission, kiddies. Go!"

11

As he didn't require sleep, Jackson took advantage and began to get accustomed to his new home. The church's basement, while not having been designed with the chance of it being a dormitory for a reanimated teenager, was to be his new home- at least for now. He had only seen Father Borbridge one other time since they first met (he came back "first thing in the morning" just like he had said). But when he came to check on Jackson, he seemed a bit rushed, like all that was necessary was that Jackson was still in one piece. He hadn't even stayed long enough to give any instruction, nor did Jackson have time to ask him about the attacker from the night before.

The basement ran the entire length of the chapel. There were two entrances to the basement, one near the front door of the church, and one directly behind the apse. Jackson decided to hang out nearer the set of stairs closer to the back of the church, so he would have more time to get out of sight when he heard people coming.

Since he had been assigned his new dwelling in the underbelly of the chapel, he had wished that

Father Borbridge would return with actual explanations and instructions. Jackson had regretted not telling him about the attack. His mind had been plagued by endless possibilities of what the dark stalker could have been, or what it could have meant. He wanted to tell the priest about his new sense of whatever it was, that he could sense the thing's presence. He hoped Borbridge could maybe explain that, too. But for now, all he could do was sit in the darkness of the basement with his theories and regret for not speaking up.

The church's basement was spacious enough, albeit dimly lit. But that was fine with Jackson. His undead eyes were impeccably good at adjusting to pretty much any lighting conditions he had come across in his second life. It also made it easier to hide from any of those altar servers that came downstairs.

Most of the people that came down there didn't linger. They would grab their candles or whatever and go on their way. But that was about to change.

Jackson heard the familiar echo made by the stairs as one of the altar servers descended. He remained perfectly still behind a set of shelves on the opposite side of the basement. Then he heard a voice.

"Hello? Am I in the right place?" When the young female voice hit Jackson's ears, he felt, for some strange reason, that those words were intended for him. Nevertheless, he remained perfectly still, hidden in the shadows.

Whoever the girl was, she wasn't going to be deterred by a simple lack of response from the darkness. She continued walking closer to Jackson, moving her head to and fro, trying to make some sense out of the pitch black. His eyes were just fine, though. Jackson peeped from around the shelf, and he saw her.

As far as he could tell, she hadn't seen him. And he doubted she had heard him. There wasn't much for her to hear. With no breath to take, or even a heartbeat, Jackson could be completely silent when he needed to be. She didn't show any sign that she could see him. Nevertheless, he saw her.

She had long, straight, brown hair. It was cut in a few layers, but the longest one went down past the waist that completed her curvy, hourglass figure. She had the kind of skin that was pale, but almost looked sickly, because she could really bronze in the sun, if she was ever out in it. Even in the dark of the chapel basement, Jackson could make out that she was strikingly beautiful. And her lost look of almost childlike curiosity she bore as she scanned the room made her that much more appealing.

Jackson had no idea why the girl had come down there. Had she come down there for him? Had she been sent by Father Borbridge? Was she someone that he could trust? Question after question about the mystery girl ran through his mind, all the while she kept fumbling around in the darkness of the basement. Whoever she was, she didn't give Jackson that dark, ominous feeling that his attacker had given him.

After a few minutes, Jackson realized that the girl wasn't just going to go away. He decided to make his presence known, but chose to remain in the dark. He forced his chest to fill with air as he prepared to speak.

"Don't be alarmed," he said softly. "There's someone down here."

Even in the dark, Jackson could see her expression change. "I *knew* there was someone down here. What are you doin' sitting here in the dark?"

Jackson hesitated a bit, but recovered soon enough. "I could ask you the same question. What are you doing down here?"

The girl became defensive. "Whatever, creep. I was sent down here. What's your story?"

At least Jackson could be honest about this one. "Same here." He hoped that she wouldn't pry any further as to why.

The two just sat in the dark for a few quiet moments. Jackson could see her just standing there, as if she were waiting for a better explanation. She finally spoke again. "Well, do you mind if I turn on the damned light? I don't really like this whole sitting-around-in-the-dark-with-a-stranger thing."

Jackson had been mere feet from the girl in the dark. He had been looking at the girl with much pleasure unbeknownst to her and her living eyes. Because of that, though, he was unable to command his body back behind a bookshelf before she found the light switch on the wall beside her. As she flicked the switched, he fearfully awaited her reaction.

There were a few moments of silence. She was even more stunning with the lights shining on her. Jackson watched in anxious horror as the girl examined him. Her gaze went from his head all the way down to his feet and back again. Her eyes grew a little wide, but she didn't seem as nearly as surprised as Jackson expected.

"Dude, what, are you goin' to prom or somethin'?" she asked. "What's with the suit?"

Once again Jackson was surprised. It was his

101

clothes that she commented on, not the fact that he had the complexion of a newspaper. "Uh, yeah, ha! This? This is all I had clean." He felt dumb for saying that. His clothes certainly were not clean. They reeked of death. He hoped that the detection of his own scent was the result of his heightened senses. He hoped she didn't notice.

"So who sent you down here?" the girl asked.

"A priest," Jackson snapped. "He's supposed to meet me down here. Wait- who are you?"

The mystery girl could not control her laughter. She was doubled over, holding her stomach. When she finally regained composure, she spoke. "So you're just hanging out in a dark, secluded basement, dressed up in a suit and tie, waitin' on a priest?! Sounds like a fun date!" She resumed her laughter.

Jackson realized how it sounded now. "Ha, ha. Very funny. It's not like that. You still haven't told me who you are."

"Oh, sorry." The girl moved in closer to him. Jackson noticed that she was about Meggie's height. She looked upward at him and extended her hand, as if for a handshake. "The name's Breann Buchanon." She locked eyes with Jackson and waited for his hand. Her eyes were the exact same shade of green that his had been in life. Now he understood why people always commented on how pretty they were. He reached out and touched her hand.

Before she could comment on it, he said, "Sorry for the cold hands. I been down here a while."

Breann nodded and raised her brow, almost in disbelief. "That's okay." She still had not broken eye contact with him. As unlikely as it was in this scenario, the human in the basement was making Jackson the zombie uncomfortable. He broke eye contact by walking over to a shelf and rummaging through some old missals.

"So, what are you doing down here, Breann Buchanon?" he asked. "Are you waiting on somebody too?"

"No, I'm not really the priests' type, ya know?" Her irreverent manner of speaking about the clergy also made Jackson uncomfortable, as they were the only people that he trusted right now. She went on, "I was just upstairs and thought I heard something, so I came down to check it out." Jackson knew she was lying. His ears were impeccable, and her footsteps had been the first thing he had heard in the church all day. At first she said she was sent down here, Jackson thought. She was clearly hiding her motivation for being down in the basement with him.

"Do you always go snooping around when you think you hear something?"

"Usually," she said.

Now it was Jackson's turn to look suspicious. He slowly forced an eyebrow to raise a little. "But you said 'Am I in the right place?' when you came down here. Why would you say that if you were just coming down here to check out a noise?"

"Why *wouldn't* I say that? That should be the question. If you're snoopin' around somewhere you shouldn't be, and there happens to be someone there doing something that they shouldn't be doing, what better way to make it seem like you're not snoopin'? When you ask 'am I in the right place?' you just seem lost."

While her reason for coming into the basement may have been untrue, her logic was sound. "Touché,

Ms. Buchanon," Jackson said.

"Well, thank you, Mr......"

"Jackson. Sorry."

"Well, Mr. Jackson. It was very nice to have met you. Now that I know you are harmless and not up to anything shady, I'll take my snooping elsewhere." Breann gave him a flirty smile before she turned and went back upstairs. Jackson tried to force his facials muscles into a smile back at her, but she had already turned before he could fully form it. He wasn't sure if she thought his first or last name was Jackson, but either way, the less she knew the better.

As he watched her walk away, he couldn't help but think of Meggie. He tragically longed to be able to see her. She was one of the main reasons he had come back, and yet, he knew that there was no good that could come from her laying eyes on him now. He was definitely feeling that main weakness that Father Borbridge had talked about. Just then, he heard the priest talking upstairs.

"Well, Hello there. What brings you here in the middle of the day?" Borbridge asked.

"Oh, you know, the usual. Praying and whatnot." It was Breann! He hoped that she didn't say anything to Father Borbridge about going down into the basement, and meeting the zombie that resided there. For some reason, whether it was because he figured she was smart enough not to divulge anything voluntarily, or because she was just generally sneaky, Jackson felt pretty confident that their meeting would remain secret from the old priest.

"Well, that's just great. Nothing wrong with coming to pray- any time of day." Jackson formed a slow smile on his face. Father Borbridge was just a happy, upbeat fellow all of the time.

"'Kay. Well see ya, padre," Breann said. Jackson could hear her steps as she exited the chapel. Then he could hear Father Borbridge's as he descended the stairs into the basement.

Upon arriving, the priest seemed a little surprised that the lights were on in the basement, almost like he had instructed Jackson to remain in the dark for security purposes. Nevertheless, he made his presence known in the basement.

"Hey, Jackson," he said in a terribly loud whisper. "It's me."

Jackson smiled again. He was still kind of taken aback by the priest's style of dress. This time it was a light brown button-down, still extra long with extra pockets. Watching the giant of a man lean down and attempt to whisper was humorous as well. "I know, Father. I could've heard you talking from a mile away."

Father Borbridge's voice reverted to its normal tone. "Really, now?"

"Yes, sir." Jackson pointed as he spoke. "The old dead ears are pretty sharp."

Borbridge inhaled deeply and used the entire breath to exhale the word "fascinating." He continued, "So, how have you been down here? Not too lonely, I hope."

"No, sir. It's not too bad at all. Anything beats a coffin." And nothing beats being unexpectedly visited by a pretty girl, he thought.

Borbridge laughed. "Well, yeah. I suppose that's true."

Jackson forced his lungs full as he prepared to start some serious talk with Father Borbridge. "Father, there is something I have to tell you."

"Okay. Feel free. That's what I'm here for. Tell me anything you want to share with me." Borbridge still seemed like an eager youngster, anxious to soak in this entire experience.

"Well," Jackson began, "last night, after I left Father Hayes' house and came here to wait for you, someone else spotted me."

"How can you be sure?"

Jackson hesitated for a moment, then responded. "Because that someone- or something- attacked me." The basement was silent as Father Borbridge looked down at the boy in shock.

"What do you mean 'attacked' you, son? Please, tell me everything." Father Borbridge no longer looked wide-eyed and ready to learn, but rather concerned and prepared to help.

Jackson wondered how he would attempt to explain the feeling he had as he walked from the cemetery to Father Hayes' house. He wondered what words he could use to describe that terrible feeling that seemed to wax and wane the whole way from the cemetery. He figured all of it would sound like nonsense, but he was in no position to assume what was or wasn't absurd.

Jackson began. "I know this may sound stupid, but- after I read Father Hayes' letter and left my family's crypt to head to his house, I felt like someone was following me. It felt like sometimes it would be so close that it was right on me, and at other times, it felt like it was following just close enough to tell where I was going."

Jackson paused for a moment to see if Father Borbridge would interject any little thing that might cause it to make sense, but the priest just nodded as if to say "go on." He continued.

"Anyway, after I talked to Father Hayes, I headed here, to the chapel. Then, when I was walking here, I felt it again. It scared me so bad that I started walking as fast as I could to the church. And right before I made it there, whatever it was knocked me into the air, and I went flying!"

"Knocked you into the air?!" Father Borbridge quickly became concerned. His brow crunched up as he looked upon Jackson.

"Yes, sir. Like some- dark- evil linebacker or something," Jackson stammered as he tried to find the right words to describe his attacker.

The priest's eyes grew wide, and his skin lost some of its color. He seemed worried about whom the assailant might be. Jackson had his undivided attention as he went on.

"And then he started to walk towards me where I landed-"

"He?" Borbridge asked.

"Yes, sir. I found out that it was a dude that hit me 'cuz he stopped from killin' me when some girls came up and talked to him. I guess he didn't want them to see him trying to kill a zombie." Jackson chuckled a little at the whole situation. Father Borbridge did not see the humor. He seemed afraid and concerned.

"Why didn't you tell me this when it happened, Jackson?" he asked.

Jackson shrugged. "I'm not really sure. I guess I was kind of scared. I landed on some concrete, and it cracked my head open-"

Father Borbridge interrupted him by grabbing

Jackson's head and jerking it around, examining it and attempting to find said crack. "Oh, my goodness, where?"

Jackson wriggled his head free from the priest's large hands and continued, "It's fine, now. I guess I'm pretty good at that regenerating thing you told me about. It was already healed up by the time you came into the church to see me."

The priest was totally stunned. His mouth was wide open, but he could not find any words.

"Anyway, so I can heal up. That's cool, especially since I got at least one enemy since I came back."

"Well, next time anything happens, please let me know. I can only help you if I know what is going on."

"Yes, sir." Jackson thought about his meeting with the Breann girl he had just had. He had full intentions of telling him about her, but he was still more concerned with whomever was trying to kill him. "So, any guesses as to who or what that might have been that attacked me, Father?"

"Oh, no guesses, Jackson. That feeling you were talking about, that you could sense its presence, and it was a malicious one, is part of being reborn. Your attacker could sense you as well. That's why he was following you."

"Wait, so I got attacked by another zombie?" Jackson was trying to imagine being strong enough to send someone flying across the sky.

"Oh, no. The Reborn, like yourself, tend to be more docile and gentle. No, you encountered one of the Dark Ones." Even when explaining to Jackson what was trying to murder him, Father Borbridge spoke in a bubbly and excited tone. But Jackson did not like the sound of it at all. It was vague and ominous.

"Dark Ones, Father? What is that supposed to be? An *evil* super zombie or something?"

Father Borbridge let out a sigh and cleared his throat. He was getting ready to say a lot. "No, not a zombie at all. You see, not only am I a Jesuit, but I also belong to an order of priests, called the Order of Lazarus. We are in charge of keeping records and dealing with cases of people coming back from the dead, be they familiars, Reborn, Dark Ones, or otherwise."

"But what *is* a Dark One, Father?"

"They are nearly the complete opposite of a Reborn. They have a hatred for life. They are dead themselves, and persist only to bring more people to death before they leave this world." Jackson listened intently as the priest continued to explain. The undead side of the world was way more complicated than he had imagined.

"Judas Iscariot was the first. He betrayed Jesus for the infamous thirty pieces of silver. His punishment was an undeath, a life of wandering and eternal separation from heaven and God. Over time, this made him bitter and angry, and he found that the only way to achieve any kind of satisfaction was through killing and consuming others' life-force by drinking their blood."

Jackson forced his zombie eyes to roll as dramatically as possible. "Oh, God. Don't tell me there's vampires too! The Dark Ones are vampires! Really?"

"Well, yes, Jackson. For all intents and

purposes, that is what they are."

"So, how vampire-y are we talking here? Since they are my enemies, I need to know- what are their weaknesses, and how do I kill 'em?" Jackson had read enough books and seen enough movies about vampires. Now that he had been told that they actually existed, he was kind of anxious to know what was real about them and what wasn't.

Father Borbridge seemed taken aback at Jackson's readiness to dispatch his attacker, but was excited to be able to share knowledge with an eager mind. Typical Jesuit.

"Well, the rosary I gave you should help. It is silver, and Dark Ones are physically weakened if they touch it."

"A Judas thing, I'm guessing," Jackson was putting it all together.

"Yes, a Judas thing. Another thing that weakens them is the sun."

"'Weakens them?' They don't burst into flames when they step out into the sun?" Jackson asked.

"No, but it does weaken them. As far as we know, it is when they are vulnerable. They do not have the speed or strength they possess during the night, and they age in the sun. This is one of the reasons that Dark Ones are able to walk among us. As long as they act like they did in their life, going out during the day, they will age- albeit slower- and they can continue terrorizing the night."

Jackson was trying to wrap his head around everything. Ghosts, zombies, *and* vampires. "What about stake through the heart? Is that how you kill 'em?"

"Yes, that would work. The wooden aspect of

the stake is what is important. They used to be alive."

"Garlic?"

"Not unless it's a stake made from a garlic plant. Otherwise, it'll just give them bad breath." Jackson and the priest shared a laugh.

"Okay, so I need to find this dude in the daylight, smack him with some silver, and stab him with a tree part?" Jackson mimed the actions as he spoke the words to Father Borbridge.

"Yes, if you could do that, that would work. Problem is, we don't know who he is, or if he even goes out during the day. And if he doesn't, then you would have your hands full. The Dark Ones are strong, fast, *and* have healing abilities much like your own, Jackson. Besides, there is a reason you were instructed to go into a church. This is sacred ground. The Dark Ones will not follow you in here. Here, they are no different than you or I-" Borbridge hesitated, "-well, me at least. They are powerless in here. I doubt you would get the opportunity to confront him. I do not want you to leave this chapel."

Jackson mulled it all over for a moment, then decided to speak again. "Well, I'm pretty sure he's a student here; and unless he only takes night classes, he goes out in the sunlight."

"What makes you 'pretty sure' he's a student here?" the priest asked.

"He told the girls he left me alone for that he was taking summer classes."

The priest grinned a bit as he said, "Well, that's just great! A limited number of students take summer classes, and all of the summer courses are during the day. We should be able to find out just who your attacker was." Father Borbridge was pleased at attaining more new knowledge.

"So, a vampire college kid is out to kill me, huh, Father?" Jackson asked. Vampires. Not Dark Ones. They were *vampires*.

"It would appear so, son."

Jackson felt powerless. He was holed up in St. Joseph's Chapel while the person that tried to kill him was out there. "Well, if you don't want me to leave the church, what are we supposed to do about it?"

"For now, Jackson," Borbridge said, "you just wait here. Until I find out who this young man is, and his schedule, I want you to stay safe in here. He will not know that I am investigating him, and he can't track me as well as he can track you. Just let me find out who he is, and we'll go from there."

It seemed to Jackson as though this was not Father Borbridge's first vampire hunt. He wondered about the depths and actions of this Order of Lazarus to which he claimed to belong. He did trust him, though. As a result, "Yes, sir" was all that Jackson dared to say.

The priest bent his tall frame down to hug Jackson before he left. "I will be back as soon as I know more. I promise."

"Father?"

"Yes?"

"Could you get me some new clothes? I think a year and a half is plenty long enough to wear a suit?"

Borbridge laughed. "Of course. I'm sure I can find you something," he said as he left.

Jackson listened to the priest's footsteps as they became more and more faint until they were outside of the chapel. I will be *so* glad to get out of what I was buried in, he thought. Then he laughed. It would definitely make that Breann girl ask less questions if I was wearing regular clothes should she see me again. "Crap! I forgot to tell him about that girl finding me." He had actually not meant to withhold the information this time. He would be sure to explain that to Father Borbridge when he saw him again.

Jackson walked over to the light-switch and turned it back off. He needed the extra line of defense and could see just fine in the dark. "Great, the story of my zombie life has vampires in it."

12

Emily had had time to bathe, change clothes, and do a considerable amount of thumb-twiddling in Meggie's absence. Maria had kept her company for a bit, but she and Ms. Paulez had since left to run errands. She had just been sitting on the couch, texting jokes back and forth to Chad about Meggie and Paul, when they pulled up and he dropped her off.

Meggie hadn't even gotten all the way back into her house before she was already being bombarded with questions from Emily. "How was the date? Where did y'all go? Come on, Meg, I gotta know!"

"Just chill, alright," Meggie said as she slipped off her shoes and put them by the front door. She then took her friend by the hand and led her into the living room, and the two sat down on the couch. Meggie had only been gone a few hours, but that was plenty of time for Emily's mind to wander what Meggie and Paul might be up to. As Meggie was fully aware of this, she sat down and asked her friend, "Now, what would you like to know?"

"Only everything, duh!" Emily exclaimed, "but

most importantly, I need to know the nature of this midday rendezvous y'all had. Is this going to lead to more dates, or what?"

Meggie smiled a little. "Well, we went out to lunch, and we caught up with each other. I told him about my first year at Auburn. He told me about his first year at Spring Hill. It was a lot of fun."

Emily raised an eyebrow and said, "I see. And do you plan on going one-on-one with all your high school friends and playing this 'catching up' game with them?"

"What? No. What do you mean?" Meggie gave her friend a confused look.

"Ah ha!" exclaimed Emily. "So it was a date!"

Meggie squirmed a little and then gave her friend a little grin. "Okay, so maybe it was date-ish."

Emily slapped an open palm on each of her knees. "Yes! So how was it? How date-ish did it get?"

"Well, not too much of a date. We were having lunch and catching up, for real, and somewhere along the way we got to talking about how much we missed hanging out. We both decided we needed to fix that, so we set something up for tonight." Meggie seemed to have a twinkle in her eyes as she concluded her statement.

"Of course y'all miss hanging out," Emily agreed. "I've seen you and all the guys. Y'all are almost sickening to be around. They're all like your big brothers the way y'all mess with each other about stuff. So, what have y'all set up for tonight?"

"We're going to a party. Alex and Ben are throwing it. He said he wanted to introduce them to me, to show that they're not bad guys." Meggie could feel her own face muscles fatiguing. She had not smiled this much in a long time.

Emily seemed surprised. "Wow, I bet Ryan and Jon will be glad of that. I mean, I don't care about Paul's new friends, but they sure seem to rub them the wrong way. Maybe this will be a chance to clear the air between all these guys."

Meggie shrugged a little. "Well... Paul didn't really say that he was going to invite all the other guys. I think this is where it gets kind of date-ish."

"Oh, I see," Emily said. "He wants you all to himself when he shows you off to his new friends. Well maybe there is something there, and something you should pursue."

"I know, right?" Meggie said.

"Well, did he at least invite me?" Emily asked. "It would be kind of rude knowing you have a friend in from out of town and all. I mean he's already taken you away for the whole day. Now he's gonna hog you all night, too?"

"Well-" Meggie shrugged. "He didn't really invite you either. I think he wants his new friends to just know me as Meggie his date, and not Meggie, Paul's date that used to date his now dead friend."

Emily was shocked at her friend's tone. Meggie had never brought up Jackson so lightheartedly. Since she had known the whole story, she had wished for Meggie to be able to talk about it; but now it just seemed wrong. Nevertheless, Emily had to brush it off in an attempt to figure out her night. "Now, what the Hell am I supposed to do while you go off to your cool party as Paul's date?" she asked.

Meggie tilted her head in contemplation. "Well, you and Chad seem to be an item now. Maybe you can make something out of that tonight. I'm sure he wouldn't mind your company. Hell, get all of the guys together and make a night of it."

Emily watched and listened in suspicion as she listened to her friend make suggestions. It seemed as though Meggie wished for nothing more than to be completely left alone with Paul at this party. She did not want her or the other guys involved at all. "Whatever, Meg. I'll figure something out."

Though Emily had lain her disdain for the situation on pretty thick, Meggie was undeterred. She was simply taken with Paul now. It showed. Emily could not help but notice that it was happening too fast for it to be innocent or natural. She wanted to get to the bottom of it, but for now, she went back to texting Chad to get something to do planned for the night.

"Hey, wanna come help me pick out something to wear tonight?" Meggie asked her friend.

"Sure," said Emily, never averting her gaze from her phone. As Meggie appeared much more concerned with Paul than the rest of her friends, Emily was more interested in making plans with Chad and the rest of the guys than what kind of outfit her friend might look best in. She sat on the edge of Meggie's bed and texted frantically away.

After about four different ensembles later, all of which Emily said "looks great" to, Meggie had settled on an outfit.

"Alright," she said as she came out of the bathroom, make-up and hair already done. "I think I'm gonna go with this."

Emily finally looked up. Meggie was wearing a dressy top with some hip-hugging jeans that really accentuated her figure. She had on a little mascara, some lipstick, and she had tamed her curls into thick ringlets that dangled from the crown of her head and bounced as she moved. She was quite a bit more dolled up than when she met Chad and Foster for going-out nights back at Auburn. It was *definitely* a date. "You look nice... skank!" Her little stab at Meggie made her giggle.

"Laugh it up, little Missy, I haven't finished giving you crap about that slut costume you wore for Chad last night." She raised an eyebrow and crossed her arms as she snapped back at her friend.

"Nah, just kidding. You really do look nice. I'm sure Paul's new friends will approve." Emily was starting to share Ryan's suspicions about Alex and Ben. Why did Paul keep the two parts of his life separate? She wondered.

"So did you find out what you and Chad are gonna do tonight?" Meggie asked. "Maybe y'all could go on your own date without the other guys, too."

Emily wasn't about keeping things separate in her life. She had even lost a few of her goth friends since she had started hanging out with Meggie and the guys. She wanted them all to be friends, but her goth friends just didn't want to. And Meggie was her roommate. It was the pragmatic decision. She had not compromised anything about her self or her personality. She was still the poetry reading, black clothes wearing, girl that she was before. But she could be friends with "normal" people too. "So what if I lose some street cred with the other Poe fans," she'd say. "No one cares what goth kids think anyway."

"I'm sure we will have time for that later," Emily said. "We decided to get together with all the guys and do something."

"Oh, okay. Well, I'm sure y'all will have fun. Those guys are a ton of fun. And the more of them there are, the time just gets better." Meggie did still love her friends, even if she was preoccupied with the new Paul.

"Well," Emily said as she stood up and grabbed her car keys from Meggie's dresser, "I guess I'll see you later. Let me know when you're gonna be back home. I don't think Chad's mom will let me stay over, and I'm not driving back to Birmingham after a night out with the Crazies."

"Okay, but Mom and Maria will be here. You don't have to wait for me to get back." Meggie appeared to be planning on being out late.

"Geez, I'm just trying to coordinate. It's not a night out with everyone. You're somebody's date. To a party. Forgive me for trying to make it at least look innocent at the end of the night." Emily wasn't sure how much Ms. Paulez trusted her daughter, but she did know the more innocent it appeared, the better.

Meggie was quick on the uptake. "Good call. I'll let you know what's goin' on."

"Good girl," Emily said as she made her way out the front door. "Behave, skank."

Meggie heard her friend's old muscle car roar to life and drive away. Now she was just waiting on Paul.

***

About an hour passed before she heard his car pull into her driveway. The sun had already gone down, and his headlights shined through the windows in Meggie's living room. She felt butterflies in her stomach. She had told her mother that she would be going out again with the guys tonight, so a simple "Bye, Mom, I'm leaving" sufficed as she went outside.

Paul was walking toward her front door when she stepped out. "You're not even gonna let me say 'Hey' to your mom?" he asked.

"Oh, don't worry about that. She's met you plenty of times." Meggie was grateful for the fact. If Paul came in to say "hi" without a loud Foster following closely behind him making a beeline for the refrigerator, any semblance of innocence about their date would be lost.

Paul laughed a little. "Okay, whatever you say." Both of them climbed into his black Honda Accord and drove away.

It was Paul that broke the momentary silence as they rode along. "I can't help but notice that you look really nice tonight."

Meggie could feel herself blushing. "Thanks. You clean up nicely too." Paul had a long-sleeve button-down shirt, with the sleeves rolled up, and a nice pair of slacks. "What's with the spiky look?" She was commenting on his strategically structured, spiked up, intentionally messy-looking dirty blonde hair. It wasn't the crew-cut Paul she remembered from high school, but she didn't mind at all.

"Well, you know," he responded, "I try to look nice." He looked away from the road and made eye contact with Meggie. It couldn't have been more than an instant; but to Meggie, it felt like it lasted much longer. She was mesmerized.

Her head was in a fog that she couldn't figure out. Normally, she would make some snide comment about his new look, and how he must have joined some frat or something. She might have said something about the other guys. She might have insisted that all of her friends hang out, because college had split them up, and summers back home were important. But she didn't say or do any of those things. She just gave him a soft smile and said, "Well you succeeded."

"Thanks."

The two rode along a little farther when Meggie finally asked, "So, where exactly are we going tonight?"

"The Fairways," he answered.

"What's that?"

"They're the apartments on Spring Hill's campus. They are right alongside the campus' golf course."

"Clever," Meggie said.

"Anyway, they're only for upperclassmen, but Alex and Ben *are* upperclassmen, so that's where they live. They're having a little get-together tonight."

Meggie thought about Chad and Foster's little "get-togethers." They were more of the t-shirt kinds of events. She wondered if the Spring Hill kids got together the same way the people did up at Auburn. "Well, I'm sure it'll be fun."

"Oh, me too," Paul said. He then placed his hand on Meggie's knee. She didn't put her hand on top of his or anything, but she didn't object to his being there, either. He had cold hands again. Even through the denim she could feel them. Somehow, though, she was comforted.

They finally made it to the Fairways. They were three brick buildings built alongside the golf course, just as Paul had said. They were each three stories high. They were built on a hill, with the last one at a noticeably lower altitude than the first. Alex and Ben's apartment was in the last building. Paul found the closest parking spot he could.

"Here we are," he said.

"Alright. Let's do this."

Their apartment was on the first floor. Some girls were outside their front door smoking cigarettes and chatting. Paul grabbed Meggie by the hand and led her past them and into the apartment. He made sure to smile at them as he passed. All of them returned the gesture. Meggie too gave an awkward grin and a wave to them as she was led indoors.

Inside the apartment were a few more girls and, as far as Meggie could tell, only two guys, one of which she recognized from the night before as Alex. His long brown hair wasn't in a ponytail tonight. It was long and wavy, down to his shoulders. It would have almost looked feminine if it had not framed his masculine face so well.

The other one was a tall, very muscular guy with short blond hair and icy blue eyes. It had to be Ben. He had a curvy brunette on his arm that was looking up at him as she rubbed his bicep that was bulging from beneath his shirt.

The one that Meggie had deduced to be Ben spotted her first. Those cool, blue eyes met hers as soon as she walked through the door. "That must be the Meggie you told us about." His voice boomed from his massive frame.

"Yeah, this is Meggie, y'all," Paul said with a smile. He walked over to his friends. He released her hand and grasped her waist as he guided her in front of him to present her.

Ben leaned down to whisper something to the girl on his arm. She tiptoed to give him a kiss on the cheek, and made her exit. Meggie turned and watched her leave, then she turned back to Alex and Ben.

Alex addressed her first. "Nice to see you again. I remember your face from the bowling alley. I'm Alex." His voice was soft and sweet. It was very soothing.

"Yeah, I know," Meggie replied. "Paul told us who ya were when you showed up. How's your uncle doing?"

"What?" Alex looked confused for a second, but quickly recovered. "Oh yeah, he's still in the hospital, but he's stable."

Meggie noticed his initial confusion. She wasn't sure if the sick uncle story was an alibi, or guy code for something more sinister, but she trusted Paul enough to let it slide.

"Well, that's good to hear," Meggie said.

"Yes, and thank you for asking," replied Alex as he gave her a half-smile.

It was then Ben's turn to introduce himself. "And I am Ben, as you might have gathered. Paul has told us about you."

"Ha! Good stuff, I hope." She felt at ease around them. They didn't seem as bad as Ryan had made them out to be.

"Just great," Ben said. He gave her a smile that must have been contagious; she couldn't help but smile back.

***

123

Inside of St. Joseph's Chapel, Jackson was feeling restless. After nightfall, hardly anyone came inside, save a few people to pray, and once a random couple looking for a getaway spot. Jackson could easily hear whether or not people were coming, so he had plenty of time to get out of sight. As a result, when the sun went down, Jackson came out of the basement and roamed the ground level of the church.

The lights in the chapel were on dimmer switches. At night, they were turned down about halfway, but never turned off. It was always open for people to come in and pray.

It didn't really matter to Jackson if the lights were on full, halfway, or off completely. His undead eyes could adjust to any level that he had come across in his second life. The light from the street lamps coming through the stained glass were plenty. But it did make him feel more comfortable being able to pace the church with the lights on. He felt more like a person, as opposed to some atrocity forced to lurk in the shadows. Because of this he had a smile on his undead face as he walked in between various pews. *I wonder if exercise is good for a zombie?* He wondered.

Ever since Father Borbridge had told Jackson about "The Dark Ones," he had been restless. He did not like having to just wait until the priest came back with instructions. Now that he knew his enemy, and his weaknesses, he wanted to get out there and fight. But then he thought about how unprepared he might be. And how strong his attacker was the last time they met. He was not ready to die again. He was certain this time it would be for good. For these reasons he paced a little harder.

Even through the thick walls he could hear sounds from outside. He could hear cars driving around campus. He could hear people's footsteps on the sidewalks. Though it was muffled, sometimes he could even hear the voices of the people walking around. When they walked close enough to chapel, he could clearly make out what people were saying. Jackson really liked his new senses. What puzzled him, however, was his complete lack of sense of the Dark One. He hadn't felt anything like that foreboding feeling he had felt since he entered the church. It was like St. Joe's was a scrambler for dead people radar. He hoped it worked the same way for the vampires.

As he paced and listened, he made out a set of footsteps that were making their way to the front door of the church. He recognized the sandal-dragging gait immediately as Father Borbridge. Hopefully he had some answers. He stopped in the center aisle of the church and faced the front door. He wanted the priest to see him, but not be startled by his presence.

Borbridge walked in and noticed Jackson immediately. He closed the big wooden door behind him as quickly as he could.

"What are you doing out in the open like that, Jackson?" he asked. "What if someone were to see you?" Borbridge made his way to the boy. He was carrying a bag.

"It's okay, Father," Jackson reassured him. "I can hear people coming from a mile away. I heard you coming. I knew it was you."

Father Borbridge sighed. "You continue to fascinate me, Jackson. But I hope that your confidence doesn't surpass your new senses."

Jackson chuckled a bit. "What's in the bag,

125

Father?"

Borbridge lifted the bag and extended it for Jackson to take. "I brought you some clothes. Go try them on, and see if they fit."

Jackson received the bag and walked toward the front of the church, where the bathrooms were located. "Be right back." the priest nodded and motioned him on with his hand.

Jackson closed the door behind him in the tiny bathroom and turned on the light. There was a mirror. Once again he looked at himself. His eyes were still bright green. He still looked dead. Other than that, it was the Jackson he always knew. He proceeded to open the bag of clothes Father Borbridge had brought him.

The bag contained a polo shirt, some blue jeans, and a pair of flip-flops. Jackson put the lid of the toilet down and set the clothes on it. It was time for him to get out of his burial clothes.

While the fine motor skills necessary for unbuttoning and unzipping made his undressing a little clumsy, it went otherwise without incident. Once he was out of his dead clothes, he looked again into the mirror.

Jackson could clearly see where the morticians had made the enormous, y-shaped incision down the front of his chest cavity, and where they had stitched it back shut. The shape was echoed by the silver rosary that draped down his chest. The incision didn't look fresh, though. It looked like a scar. Had it healed? What did they stuff me with when they took out my organs? I've felt the presence of some of my organs since then. Where did the stuffing go? Was it consumed in the regrowth of my new ones? Questions

126

flooded the boy's mind as he gently traced the shape of the "Y" on his front.

After a moment, he thought that Father Borbridge might become concerned; so he began putting on his new clothes. Except for the shirt being a little too long, everything fit well. Jackson stuffed his old clothes into the empty bag and left the bathroom.

Borbridge looked at him as he closed the bathroom door behind him. "I'd have to say I did pretty good at picking out your sizes."

Jackson nodded in agreement. "Yes, sir, you did. But do I even need to ask where they came from?"

"Jackson I'm a Jesuit priest in the Catholic Church," Borbridge said. "We get charitable donations all the time. Food, clothes, money, you name it. And I can't think of someone who might need new clothes more."

"Good point. So... any news on the vampire?" Jackson asked quizzically.

"Well, no. Not yet." Father Borbridge rubbed his hands together and began rocking back and forth on his heels. "But I did get an exact count- and names- of the male students who are attending classes for the summer term. I'd say that's a good start. There's less than a hundred of them."

Jackson was hoping for better information, but it was still better than nothing. "Well, alright then. Just keep me posted, I guess. I don't like knowing there's someone out there that wants me dead, and me *not* knowing who he is!"

"I understand, son." The priest put a hand on Jackson's shoulder. "But you're safe here. And that is what is important. He can't harm you if he can't get to you."

Jackson shrugged. He knew Borbridge was right. "Yes, sir."

"Okay, well I'm going to get out of here. I've got some things I have to take care of. Is there anything else I can help you with?"

Jackson thought about it. He wanted to know exactly what his vampire attacker was capable of. He asked the priest, "Are there any books or anything about vampires and zombies? I'd like to know all I can about it. Like, does your Order of Lazarus have some cool, secret library I can check some books out of?"

The old priest smiled. Jackson yearning for knowledge, of any kind, warmed his heart. "I'll see what I can do." He then turned and exited the church.

Jackson resumed his pacing of the aisles in the chapel. As he paced he examined his new clothes. They were pretty much his style, not that a zombie had any reason to be fashionable. He could hear the outside noises again. Some cars were being driven about campus. Some people were having conversations. He made his way to the entrance of the church and stuck his ear to the wooden door.

The sounds from outside became clearer. There was still at least some scientific basis to his supernatural senses. Just being able to hear the things clearer made him feel better. It made him feel somehow in touch with the world again, and not a prisoner in some holy cell. His leaning on the door pushed it slightly open. Jackson could smell the fresh air from outside as it leaked through the crack in the door. Through the crack the sounds became even clearer. The voices he heard were clearer. He was able to discern their genders and each voice's point of origin. Off in the distance to the West, he heard a laugh that he recognized. If he had had a beating heart, it would have stopped it. He knew that laugh anywhere. It was a girl. It was Meggie.

Jackson backed away from the door and stood motionless. Were he alive, he might be gasping for air. But he didn't. He stood in place for a while, thinking.

Meggie was near. How close was she? Was she on campus? He couldn't help but recall the face of the girl he had fallen in love with during his life. He desperately longed to see it again. He knew it was foolish. He knew it was irrational to even think that she might want to see him like this, even for a second. None of that mattered. Going against all logic had gotten him this far, and going against it once more would determine his next decision. He opened the chapel door and stepped outside.

13

Jackson stood just outside the chapel doorway. He couldn't believe what he had just done. Stepping outside of his crypt after coming back to life was one thing, but this was something much more dangerous. Leaving the safety of the chapel, despite repeated warnings from his only ally, besides Father Hayes, was basically suicidal. The only other person that knew of his existence could sense his presence *and* wanted him dead again. Jackson's only real defense outside of the church was the silver rosary around his neck. If they get close enough to touch it, he thought, I'm probably already screwed. Regardless of the circumstances, his compulsion to locate Meggie surpassed any rational thought that might have kept him safe.

Jackson was first attempting to feel his attacker's presence somewhere close by. He could not. Luckily, the vampire had not been lurking about St. Joe's, patiently waiting for Jackson to be dumb enough to come outside. He figured he was somewhere on campus simply because he was a student taking classes. But the Dark One was not on his trail, which came as a great relief to Jackson.

The next thing to do was to try and pinpoint from where he had heard Meggie's laughter. He faced westward and tried his best to focus. He could make out some voices coming from that direction. Some of them were male. Most of them were female. They all seemed to be in good spirits. Had to be a party, he thought. Perhaps Meggie was at the party. He turned slowly in that direction. There was a brick path lined with tall azalea bushes on both sides that went in the direction he wanted it to go, so he started down it. The pathway seemed to serve as a tunnel for sounds to reach Jackson's ears. All of his focus was on listening; his body was moving slower than it could have been. But he kept walking toward the sounds.

He could hear the sounds of the city well enough to know that they were there, but he couldn't make out anything specific. All of his attention was being paid to the sounds of festivities west of him. Then he heard it again. He heard her laugh again, this time accompanied by a male's laugh that he recognized. He wasn't sure exactly who the man was, but he *knew* that he had heard Meggie's laugh a second time. Jackson sped up as best he could in that direction. He had only been able to walk about thirty feet with so much of his focus and energy being on making out the noises. As he was assured now that it was Meggie, he focused less and was able to quicken his pace.

Up ahead to his right, a second paved path intersected his own. He could hear footsteps coming from it. At first he wasn't sure whether to slow down or speed up. But as the back of his head probably looked more normal than the front, he chose to walk faster. Even if they took a turn onto his path, at least they would be behind him.

By now Jackson could hear her having a conversation with people. He wasn't completely sure how far away he could hear people talking, but he figured he had to be getting close. Just as he crossed the intersecting path, he heard the footsteps coming from it stop- and then start again. The person had seen him. He didn't hesitate, though. He just kept walking toward Meggie.

As he continued his journey, he heard the person who had spotted him start walking in his direction. They were behind him. Jackson didn't know just how fast he was walking, but the person following him was closing the gap. It wasn't a vampire. That dreadful feeling didn't accompany this person's attention, so he chose not to alter his pace. Before he knew it, the steps were right behind him. "Jackson?" he heard it in a voice he recognized.

He turned around and faced her. It was Breann Buchanon, whom he had met earlier in the day. Even if he was perturbed by her interruption, he was somewhat relieved that he hadn't added to the list of people that knew he existed. "Hello," he said.

"I guess your date's over."

"Huh?"

"You're not in your tux anymore, so I'm guessing that you're through with your date." She was dressed in a t-shirt and some short shorts. If anyone saw them talking in the moonlight, with Jackson now out of his suit, they would just look like two normal teenagers having a conversation.

"It wasn't a tux. It was a suit. And it wasn't a date."

Breann laughed. "I'm just fuckin' with you, dude. Lighten up," she said. She then proceeded to give him a playful punch in the arm. It didn't hurt, but he judged that if he still could feel things properly, he would definitely have felt it. So he rubbed his arm.

"Okay, okay," Jackson said, still rubbing the spot she had tagged. "What brings you out walking around in the middle of the night? Doing some more snooping?" As he waited for her response, he tried to hear Meggie again. She was still talking.

"Nah, just walking tonight. What about you?"

"Same here. I thought I heard something," he told her. "You know how that is." He hoped that he could close just one eyelid properly to make a wink. It was his first attempt as a zombie.

"Yeah, I guess I do. Mind if I tag along?" she asked.

Jackson looked at her as he decided. She was so pretty with the moonlight shining off her long, brown hair. He could see individual stars reflecting from her big, green eyes. His answer came out before he even had a chance to fully think about it. "Not at all."

Breann gave him a smile. He turned back toward the direction he had heard Meggie and began walking again. Breann shuffled up next to him and walked alongside.

Jackson tried to listen intently to make out more specifically where the voices were coming from. Like before, it made him walk slower. He still hadn't figured out how to completely multitask as a zombie. But Breann must have thought he slowed down because he was being sneaky like herself.

"What are we listening for?" She whispered

into Jackson's ear.

"I heard a voice I thought I recognized up this way," Jackson said. With listening and responding to her question, he had almost come to a complete stop. He could hear Meggie in the distance talking, but he knew there was no way to explain that to Breann. The two just inched slowly further toward her.

"Mind if I ask who it is?"

Just thought about how to respond. "An old girlfriend."

Breann snorted as she tried to stifle her laughter. When she regained her composure she whispered, "Man, you really are a creeper."

Jackson gave her a look for a second, then focused once more. There was something else he was sensing. "Stop!" he whispered as loud as possible while still maintaining a whisper.

Breann grabbed Jackson's arm and hugged up next to him. "Now, you're scaring me."

He felt it again. The dark presence. It was coming from the same direction as Meggie's voice. He began to worry for her, but she laughed again. The vampire was not harming her, nor had the vampire seemed to notice Jackson. "Just wait a second," he said to the living girl on his arm.

Jackson was scared to move, afraid that any movement might give away his position to the Dark One he could feel nearby.

Breann hugged his arm tighter. "Jackson, this isn't funny. What's going on?" She wasn't whispering anymore. She was legitimately frightened.

"Shh!" he snapped back at her. But it was too late. What he feared the most had happened. The vampire noticed him. Jackson could feel the vampire's familiar presence taking notice of his. He felt it turn his way as it attempted to home in on his location. The Dark One had locked in. It didn't seem as close as before, but it was heading Jackson's way.

Jackson turned around as fast as he could. Breann was still holding onto his arm. He tried to gentle brush her off. She tightened her grip. "Breann, let me go!"

"Not until you tell me what you're trying to pull on me." Her fear had raised the volume of her voice.

Jackson began making his way back to the church as best as he could with her hanging from his arm. "I'm not trying to pull anything. You're pulling *my* arm. I have to get back to the church." The Dark One was getting closer. The chapel wasn't far away, but he would never make it back there in time if Breann didn't let him go. He had managed to get a little closer to St. Joe's with her still holding on. But it was not enough. His attacker was bearing down fast upon them. Jackson knew what the monster was capable of. He knew that the vampire intended to kill him. Fear set in on the zombie's mind. As he inched closer and closer to the chapel's front door, fear became all that he could feel. He couldn't think straight. He wasn't actively commanding his body to press on anymore. He no longer even felt the dark presence pursuing him anymore. There was only fear.

In the fog of that fear, Jackson witnessed himself move as he had never moved since coming back to life. With strength he never knew as his own, he scooped Breann up into his arms and headed toward the chapel. Even with the burden of the girl, he was running! He was not sure what was going on, or why; but he was in no position to object. Jackson held Breann in one arm and flung open the church door with the other. He walked over the threshold and collapsed on the floor. He fell so as to break Breann's fall. In his state, he had lost any sense of the vampire's presence behind him, but he knew it had to be a close call. Jackson could hear him screaming and grunting outside the door. He recognized the attacker's voice from the first attempt on his life. After a moment, he conceded and walked away.

Breann let go of the zombie arm that she had been holding and stood up. "What the Hell just happened!"

The situation had caused her to pant and take deep breaths. No such panting came from Jackson, just a cool, calm response. "Are you okay?" He avoided explaining what had transpired. He was not ready to introduce her to the world of the undead.

"I'm fine. Just tell me what's going on. I've never seen anyone move like that."

Great, he thought. Breann saw the vampire. Perhaps she could tell him what he looked like. "So you saw him?"

"Saw who?" she asked. "Whoever was chasing us? No, I didn't see anything. I was talking about you. I've *never* seen anyone move like that."

He recalled running, which was strange enough; but he didn't remember running unnaturally fast. Obviously he was mistaken. "Must've been adrenaline, I guess," Jackson said. He wasn't even sure he had adrenaline as a zombie, but he hoped it would satisfy her curiosity.

"Well that was some adrenaline, then. I know who to call when I'm pinned under a car." Breann and

Jackson just stood in silence for a few minutes, just looking at one another. She was catching her breath; and he was hoping she didn't ask any more questions. He didn't want to have to lie in a church.

Before looking at one another became awkward, Jackson walked past her, genuflected, and sat down on one of the back pews of the chapel. Before Jackson could even properly process what had just happened to him and Breann, he heard her taking footsteps toward him.

"Oh, my God. Did you always have a giant gash on your back?" she asked Jackson.

"Huh?" he responded frantically as he stood up and tried to crane his neck around far enough to see the wound. Breann was correct.

The vampire must have been closer than Jackson ever thought to be able to leave such a mark. It started on the back of his right arm and stretched across his shoulder almost to the middle of his back. His shirt was slashed, and it revealed the wound underneath. Breann looked on curiously as Jackson assessed the damage done to him.

The claw marks across the top of Jackson's back were slowly leaking a dark red, almost purple, liquid. Like the fluid that had leaked from his head, it was kind of oily. So that's what zombie blood looks like, he thought.

"You should probably get that looked at, Jackson," Breann said. "That looks pretty bad."

Jackson didn't want to tell her that there was nothing to worry about. He was pretty sure he wasn't going to bleed to death. But he also didn't want his wounds to start healing in front of her. "I'll be alright."

"Um- okay." Breann seemed unconvinced.

"What the Hell just happened anyway? I didn't hear anything, and you just started running. How did you know something was chasing us at all?"

Jackson didn't know how much longer he could keep his secret from Breann, but he also didn't really see a point in it. She was sneaky enough, and he had already given her more than enough to make her suspicious. She would eventually investigate and figure it out. "Don't worry about it. We're safe now." he stood up and faced Breann. He could see all over her face that his response was not enough to satisfy her.

"So, you gonna tell me what was chasing us- and what did that to you?" Breann asked.

Jackson walked over to the marble basin full of holy water. He scooped some out and rubbed it on his wounds. They had already begun healing. "I'm not really sure you would understand."

The young girl seemed offended. She walked around to the other side of the basin so she could stare straight into Jackson's eyes. "I understand a *lot* more than most people," she said.

Jackson didn't respond immediately. He just kept attending to the cuts across his back, which were almost completely healed at this point. Jackson was more concerned with finding another shirt to wear. He really didn't want to have to put his suit on again.

As he was examining himself, Breann became frustrated. She moved to his side and positioned her head perfectly, forcing Jackson to look at her if he turned his head around to look at the scratches. "Well? I'm not going away." She was close enough for Jackson to smell her. He could recall the scent from earlier.

She was too curious. It was clear to Jackson

138

couldn't keep her in the dark. Telling her something would be better than having her snooping around trying to figure things out on her own. "Okay. I know. But let's sit down for this."

"Fine," she said. Breann sat down on one of the pews.

Jackson took a seat on the same pew, but several feet away. He kept his head looking forward, even though he could feel Breann's eyes boring into him. "How much do you know about that man?" he asked, pointing to the big crucifix behind the altar?"

"What? Jesus?" she asked. "We got chased by Jesus?"

"No, no. How much do you know about his story from the Bible? The gospel stories and all that?"

Breann leaned her head to the side and pondered on the question as she looked at a Jackson who was still not looking at her. "I dunno. I guess I know the basic stuff: baby in a manger, three wise men, disciples, died on a cross, came back on Easter. I'm from the South, so all that is just shit everybody from here has heard their whole life. My family never really went to church on a regular basis."

Jackson didn't think he would ever get used to her irreverence toward God or the church, but she had at least explained to him why she was that way. "Well, I *did* grow up
going to church. And the Jesus story is a little more interesting than you might think."

"What do you mean? What does that have to do with whoever did that to your back?"

"Well," Jackson went on, "you know that part about coming back on Easter?"

"Yeah?"

"That part, to me, is the most believable now."

"What are you talking about, Jackson?" She was clearly confused.

Jackson inched closer to Breann on the pew and turned to look at her. "People can come back from the dead."

Breann looked at Jackson. "What does that have to do with anything?" she asked.

"Not everybody that comes back from the dead is as nice as Jesus." He thought about what Father Borbridge had said about the Dark Ones, them being the more malignant of the undead. "Some of them are bad. That's what was chasing us tonight."

"An- an evil undead?" she stammered.

"Yes." He hoped it would be enough to sate her curiosity.

"Do you really expect me to believe that somebody came back from the dead and chased us into a church?" Breann did not seem as willing to accept the supernatural as Jackson was. But then again, she hadn't woke up in a coffin after a year.

"I know that it's a lot to take in," he said, "but I'm being serious. That's what it was."

Breann looked at him like she was waiting for him to burst into laughter from the joke. But he didn't. "You're not fucking with me, are you?"

"Not at all."

Breann looked skeptical and bewildered. "Well, what's up with the church then? It's not chasing us anymore."

"They won't come in here," he said. "It's holy ground."

Breann gave Jackson a suspicious look. "So, we're safe in here?"

"Yes, as far as I know." Jackson wasn't completely certain about all the rules governing zombies and vampires, but he was pretty sure about them not coming into the church.

Breann stood up and started walking slowly toward the altar. As she approached it, she turned around to Jackson and said, "Well, I guess that means I'm staying in here tonight. You can go back out there if you want to, but I'm gonna wait this out until morning."

Breann was unaware that St. Joe's was Jackson's new home anyway. "I'll wait here too," he said.

"How long do you think we really need to wait in here?" she asked.

"I think it would be best if we at least stayed here for the rest of the night." Jackson pulled the slashed part of his shirt over his shoulder. "If he'll do stuff like this, I think I'll hang out at least until the morning, when other people might be around." He didn't want to tell her the real reason he was waiting was for the sun. The vampire probably would not be capable of such speed and violence in the daylight. The reason he gave her was plausible enough. And now he didn't want to turn his back to her for fear she might see that, underneath the blood-soaked slashes, his wounds had already healed shut.

"I guess you got a point." Breann let out a little laugh.

"What's so funny?"

"I don't think I've been in church that much the whole rest of my life," Breann said. "A whole night's worth of time in a church. Ha!"

Jackson laughed a little too. "Well maybe it will

do you some good."

"Who knows," she said, making her way back closer to Jackson. "So what's your story, Jackson? If we're gonna be here all night, we might as well get to know each other."

"Oh, by all means, ladies first."

Breann let out a sigh. "Fine. What do you want to know about me?"

Jackson shrugged at first, but then decided to keep her talking as long as possible. As long as she was talking, he wouldn't have to tell her anything about himself. He leaned casually against a pew and said, "Everything. Tell me the whole story. How did I go my whole life without ever seeing you, then you run into me twice in one day?"

Breann mimicked Jackson posture and stance perfectly and leaned on a pew as well, as if to mock him. "Maybe it's fate. Maybe it's God. Maybe *you* just popped up outta the blue into my universe. I'm from Mississippi originally; so that would explain why you haven't seen me before. But I've been going to Spring Hill for a year, and I've never seen you. Maybe I should ask you *your* story."

Jackson ignored her attempt at diversion. "So you just finished your freshman year here?"

"Yeah."

"So that would make you what? Eighteen? Nineteen?"

"I just turned nineteen," she answered. "What about you?"

Jackson wasn't sure exactly what the day was. School was out, though. He assumed his birthday, May 3rd, was soon to pass, or had recently done so. "Yeah, me too." He was buried as a seventeen-year-old. Other than his pallid complexion- which Breann still had said nothing about- Jackson figured nineteen was believable.

"Cool. So what's up with meeting the priest and hanging out on campus?" Now Breann was asking the questions. "You gonna transfer here or something?"

"No. The priest I was meeting is just a friend. I needed to ask him for some advice." Jackson was doing a pretty good job at remaining both honest and vague.

"Oh, okay. Well, where *do* you go to school? Are you in college?" she asked him.

"Well, I went to Mcgill-"

Breann interrupted him. "That's the Catholic school here in Mobile, right?"

"Yeah."

"A lot of folks from there go here now."

"Yep. That's us." Jackson remembered that Ryan and Paul had decided to attend Spring Hill. He wondered if she knew them. But then he really hoped she didn't. If she knew them too well, it might get back to them that Breann had been having conversations with their dead friend. "Anyway, I got into 'Bama, but I kind of took a year off."

"A year off?" she asked. "What for?"

Jackson wondered how he could answer within the confines of the truth. Then it came to him. "A new lot on life. There's a lot more to it than just going to school, you know?"

"Sounds good, man. So how has this year off treated you? What new insights on life do you have?" Breann still seemed to be mocking him.

"I'm not really sure. I just know I feel a little

left behind." Jackson thought about his friends that had moved on a year later into their lives. It made him sad. He knew that it was inevitable, though. He couldn't judge them for that. The fact that he was dead to them hit him hard and suddenly. "I mean, I really think that it has broadened my horizons, but to the rest of the world, I'm nothing more than I was a year ago. Less, maybe..."

Jackson thought about his friends. He thought about how they might have spent their freshman years. His friends went on to different colleges and got on with their lives. He was glad they did. It would have been a bigger tragedy if his death had stopped that. But it didn't make it hurt any less. Breann must have been able to see that on his zombie face.

"Dude, don't sweat it. I just finished my freshman year, and I ain't any closer to knowing what I want to do. You just took the cheaper route." Breann was trying to cheer up the dead kid. It cracked him up a little. Jackson wasn't sure a funeral was any cheaper than tuition, but he knew what she meant by it.

"It's okay," he said. "There's nothing I can do about being a year behind now. I just have to make my own way."

Breann moved in close and put a hand on his shoulder. He could feel the warmth of her living breath on his skin. In his life, he might have jumped at the sudden touch, but he didn't flinch. He just looked into her eyes. "I'm sure your way will do just fine if they love ya," she said. "You seem like a solid guy, Jackson."

"Thanks." He wanted to place his hand on top of hers that she placed on his shoulder to let her know the affection was well received. But he had made it this far with his dead appearance without any question from her. He didn't want to make her any more suspicious. He gave her a nod of acknowledgment. After a few seconds she withdrew her hand and resumed a congenial distance.

Breann raised a hand to her mouth as she yawned. The living necessity of sleep was beginning to affect her. He wasn't sure of the time; from her body language, though, it had to be late. Jackson knew that no such affliction would befall him, but he did not want her to know that. "You must be getting tired," he said.

"Fuck yeah, dude. I got up too early, and it's too late. I wish I was in my bed."

"Well, feel free," Jackson said. He motioned his hand toward the front door of the church. He half-hoped she would leave. If Father Borbridge came back to see him tonight, he did not want to have to explain anything to him.

"Nah, man," she said. "I'm cool. On the off-chance that you're right- that there are dead people out there ready to kill- I don't mind crashing here in the church." Breann took a seat on one of the back pews.

With no chance of her leaving, Jackson decided it would be best to wait for her to fall asleep, then get out of sight before she awoke the next morning. "Alright. Well do you want to see if there is anything we could use for blankets and pillows? Maybe there are some extra robes or something." Jackson knew that there were.

"Sure." Breann knocked on the wooden pew. "Anything has to be more comfortable than these." She stood up to follow Jackson.

There was a staircase near the front door of

the church that led down to the basement. Jackson walked down them, with Breann not far behind. To the living, it was pitch dark in the basement. But he could see just fine. Jackson had spotted the shelf full of robes for altar servers the moment he was down there, but chose to turn on the lights for Breann's sake. He walked over to them. They were black and white, and in various sizes. "Here we go. A few of these should be cushion-y enough."

Breann walked over to them and grabbed a handful of her own. "Well, I'm going to take a couple extra. You can never be too comfortable."

Jackson watched her take some of the robes and ascend back up the stairs. He turned off the light and followed after her.

By the time he was up to the main level of the chapel, Breann was already laying the robes she had grabbed down onto one of the back pews. He put down the robes he had onto a pew near her.

Even though he knew he was not going to want or require any sleep, Jackson began assembling his makeshift bed for the night. Breann, having completed her own, walked over to him.

"What is it?" he asked.

"You ain't half bad, Jackson." Breann tilted her head a little and gave him a smile. After he gave her an uneasy smile in return, she leaned in and gave him a kiss on the cheek. Jackson wasn't sure if zombies could blush. He hoped not.

"Thanks," he said.

"No problem."

He watched her as she made her way to her own pile of robes, using the topmost one as a blanket when she laid down. Jackson couldn't help but notice the curves of her body beneath the cover of the robe. She was appealing from any angle. He laid down in his own pile of robes.

Lying down in the pew, he looked forward. In the backside of the pew in front of him, he saw a small pencil and an envelope. These were usually used for church patrons to write out amounts of money they were giving, or to specify which social justice cause they might want to offer money to on Sundays. Jackson took them and just doodled on the envelope. He traced the seams of the envelope and drew swirls seamlessly as he waited for Breann to fall asleep.

After a while he heard the cloth above and beneath her rustle swiftly. She must have twitched. Jackson recalled those random, full-body twitches that happened just before falling asleep. Before long, he heard the beginning of the sounds of sleep. Breann's breaths became slower, but deeper. Eventually he could hear her softly snoring. That was his cue.

Jackson instinctively stuffed the pencil and envelope in his pants pocket and arose from the pew, as quietly as possible. He did not want to wake her. He gathered up his pile of robes and began to tiptoe past the pew where she was sleeping. As he made his way to the staircase that led to the basement, he heard something outside. Jackson gently placed the handful of robes on the closest pew and walked back toward the side door of the church, where he had heard the noise.

It sounded like people were talking just outside the door. As Jackson stepped closer, he could make out that the voices were male. He looked back to make sure Breann wasn't stirring. She was still snoozing in the back pew, so he crept closer to the door.

By the time he made it to the door that was the side entrance of the chapel, he could hear them talking.

"He's in there." Jackson recognized it immediately as the voice of his attacker. It was a young male voice, but it was deep and commanding. "I saw him go in there, and I haven't left since. He's still in there."

"Well, go get him." The second voice made Jackson's undead heart sink down to his feet. It belonged to his friend Paul. Just hearing it made Jackson recall times when he had been alive. He remembered hearing that voice during some of the most fun times he had ever had. It didn't seem as endearing now. It didn't sound like the voice of a friend. Paul sounded annoyed. Even worse, he seemed to be friendly toward this person who was determined to see Jackson re-terminated. Jackson was scared and confused.

"Father told us we can't go into churches," the other voice said. "So I'm just gonna wait and see if he comes out."

Jackson's attacker was not going to just go away. He intended to stalk and kill him. The dawn could not come soon enough for him.

"Fine," Paul said. "But I'm going home."

Did Paul know that it was his old friend cooped up inside a church hiding from a killer? Jackson wanted to burst through the door and let his presence be known. If he could just get Paul to see him, maybe he could talk some sense into the other one; maybe he would leave Jackson alone. Maybe Jackson wouldn't be confined to St. Joe's anymore.

"What happened to that chick?" the other

voice asked Paul.

"Meggie?" Paul had been with Meggie earlier. "I took her home a while ago. I didn't feel like having to explain any of this shit to her."

"Well she's going to find out eventually, one way or the other." The other person sounded as if he had said those words with a smile.

"Whatever, man," Jackson heard Paul say. "I'm done for the night."

"Hey," said the other voice. "So, you don't care if I kill him?"

The thought of dying again was not appealing to Jackson whatsoever. He did not want to have to die again. Then he heard his friend Paul say, "Technically, he's already dead. He's just walking around for some reason."

Those were the last words he heard Paul speak. After that, he was able to make out the sounds of his friend walking away into the distance. Jackson crumbled into a pile of dead flesh next to the side door of the church. He saw undead tears fall onto the floor in front of him as he listened, defeated, to the sounds of his killer stalking around the chapel.

14

Jackson wasn't sure how long he sat there next to the side entrance of the chapel. It could have been minutes. It could have been hours. All he knew was that he felt every tear that dropped, from the tear ducts in his eyes, to every cell that they touched on his face as they fell onto the chapel floor. Zombies could cry, he thought. They fell freely as he reflected on what he had just heard. Not only did one of his friends know that he had come back from the grave, but that friend, Paul, was completely fine with him dying all over again, even if it meant at the hands of a Dark One. A vampire. Jackson contemplated doing everyone a favor and just dying again. He may not have been able to feel the physical pain of his head bouncing off concrete or his back being slashed, but Jackson was feeling this hurt.

How does one simply will themselves back to death? Jackson wasn't sure, but he thought about how he might go about doing such a thing now. He was feeling the full force of a "Reborn's biggest weakness" now. As he knelt beside the door, he heard the other one, the vampire that wanted him dead, circle around to the front door of the church. Aside from an occasional audible inhale or exhale from Breann, it was all Jackson had to listen to.

Just then he heard a second person approach the front of the church. It was a set of footsteps he recognized. It was Father Borbridge. All at once he feared for the priest being mauled by the vampire; he thought about him walking in and finding Breann nestled in a pile of robes. He thought of some "Father" telling his attacker not to step foot in churches. He thought of springing to action to defend the priest, and the girl if he had to. He thought of having to defend himself against Borbridge and the vampire. But he did nothing. Defeated, he just remained on the floor, listening.

"Hello, Father," Jackson heard his attacker say. "What brings you here at this hour? Is it a late night or an early morning?"

"Oh, a little bit of both, I might say." The old priest spoke as chipper as ever. "What about you, son?" Jackson recalled Father Borbridge calling him "son."

"Nothing, just a late-night stroll, Father." Jackson's attacker appeared as innocent as anyone.

"Well, unless you want to join me in the sanctuary, I guess you'd better head on back to wherever home is for you. There's no business, but bad business, out this late at night."

The vampire must have heeded the priest's warning, even if it was reluctantly. He let out a sigh and said, "I guess. Good night, Father."

Jackson could hear his footsteps fading away

into the distance as Father Borbridge's came closer to the front door of the church. Was Borbridge this "Father" that had instructed the vampire to stay out of the church? Was he sure the priest had been completely truthful with him? As he pondered, Jackson heard Father Borbridge's hand touch the handle on the door as it creaked open. The zombie rose to his feet.

Jackson wasn't sure what to expect when he turned to make eye contact with Father Borbridge. He wondered if his eyes were red from crying recently. But he didn't really care. He wasn't sure what to trust or believe anymore. One of his best friends from his life had just denounced him; and he had overheard the one person he thought he could trust, Father Borbridge, order a vampire away without any difficulty. He almost welcomed eye contact with the priest.

Father Borbridge came walking in with a leather-bound book under his arm. He peered around the chapel until he found Jackson looking back at him. He quickly began making his way to him.

Jackson lifted a finger to his lips, signaling Father Borbridge to be quiet. The priest obliged the request and was as silent as possible as he walked up to Jackson.

"What is it, son?" Borbridge asked in a soft whisper. Jackson wasn't sure if he had actually turned up his lip, or if he had just thought it. The fact that the priest had called both the vampire and him "son" in the same instance disgusted Jackson.

Jackson pointed in the direction of the sleeping Breann. "We have company," Jackson whispered. While it was technically a whisper, Jackson's current disdain made it a pretty loud one.

"What's wrong son? You seem distraught."
While Jackson was not currently trusting him, Father
Borbridge did appear to be truly concerned.

"A few things. What day is it? I need more
clothes. And I need weapons. I'm not staying in here
anymore." Though he maintained a whisper, so as not
to awaken Breann, Jackson spoke briefly and
deliberately to the priest.

Father Borbridge seemed shocked. "Well, it's
Saturday, May 19th, I'll get you some more clothes, and
something to defend yourself, since you are
determined to leave this chapel."

"Thank you... Father." Jackson put a deliberate
pause in his speech. He wasn't sure who to trust
anymore, not even Borbridge.

The priest offered him the book he had. "This
is that other thing you asked for," Father Borbridge
whispered. "This is a collective journal kept by
different members of the Order of Lazarus. It's all the
firsthand knowledge of Dark Ones and the Reborn
that we have."

Jackson took the book. "Thank you."

Borbridge looked bewildered. "Jackson, what
happened? Are you sure you are alright?"

"I'll be fine. I just know that I can't stay in here
anymore. If I have to fight, then that's what I'm going
to do. If I have to die again, so be it. But I won't sit in
here hiding anymore." Maintaining a whisper was
becoming increasingly difficult.

"I'm not completely sure I understand, but
okay." Jackson did not want to tell him that the person
he had just spoken with outside of the chapel was the
vampire they were looking for. He didn't tell

Borbridge that his attacker had been stalking outside most of the night. He didn't know if Borbridge was in cahoots with him or not; so Jackson kept those facts to himself for now and just glared at the priest.

Father Borbridge had not walked into the chapel expecting such tenacity from Jackson. "Please, just wait until the sun is out. After that, come to Father Hayes' house. I'll meet you there. But don't be too long after the dawn, though. People will be about tomorrow. They will be having Mass in here."

At least he offered a rendezvous point Jackson could trust. Even if Borbridge was in question, Father Hayes had always been straight with Jackson. "Okay," he said.

"Okay." Father Borbridge was uneasy about Jackson's entire demeanor, but he did not want to further upset the Reborn. "Well, I guess I'll be on my way. I'll be sure you have what you need tomorrow morning." The priest, unsure of what exactly had set Jackson off, turned and promptly exited the chapel.

As new doubts filled his head about Father Borbridge and his Order of Lazarus, Jackson looked down at the book he had just been given. It was pretty thick, and the pages were kind of floppy, apparently from years of use. It was bound in brown leather that had developed a very weathered patina since the book's beginning. There were no words on the cover, only metal adornments. On every corner, front and back, there was a silver rivet. On the front, a thin silver crucifix, almost the height and width of the book, was sewn onto the cover. Jackson turned the tome over and over in his hand, examining it. A small piece of the leather had worn off bottom of the book's spine. The missing leather exposed another piece of silver. A slat of silver ran the whole length and reinforced the spine. Jackson wondered how floppy the book might be if not for that. While he was not completely trusting of Father Borbridge, he had seemed to come through for him again with some form of reading material on his new enemy. As he awaited the safety of the sun, Jackson sat down in a pew and opened the book.

At first he just thumbed through it, without really reading anything. It was as the priest had said, a sort of heirloom journal. After several pages of one person's handwriting, the book obviously changed owners. It was apparent by the complete change of penmanship on subsequent pages. This book had changed hands many times. Jackson could feel his eyelids open wider as he thought of the wealth of knowledge this book could contain. Numerous firsthand accounts of the undead were at his fingertips. Some of the authors even included graphs and drew sketches of things. This was certainly what he wanted.

Jackson heard Breann stir behind him. From the sound of it, she was just mumbling gently in her sleep and readjusting. Nevertheless, Jackson hunched over protectively to further guard the book from view. He was sure it would keep him busy until the sun came up, and he could leave the chapel safely.

The first few pages of the book were in a language other than English. He was only able to make out dates. The books first entries were from the late 1600s. Other than that, Jackson could decipher nothing from the faded ink on the pages. He skipped a couple journal owners until he found something written in English.

The first pages he could read were from a priest signed each entry "J. Coghlan." He was an Irish priest tracking a Dark One from Lithuania in the South of France. From what Jackson read, the vampire Coghlan was following was strong, fast, and adhered strictly to only coming out at night.

Jackson already knew these things. He didn't want some anecdotal account of some powerless clergyman observing one of these monsters from afar. He wanted data, facts, something he could use on the vampire that was hunting him presently. He skipped ahead for what felt like most of the book until he saw a list with bullet-points. It looked promising.

While anyone worthy of being the bearer of this codex will surely already know the vast majority of what I am about to write in it, I do believe it bears repeating- and ink-to-paper documentation of what we know about the undead that inhabit our world. I will now, to the best of my abilities, list briefly what we know- and do not know, about them.

Dark Ones can be killed by the following:
-severing of the head
-silver, or wood, driven through their heart (while a wooden stake driven through the heart of a Dark One will instantly kill him, silver is not as quick. Silver must be kept in contact with the Dark One's heart to

prevent healing of the organ in order to kill him.)

Dark Ones are vulnerable to, or weakened by:

-contact with silver. Prolonged exposure will burn them, and silver chains can be used to bind them. It should be noted that a wound caused by silver upon a Dark One will counteract their rapid healing ability. (also, a necklace of silver will protect the wearer from becoming mesmerized by the Dark One)

-sunlight. They lack their tremendous speed and strength in the daylight. Also, exposure to the sunlight is the only thing that will cause them to age. A Dark One who never sees the sun can live forever.

-blood. The Dark Ones must feed on the living to maintain their strength. If they do not feed, they are noticeably weaker.

-fire. It can be used to subdue them temporarily, or it can be used as a means of escaping one.

-holy ground. Churches, chapels, cathedrals are safe places. Here, the Dark Ones have no supernatural power. It should be noted, though, that they do not age in these places.

-holy symbols. From personal experience, these seem only to taunt the creatures. While they do produce a reaction from them, the reaction does not physically cripple the Dark One, merely distracting it momentarily at best.

-One of your best defenses is your own home. Dark Ones will not set foot in a dwelling which they have not been invited, I.e. not welcome.

The author continued with a similar list for Reborn, like Jackson. It was a much shorter list. It did not appear that the Order of Lazarus had had nearly as many dealings with zombies as they had with vampires; or perhaps the Reborn were not threatening.

The other undead are the Reborn. Their ranks include our order's patron, Lazarus, and even our

Savior, Jesus Christ. They are the people that have died and have been resurrected by means other than the abominable method of the Dark Ones. While they are rarely welcomed back by their loved ones, the Reborn are excellent as tools for tracking Dark Ones. Members of the Order should respect them and do their best to protect them. Their resilience varies, unlike their evil counterpart, but as far as my own experience can attest, these are their strengths and weaknesses.

Strengths
-heightened senses. All five senses are extremely sharp. The only exception is pain. Reborn do not appear to feel physical pain.

-speed. While this varies greatly, some of the Reborn have the capability to employ great alacrity should the situation call for it.

-being able to sense the presence of a Dark One. This is their most valuable ability.

Then there were the weaknesses.

Weaknesses

-decapitation

-consumption by fire

While the list was shorter, it seemed accurate enough to Jackson. He definitely had heightened senses. He could identify Breann and Father Borbridge by scent now if he had to. He could see just as well in the dark as midday. The speed thing worried him, though. It was like it was some form of zombie adrenaline that he couldn't control like his enhanced sensory perception. And he definitely knew about being able to sense the presence of vampires. The fire thing Borbridge had told him about, and the decapitation made natural sense. He did notice, however, the distinct lack of healing and regeneration in the list of Reborn strengths. Jackson added them in with the pencil he had in his pocket.

He was also unsure of the "abominable method" of creating a Dark One, but he wasn't too concerned with creating one. He was set on killing one. Get some wood. Get some silver. Starve them if you can. Get them in the sunlight, and don't stop stabbing until you hit the heart.

Day was breaking outside. Jackson could see the sky becoming a pale blue through the clear portions of the church's stained-glass windows. He could hear birds chirping. He was more than ready to walk outside without fear of being attacked. He gathered up the pile of robes he pretended to sleep on for Breann's sake and headed down into the basement to put the back where he got them from. Once he made his way back to the ground-level of the church, he took one last look at Breann, who was still sleeping soundly, and walked out the front door of the church.

As soon as he was outside, he could smell the dew that was still on the ground. He could feel the warm humidity of the Mobile air on his dead skin. He began walking, with the leather-bound book under his arm. Except for the back of his shirt being slashed and blood-stained- and his pale, dead complexion- Jackson might have looked like any college kid walking around Spring Hill's campus. But he wasn't. He was a Reborn, a zombie, and he could feel someone else.

Off somewhere to the North, where he had to go to get back to Father Hayes' house, he could feel the presence of the Dark One. He had not gone home like Father Borbridge implored him to do. He had crept out of sight, while he still waited for Jackson. As the day grew brighter, Jackson's confidence grew stronger. He did not fear his attacker with the light of the morning upon him.

The vampire's presence grew stronger and stronger as he walked closer to the priest's house. There was no one else around to see the zombie walking around; but the vampire was near.

"I know you're there," Jackson said. "I can feel you just like you can feel me."

The road to Father Hayes' house was built into the side of a hill. To Jackson's right, the hill climbed higher and led to dormitories. To his left there was a steep drop-off filled with kudzu. He heard the kudzu

161

rustle as a figure emerged.

The young man that Jackson saw was definitely the source of the darkness that he was feeling. He was a tall, muscular fellow. He was dressed well and had his short, blond hair styled. His body looked like a hairless, Nordic version of Jon's to Jackson. He was not the dark, ominous monster that he was expecting. He moved in close to Jackson and stared at him.

"So you're the one that keeps trying to kill me? Well, Hell, at least you don't sparkle." Jackson feigned laughter.

"Funny words coming from someone who's already dead." his voice was deep and loud. His voice, coupled with his rather large frame, might have intimidated Jackson in his life. But since he had endured death, along with everything else that he had survived, the zombie had no fear.

"Do ya mind telling me your name?" asked Jackson. "I'd at least like to know who has been keeping me trapped in that church."

Jackson saw the young man smile. His second incisors and canines looked unnaturally sharp, but not overly obtrusive. Normal people might not even notice that these teeth were that much different. But Jackson took notice. They were fangs. "I'm Ben," he said. "And I *will* kill you."

"Well, I don't know about that, Ben." Jackson made sure to restate his name. His attempted murderer had a face now. He had a name. He knew who he was. He was no longer some scary, shadowy figure that would attack unbeknownst to Jackson. He was looking on the entire measure of the monster that would see him dead. "You sure won't in this light," Jackson remarked.

162

Ben growled under his breath. "Your time will come, dead man. You should be gone to this world, and I will see to it that you get that way."

Jackson knew full well that he had the upper hand in the daylight. He reveled in the fact. "I know you won't attack me now. You aren't near as strong when the sun's out."

"The sun's not always out, Jackson." Ben knew his name.

"Whatever you say, chief," Jackson said with a grin. "But I'll be ready when you are."

Ben grunted and walked past Jackson, headed in the opposite direction. Jackson turned around to face him.

"Take a good look, Ben. I want you to see my face, because I promise I won't be trying to run away the next time we meet." Having seen his attacker, Jackson no longer feared him. He was ready to face him.

Ben was not willing to fight him now. "Whatever, dead man. You'll get your chance to fight us." Ben walked away. Jackson watched him as he walked away until he was out of sight.

Who was "us"? Jackson thought. There was more than one vampire. He was pretty sure that Ben had been the only one that had tried to attack him, but he hadn't even considered that there was more than one. Undeterred, he pressed on to Father Hayes' house.

Once he made it to the front porch, Borbridge opened the door and met him out there. "Did you make it here without any trouble? Did anyone see you?"

Jackson still didn't want to fully trust the priest,

but he felt he needed to give him the benefit of the doubt. "Only the vampire saw me," he said."

"What?!" Borbridge asked.

"Yeah, he saw me. I talked to him. I know who he is."

Father Borbridge was fascinated. "Really? So, what did you talk about?"

The question bothered Jackson. "That's what you want to know? What we talked about? Don't you even find it weird that you couldn't figure out who was trying to kill me, and I could do it just by walking here?"

"Well, with all due respect, I have student records. You have whatever it is that you have. You can sense him. I cannot." He really didn't seem to be hiding anything. "What is his name?"

"Ben," Jackson said. "That's all he told me." He still hadn't mentioned to the priest that it was in fact Ben that Borbridge had spoken with outside the chapel earlier.

"Well, that I can work with," Borbridge said. "Now come inside, son."

Jackson followed the priest into Father Hayes' house. Father Hayes was already sitting in his recliner. Borbridge took a seat on his sofa. Jackson remained standing across the room from them.

"I see Father Borbridge has given you our journal, Jackson," Father Hayes said as he pointed to the book that was in Jackson's right hand."

"Oh, yes sir." Jackson brought it to his other hand and played with the weight of it. "I haven't read all of it, but what I have read has been eye-opening."

"I wasn't completely honest with you before, Jackson. I sent you to the chapel to make completely sure that you were, in fact, a Reborn."

"No big deal, Father," Jackson said. "I understand you had to cover your bases." Jackson was still eyeballing Father Borbridge suspiciously. "So did you bring me clothes and weapons like I asked?"

Father Borbridge stood up. "Oh, yes. Yes. I've got a box full of clothes, and I got some weapons that, I think, you will be able to use." He motioned to a box on Father Hayes' dining room table.

In the box were numerous shoes and jackets. Jackson found a pair that looked like they would fit him. They were some leather, steel-toed work boots that looked serviceable enough. He also found a thick jacket. It was a dark blue jacket that zipped up in the front, had a hood, and looked very durable. Jackson put it on immediately. It seemed to be made for him. It even had an inside pocket in which the journal fit perfectly.

Jackson rustled through the box to find some socks. Once he did, he put them on and topped them off with his new leather boots.

"What about a weapon?" he asked. "I read enough of that book. I need a lot of silver and a lot of wood."

Both of the priests laughed. "I think he might be ready," Father Hayes said.

"I fear you may be right, Gerald," Borbridge replied. "Well, I brought this dagger." Father Borbridge presented to Jackson a small, silver dagger in a leather sheath. Jackson took it readily. He pulled it out of the sheath to examine it. It was pretty sharp. Jackson put it back into its leather holder and placed it in one of his jacket pockets.

"Thanks," Jackson said.

As Jackson stood there, armed with the Order of Lazarus' journal and a handful of silver, the priests looked at him with equal parts fear and amazement.

"Well, what are you planning to do now, Jackson?" Father Borbridge asked.

"I have to kill them."

"Them?" Father Hayes asked.

"Yes, Father," Jackson said. "Ben said that there was more than one of them."

"Then, no. You won't do anything yet." Father Hayes was getting worked up. "If there is more than one, I forbid you to just go after a whole lot of them. I've seen what happens when they fight in numbers, and I will not let you do that."

Jackson looked defeated. "Well, what am I supposed to do?"

"You will wait here until we can find out more details." Father Borbridge's interjection was stern and deliberate.

"Yes, sir," Jackson said reluctantly. He was still respectful of the old priest.

"I have to go now. I have to say Mass at St. Joe's in a few hours. Gerald, look after the boy."

"You know I will." The priest's words were nothing but comforting. There was someone who cared about him still.

As Borbridge left Father Hayes' house, he gave nothing more than a nod to Jackson. Jackson was immediately restless and plopped down on the sofa.

"He said we was going to kill me, Father," Jackson told Father Hayes.

"Well, that's simply not going to happen as long as you stay here. You're safe here." Jackson thought about what he had read in the journal. If they haven't been invited in, they won't be able to get in here, he thought.

But he also thought about leaving. He hated just sitting around in any kind of safe-house waiting on his enemy to make a move. Jackson hoped that the fact his zombie body required no sleep would serve him in this instance. He would wait until his old parish priest dozed off; then he would make his move.

It didn't take too long. Father Hayes was out before he knew it. Jackson arose slowly and quietly. He crept by him and out of his door. Once he was outside he wondered where he might go. Part of him wondered what Father Borbridge might have to say about a young girl sleeping on robes in a back pew. Another part of him wondered about the other people he cared about. Where were Jon and the other guys? Where was Meggie? Was she really okay? Jackson just knew he couldn't stay in any safe place waiting for his enemy to make a move. He left Father Hayes' porch and set off in an all-too-familiar direction.

15

Meggie was walking around her room, deliberately making as much noise as she could. It had been so late when Chad brought Emily back, that Meggie was already asleep. Paul had called it an early night and brought her back before midnight. Meggie had told her mom that it was because she wasn't feeling well, so she wouldn't wait up to interrogate Emily.

As she picked out some clothes to wear to Mass, she opened drawers and closet doors, being as loud as possible. After slamming her sock drawer closed, she finally heard her friend stir.

"Ughhhhh! Be quiet, slut." Emily groaned from underneath the comforter.

Meggie jostled her friend. "Get up, girl." Emily rolled over, away from her.

"Leave me alone. Sleepy time."

Meggie wasn't taking "no" for an answer. "Wake up!"

Emily accepted her fate. Her friend wasn't going to let her sleep. She sat up. Her hair was a mess, and her eyes were barely open. "What can I help you with, stupid?"

Meggie laughed. "How did it go last night? My night ended pretty early, so I was asleep when you finally decided to come home."

Emily grunted. "It was the guys. How do you think it went? It was fun. Foster was dumb. Chad was sweet. Ryan and Jon were nice, even though they were mad at Paul. And Brandon was all muscly and beautiful. What more do you want to know?"

"Brandon?" Meggie asked. Meggie had not expected to hear anything about him.

Emily scoffed. "Yeah. He told you he was gonna be home. He went out with us last night."

Meggie immediately felt guilty. She had forgotten all about Brandon telling her back at Auburn that he was going to be in Mobile before he had to deploy. "I forgot all about him."

"Yeah, I know you did," Emily said. She was not amused with her friend's infatuation with Paul that made her dismiss everyone else. "They kept asking about you all night. But don't worry, skank. I gave them an excuse besides Paul."

Meggie felt bad about ditching all her other friends to hang out with one of them. "What did they say?"

"I don't know, dude." Emily was not much of a morning person, but even if she was wide awake, she wouldn't have been able to recall everything the guys had to say. In her current state, though, she couldn't remember anything. "If you cared so much, you probably should've been there."

Emily's words were more of a cranky response for being awakened too early than an actual stab, but

169

they affected Meggie just the same. "Look, I'm sorry I missed Brandon- and everybody else- but I can't do anything about it now. I just want to know how it went."

Emily was beginning to actually wake up by now. She rubbed her eyes and prepared an actual statement for her friend. "Look, Meg, the guys were hoping you would be able to bring Paul back around more; instead, he just took you away, too."

Emily's words made Meggie sad. But she couldn't help it. When she was around Paul, she didn't care about anything or anyone else. He made her forget. Now that he wasn't around to make her forget, she was able to think about it. "I'm gonna have to talk to them after church today."

Before they all graduated and went their separate ways, Meggie and all of the guys went to the same church. This was her first weekend home from college. She wasn't sure if their parents would make them go to Mass, but she hoped so, since she knew her mom would make her go.

"So how do I need to dress?" Emily asked.

"Oh, you don't have to go," Meggie said. "Mom knows you're not Catholic. She won't make you go."

Emily scrunched her brow. "Then why the Hell did you wake me up?"

Meggie laughed at her sleepy-headed friend. "Believe it or not, I really wanted to know how last night went."

"Well, it went alright. We had dinner at Brandon's house with his family. Then we went and played some beach volleyball on the South Alabama campus."

Meggie thought about how much fun her friends must have had without her. She now wished she would have gone with them. "Typical. It's always sports or booze with those boys."

"How about your night, lover girl?" Emily asked. She was finally awake enough to be talkative.

"Oh, it was fine. I got to meet Alex and Ben. They're not too bad. If you think Brandon is all buffed up, you should meet Ben. He's got Brandon's muscles, but he's as big as Jon."

"Sounds like somebody I don't wanna piss off," Emily said. "But what are they like? If they're not bad, maybe they *should* come around the other guys."

"I think so too. I don't know why Paul won't do it."

"You should work on that. So, how about Mr. Paul? How did things go there?" Emily got out of her friend's bed and grabbed her phone from Meggie's nightstand to check her messages.

Emily was texting someone back as Meggie responded. "We had fun. We hung out at Alex's and Ben's apartment and had a few drinks."

"So you were drinking in an apartment with three dudes!" Emily sounded a little upset.

"No, there were other girls there too." Meggie laughed. "It wasn't anything like that. It was just a party."

"And?" Emily wanted to hear more details.

"Something came up with the other guys, and Paul said he had to take me home. He dropped me off and kissed me good night."

"He did, huh?" Emily gave her friend a wink. "How was that?"

"It was alright." Meggie's response came out

before she could even think about it. At the time of
the long kiss goodnight, she remembered feeling
lighter than air, with a stomach full of butterflies. But
now all she could think about was how it was not
Jackson. His kisses were the best. Just as she forgot
everyone when Paul was around, she had also
forgotten about Jackson and his kisses. Now she could
only think to compare it to them and how they didn't
stack up.

"You sound let down," Emily said. She could
read her friend. "He's not Jackson, and he's not going
to be. Be happy, girl." Secretly she was relieved that
Paul's smooches were a letdown; but she did want her
friend to be happy, even if it was with Paul.

"Yeah, I know." Meggie went back to getting
ready. Emily got back in the bed. "Who ya texting?"

"Chad. He's the only person I told where you
really went. I'm just filling him in." Emily answered
her friend without stopping her thumbs.

"Oh, okay."

Once Meggie was dressed, she stopped in her
doorway before leaving. "We're heading out. I'll lock
the door behind us so nobody can come get you while
your lazy ass goes back to sleep. If I get up with the
guys after church, I'll text you and let you know."

"Sounds like a plan." Emily smiled and gave
her friend a thumbs-up. She heard the front door close
behind Meggie's family. She was alone in the Paulez
home.

***

Emily lay in the bed for a while, until she
couldn't take her morning breath anymore. She got

herself out of the bed and dug around in her bag until she found her toothbrush. Once she had it, she made her way to the bathroom across the hall.

After she finished, Emily splashed some cold water on her face. She was refreshed and ready to face the day. When she walked back into Meggie's room, though, she heard a noise.

Emily could hear the front door open. While she thought that Meggie and her family hadn't been gone long enough to be back already, she had definitely heard the door. Then she heard a slow and steady male voice.

"Emily, I know you're here. Just don't freak out. I don't have a gun or anything." The voice's request was useless. Chills immediately ran up her back, and Emily's arms were filled with goosebumps. Her keys were on Meggie's dresser. As quietly as she could, she picked them up and opened the protective cap atop her pepper spray.

She could hear her heart pounding in her ears. It muffled the sounds of the footsteps making their way to Meggie's room. Before she could even think, she ran toward the sounds with her key-chain pepper spray out front, ready to blast the unwanted visitor.

Emily unloaded the canister on her assailant. Amidst her blood-curdling screams and frantic waving of the pepper spray, she could make out the figure hiding his face. He was wearing a dark blue jacket. She could tell her pepper spray was running low, but it just made her shake her hand more frantically. As it sputtered its last bits of defense, the man turned to face her. The final bits of pepper spray landed directed on his unprotected face as Emily looked upon him. When she saw him, she tried to place him. She recognized his face, but she couldn't figure it out. Then she did, and her vision blackened as her legs buckled beneath her.

When she came to, she saw him again. Knelt at her feet was someone she *never* expected to see. She looked into the dead green eyes of none other than her friend Meggie's belated boyfriend, Jackson Hughes. She let out another terrified shriek as she scrambled back to her feet and backed away from him.

"Please, calm down," Jackson said. He never stopped staring at her, only watched her intently as she panted from fear. "I promise I won't hurt you."

Emily attempted escape. He was blocking the fastest way out of the house. She ran as fast as she could toward him. She had enough room to pick up a pretty decent amount of speed. As she tried to run past him, Jackson sidestepped and blocked her path. It was like hitting a wall. While Jackson didn't budge, Emily fell backward onto the floor again. She sprang to her feet and backpedaled.

Cold sweat had filled Emily's palms and covered her forehead. She could hardly breathe. Emily felt as though she may collapse again when she tried to catch her breath again. For some reason, though, she seemed to believe that this person, whom she *knew* was supposed to be dead, meant her no harm. "What the Hell, dude?"

"I'm sorry I frightened you," Jackson said. "You weren't supposed to be here."

Breathing became a little easier. "You're Jackson. You're dead. How is this even possible? And how do you *know* me?" Emily leaned against the wall in the hallway. She didn't have complete faith that her legs would fail again.

"I came back from the dead. I'm a zombie. And I remember you from when you visited my grave."

Emily looked at him. She had just sprayed him with an entire can of pepper spray, some of which hit him directly in the face and eyes. She became frightened again when she noticed that he hadn't even flinched. There was enough of it in the air that Emily's eyes were burning, and the back of her throat itched. But his eyes weren't watering or red; and he didn't look to be any worse for wear. He just looked back at her as the liquid dripped down his pale skin.

No amount of Gothic literature prepared her for a face-to-face with Jackson. Reading and fantasizing about the dead could not compare to this. A zombie, in the flesh, was staring back at her. She turned her back to the wall and slid down it until she was sitting on the floor. Emily used both of her hands to pull the skin of her face back, causing her eyes to widen. She thought about her visit to the cemetery over winter break. How long had Jackson been there, reanimated? How long had he been walking around again? She tried to wrap her head around the situation. It was no use. Emily looked up at Jackson. There he was. She looked at the dark blue jacket that she had noticed earlier. Beneath it, he had a polo shirt and a rosary around his neck. After she took note of his blue jeans and big, leather boots, Emily looked back up at his face. It was the same pretty face she remembered seeing in the picture that Meggie kept in a box under her bed back at Auburn. But it was paler. It was a dead face.

"S-s-so you're a zombie?" Emily stammered.

Jackson nodded. "Yes. Some people prefer to say 'Reborn,' but, yes, I am a zombie." He refused to use the watered-down term preferred by the Order of Lazarus.

"And you're not here to eat my brains?" Emily was still worried. Zombies weren't usually the nicest characters in the books she had read.

The comment made Jackson smile his crooked smile. "No." He had not experienced any form of thirst or hunger since his return, for brains or otherwise. "I haven't had anything to eat in over a year. And I'm not hungry. You're safe there."

"Okay." Emily got back to her feet. She stood where she was. She was still not ready to be any closer to him. She rubbed her eyes. Unlike Jackson, the pepper spray *had* affected her. "So what are you doing here?"

Jackson had not expected Emily to be at Meggie's house. He had banked on her family being at Mass, like they always did. "I came here to leave a note for Meggie. I didn't expect you to be here, though."

Jackson's words confused her. "Ain't you afraid of freaking her out with that? You are supposed to be dead. A letter from you might not be the smartest thing." Emily was surprised at how human Jackson was. She never expected a zombie to be so personable. He wasn't scary. If she didn't know for sure that he was supposed to be buried, it would have felt like a normal conversation.

Jackson understood her concern. "I wasn't going to make the letter from me. I was just going to warn her."

"Warn her? Warn her about what?" Emily was concerned about what a zombie might know that

176

compelled him to warn anyone about anything.

"About Paul."

Emily stepped closer to him. "Paul? For real? Man, none of y'all want her to be with him."

"What do you mean, 'none of y'all'?" Jackson's protective nature toward Meggie overtook him.

"Th-the other guys." Jackson's tonal change scared her a bit. "Chad, Jon, Ryan, Foster, Brandon. None of them trust Paul."

Just hearing their names brought back a wave of memories and emotions. He longed to be reunited with his friends, but he knew that that couldn't happen in any real sense. He could never be the Jackson they knew again. "You know all of them?"

"Yes," Emily said. "I've met them all, including Paul."

Emily could see emotions showing up on Jackson's face. Was she feeling pity for a zombie?

"Anyway, I came to warn her about Paul. But since you are here, you can do it for me." Jackson moved in closer to Emily. She didn't back away.

"What do you need me to do? What were you gonna tell her?" Emily found herself anxious to help the zombie. She was no longer afraid of him. It was more of a fascination now.

"Paul has a friend that is bad," Jackson said. "And it's affected Paul too."

Emily sighed. She had heard this from the rest of guys enough. "Is it Ben or Alex?"

Jackson was taken aback. Did Emily know about Ben being a vampire? And who was Alex? While he wasn't sure of what Emily might know, or who this Alex was, he was sure that it was Ben that he needed to warn Meggie about. "It's Ben. He's evil." He left out the blood-sucking aspect.

"Ryan and Jon don't approve of him either," Emily said. "They don't like him because he keeps Paul away from them. What's your reason?"

Jackson wasn't in the chapel anymore. He could tell her a bald-faced lie, and he wouldn't feel as guilty about it. But he didn't lie to Emily. He didn't mention any Dark Ones or vampires, but he didn't lie. "He knows I'm back from the dead. And he has tried to kill me- twice."

Emily chuckled a little. "Does that really make him bad?"

"What are you talking about?" Jackson asked.

"I mean," Emily went on, "You're already dead. It's not like it's murder."

Emily's words angered him. He may have died, but he was most certainly alive now. His new life had just as much value to him as any life. "This Ben never knew me when I was alive." Jackson peered into Emily's eyes with disdain. His deliberate speech intimidated her. Jackson did not like his second life being marginalized. "I know I died once, but he tried to kill me. Twice!"

Emily could sense that Jackson was upset quite clearly. Though she wasn't necessarily afraid of him, she did not want to upset anyone that had already defeated death once. "Okay, okay. So he's bad. What do you suggest? We've already expressed our opinions. How am I supposed to get her to stop seeing him?"

Jackson hadn't really thought about *how* he would warn Meggie. He wasn't even sure what he would have written in the note. He just knew that he had to get to her. "We need to keep her away from Paul. If she stays away from him, she won't have a reason to be around Ben."

Emily had a way that was simple enough. "I guilt-tripped her this morning. I'm sure I can get her to hang out with me and the rest of the guys today. She had kind of planned on it anyway."

"That's good," Jackson said, delighted. "That will buy me some time."

"Time for what?" Emily asked.

"Nothing. Don't worry about it."

While Emily wasn't afraid of Jackson, she certainly wasn't about to ask a zombie the details of his comings and goings.   "Okay."

"Thank you, Emily." Jackson extended a hand for her to shake. After some hesitation, she shook it. His grip was a cold, firm one. Jackson took notice of the silver necklace she was wearing. It seemed to relieve him. Jackson turned to leave.

When he was almost to Meggie's front door, he heard Emily's phone vibrate in her pocket. He stopped and turned his head. "Who is it?" he asked.

His question surprised Emily, and it scared her a bit. How did he know her phone was ringing? It was on silent. She pulled it from her pants pocket to see the identity of her caller. "It's Meggie."

"Answer it." Emily obeyed his command.

"Hello?" Emily answered. Jackson stood in place and awaited Meggie's voice come from the phone. It was loud and clear to his undead ears.

"Hey, girl." Her voice was sweet and melodic to Jackson. She went on. "We just got out of Mass. The guys wanna meet up at Jon's house. Brandon's gonna come too. I'll text you the address. You can meet us there."

Emily listened as she looked at Jackson. He

nodded at her. She gathered that he could hear what Meggie was saying. Emily shrugged and widened her eyes at him.

"Tell her 'okay.' Tell her you'll meet her there." Jackson whispered very softly. As he slowly forced out the words, he hoped they were audible enough for her to hear.

Emily could hear almost all of his whispered words, and she was able to read his lips for the rest of them. The message was properly conveyed. "That's fine. Just text me the address. I'll meet y'all there."

"Alright. Lock up behind you. Bye." Jackson heard Meggie hang up.

"How did you hear her?" Emily asked him. She was way too far away in the house for it to be humanly possible for him to hear Meggie on the phone.

Jackson smiled at Emily. "My zombie hearing is pretty good."

"I guess so," she said. Emily thought about Meggie telling her to lock up. "How did you get in here anyway?"

Jackson smiled his crooked smile at her again. "They used to keep a key under the big plant pot by the front door. They still do."

"Well, what are you gonna do?" she asked the zombie.

"I'm going with you."

Emily raised an eyebrow. "Ain't that gonna be a little awkward when everybody sees you?"

"Well, I'm not gonna go to Jon's with you," Jackson said. He wished he could, though. "But I wanna show you where to bring Meggie." He had to make sure she ended up in St. Joseph's Chapel before

180

nightfall. It was the only way he knew that she would be safe.

"'Where to bring her'?" Emily asked suspiciously. "What is going on?"

Jackson closed the gap between them. Emily got chills again as he moved in close. "Emily, please trust me. I know how to keep her safe from Ben. But you have to do what I say and take her to where I tell you."

Emily was close enough to Jackson that she had to look up at him. His piercing green eyes reinforced the chills she had. She was scared. But she was willing to trust him. "Alright."

As she continued to stare at him, Emily's phone vibrated again. Jackson had heard it. "I guess that's the text with the address." She pulled out the phone and looked at it. It was. "And we need to go ahead and get out of here before Ms. Paulez and Maria get back. I don't feel like having that conversation yet. Do you need anything else? I mean, you already have your keys, for sure."

Emily looked down at the car keys that contained the empty pepper spray canister. She looked back up, and the zombie was smiling at her. "It's okay," Jackson said. "You just let me know that it doesn't affect me."

She grinned. "At all?"

"Not at all," Jackson said. "At first, I flinched and covered my face out of some survival instinct or something. Then I realized that it didn't hurt me one bit."

"That's kind of awesome," Emily said.

Jackson smiled again. "I guess it is pretty awesome."

Emily was beginning to see why Jackson's friends loved him so much. Even as a zombie, he was quite likeable. "I guess we better get out of here then. Just let me put on some different clothes first, okay?"

"Okay."

After a few moments, she reemerged from Meggie's room in new clothes. She was wearing a pair of jeans and a black shirt with some band he had never heard of. Emily went to walk past Jackson to head out the front door. This time he let her. As she passed him he turned to follow her out the front door.

Emily and Jackson were outside. "Did you lock it?" she asked him.

"Yes. By the way, I saw your car when I walked up," Jackson said. "Freakin' sweet ass car!"

"Thanks. Not everyone appreciates a classic."

Jackson shook his head. "I don't know why. This old car looks like a beast! I mean, I don't know nothin' about cars, but I know enough to know that this car rocks!"

"Thanks, dead man." Emily smiled at Jackson as they made their way to their respective doors. Unlike when Ben had said it to him, it sounded more like a term of endearment than an insult. Jackson returned the gesture and smiled back at her.

Emily found the right key and unlocked her car door. Once she was inside, she unlocked the passenger side so Jackson could get in. She buckled her seat belt and turned the ignition. The Dodge Dart roared to life.

"Oh, it sounds as good as it looks," Jackson said. He buckled his own seat belt.

As Emily put the car in reverse and started creeping slowly, she slammed on the brakes, bringing her backing out of Meggie's driveway to a sudden halt. She bent over and started wheezing.

"Are you okay?" Jackson asked.

Emily wheezing changed as soon as she caught her breath. It transformed to uncontrollable laughter. "Yeah, it's fine." Emily was laughing so hard, she had to wipe tears from her eyes. "You just put on your seat belt."

Jackson grasped his shoulder strap and chuckled a bit himself, as he also grasped the irony.

"I guess that's those survival instincts again," Emily said as she drove out of Meggie's neighborhood.

"Take a left here." Jackson pointed at a road just up ahead of them.

"Okay." Emily obliged and made the turn. As she rolled down her window, she asked. "Mind if I ask you a question?"

"Sure. Go ahead." Jackson was feeling and hearing the air whip into the car. They were pleasant sensations. He rolled down the window on his side as well.

Emily waved her finger toward Jackson, pointing out all of his clothes. "Is that what your family buried you in?" She giggled.

The zombie looked down at his garb. His jacket and big, steel-toe boots didn't really look right on him, especially in the balmy Mobile heat. He looked pretty silly to Emily. But then again, he was supposed to be dead. Fashion was not his primary concern.

"No," he said. "I found these clothes later. Okay, take another left." Jackson's memory of the roads in his city was still just as good as it ever was when he was alive.

"So what's with the coat?" she asked.

"What do you mean?"

"It's too hot for long sleeves, let alone a jacket!"

While Jackson thought about the rips and blood stains on the back of his shirt that the jacket concealed, Emily could only think of how hot it was. "It's more functional," he said. "Lots of pockets."

Emily scoffed. "Well to Hell with function. It's too hot for all that."

Jackson thought about how he would attempt to make her understand his relationship with his sense of touch. He could feel things. He could even feel things well. He could feel the wind on his face. He remembered feeling the warmth of Breann's breath. He could even feel the slightest vibrations made by people walking and talking. But when it came to pain, Jackson felt none. He felt the warmth of the sun, and the extra warmth caused by his jacket, but there was no discomfort. "I don't really *feel* hot like that."

"Oh, yeah. I didn't even think of that," Emily said. "But why would I? It's not like I get to talk to a zombie every day."

Before Jackson could say anything back, he felt the back of Emily's hand press up against his left cheek. She rubbed it around a little and then moved down to his shoulder, where the sun had been shining on it through the windshield.

"You're like, room temperature," Emily said. "That is so weird. But your shoulder's all hot from the sun. I wonder- if we left you shut up in the car, if you would cook."

He thought about what Father Borbridge had

told him, about how fire was the only thing that could completely end a Reborn. Baking slowly in a car in the midday heat was too close for comfort. "Let's not find out."

Emily smiled at Jackson. "Yeah. Let's not."

16

Emily tried with all her might to remember everything that Jackson had told her. He laid out very specific instructions about how to get Meggie safely to St. Joseph's Chapel. He was very clear about what to do and how to handle it. Whether it was her affinity for the Gothic or fear of offending an undead man with nothing to lose, Emily did not want to let him down. She wished she had written down his instructions as she went frantically through her mental checklist. Driving to Jon's was a distant second to remembering everything she had to do.

Jon's house was in a subdivision in Mobile called Sugar Creek. Most of the houses had been built in the 1970s, so they were a little dated. They were still very nice, though. Emily looked down at her phone once again to confirm that she had arrived at the correct address from the text she had gotten from Meggie. When she was sure the numbers on the mailbox matched the numbers on her phone, she parked her car in his driveway. Once she was parked, she made her way to the front door of Jon's big brick house.

Before she could even ring the doorbell, the door opened to reveal a man that *had* to be Jon's father. He looked just like him, plus about thirty years, complete with the same kind face, and the same bull-in-a-china-shop disposition. The man looked down at Emily with a grin. "You must be that heathen roommate of Meggie's up at Auburn."

Emily was a little shocked by the salutation, but quickly caught on that he was kidding. "That's me- didn't go to church with her this morning. I was afraid somebody would burn me at the stake."

Mr. Williams put his hand on her back and welcomed her into the house. Like Jon, he was unaware of his own strength, and he jostled Emily a bit. After feeling halfway shoved, she was inside the house. "Come on now, us crazy Catholics, we ain't that bad."

"Oh, I know."

Jon's father pointed toward the back of the house. Through a big window, Emily saw Meggie and all her friends. "I'm sure they're the ones you're lookin' for." Mr. Williams gave her another exuberant nudge.

"Thanks," Emily said, making her way out of the back door that opened to Jon's patio.

Except for Meggie, everyone else was swimming. All of the guys were swimming around and splashing. Having just seen their fallen friend, Emily tried to picture Jackson right there with them, enjoying the pool. Only being able to picture him in what she had seen him wearing, the mental picture was comical. After a little soft laughter, Emily returned her focus to the real world.

Meggie was the first to notice her. As she approached Emily, the guys hadn't even realized her arrival. "What's up, skank?"

"Not too much," she said. "You didn't tell me

it was going to be a pool party."

Meggie laughed. "They didn't tell me either. I don't have my suit."

"Ha!" Emily exclaimed. "Well, as your roommate, I've seen your underwear and your bikini. There's very little difference."

"Keep it up," Meggie said with a grin. "I'll throw you in with everything you're wearing."

Matching metal chairs and tables were scattered about the perimeter of the swimming pool. Emily and Meggie grabbed a couple and sat down.

"So, I noticed there's no Paul here," Emily said snidely.

"Yeah, he didn't come to church today."

After spending her morning with Jackson, Emily was in no way surprised by that. "Uh huh. Are his parents not as strict about it as y'all's are?"

Meggie laughed. "Except for my mom, none of our parents are really strict about going to church. It's just what we do. We all believe in God, and it's another reason for all of us to see each other."

"And Paul not being there didn't bother you?" Emily asked suspiciously. "It would seem that, if that was the reasons for going to church, him not being there would bother you more."

Meggie tried to reassure her friend. "He told me last night that he might be out late with whatever came up with the other guys. He probably just slept in."

Meggie seemed captivated by Paul. It was as though he could do nothing that might warrant suspicion, let alone any wrong. Emily wanted to press her more, but they were interrupted.

The girls felt several drops of cold water fall on

them. They had come from Foster's direction. "What up, Emily? How's the show?" he asked as he flexed his arms. Foster was tall and lanky. The only thing that would have made it funnier was if Foster had been serious.

Emily gave him a thumbs up. "You know it, Foster." She leaned in to whisper to Meggie. "Though, I must say, that Brandon ain't bad to look at."

Emily had just finished making her remark about the musclebound marine when her new boyfriend, Chad, walked up. "What is happening, ladies?" he asked.

"Oh, just hanging out with my friend, since y'all can't tell somebody to bring a bathing suit," Meggie said, elbowing Chad in the ribs.

Ever polite, Chad lowered his head. "You're right. We should have told you. I'm sorry."

"It's okay, dude. We'll be here when y'all get out." Meggie didn't want to make Chad feel bad.

Chad put his long, wet hair behind his ears and leaned down to hug Emily. She wrapped her arms around him and also gave him a kiss. "My boyfriend. The sweet one," she said as they crinkled their noses and rubbed them against one another. Meggie grimaced at their sickly sweet exchange.

"We'll be out soon, okay?" He backed away from Emily so he wouldn't drip any more water on her.

"Take your time."

"Alright," Chad said as he turned and ran toward the pool. Before the girls knew it, he was midair in the shape of a cannonball aimed at Jon.

"Heads up, sweater vest!" Foster shouted as Chad landed on Jon, slamming him underwater.

Jon emerged from under the water. He rubbed from his chest to his navel with both hands, smoothing out his hairy torso. "Don't hate! This is what a man's supposed to look like." The girls shook their heads and got back to their conversation.

"So, is Paul coming over too?" Emily asked.

"What? No. He called me just before you got here. I'm probably just gonna hang out with him later."

Emily really didn't like the way Paul could control her friend. "And that didn't strike you as odd?" she asked.

"What do you mean?"

"I mean, once he got you alone, he just wanted to see you, and doesn't want to hang around the guys." Emily was trying to make her see. It was no use.

Meggie became defensive. "Well, Jon and Ryan say that Paul has changed. Maybe they have changed, and he doesn't want to hang out with them anymore."

Emily looked at the boys swimming in the pool as their horseplay ensued. She looked back her friend and raised an eyebrow. "Do they really seem *that* different?"

Meggie knew she was right about that. They were the same fun-loving guys she always knew. She prepared her next defense. "Well, something did change. I'm not just Meggie, that girl that always hangs out with the guys. I'm Meggie, the girl that went on a date with Paul."

Emily laughed. "Meg, did you forget that Chad and I are an item now? I don't think it would be *that* weird."

"Did you forget that I used to date Jackson, and he died!" Meggie almost shouted. It was loud enough that all the boys heard it and stopped what they were doing. Emily prepared to retort, but Brandon hopped out of the pool and hustled over to the girls.

"Whoa, whoa, whoa. What's goin' on over here?" he asked.

Emily couldn't respond. The secret she was keeping from Meggie was burning her insides. Jackson was alive, or at least not dead. She could see the anguish on Meggie's face. It was the familiar look she got when she talked or thought about Jackson too much. Emily wasn't sure the knowledge she possessed would help or harm her friend, but it was definitely difficult to contain. Meggie, although distraught from bringing up her old, dead boyfriend so dramatically, seemed to be deep in thought.

"Hello?" Brandon asked again. All of the other guys were waiting for any sort of response. No longer was there any splashing. They were awaiting her response.

"It's fine," Meggie said. "I just got a little worked up being back here with all of y'all." It was a half-truth. Bringing up Jackson did get her upset, but she was equally upset at the thought of creating a new dynamic amongst her friends because of Paul.

Brandon bought it, though. He put his hand on her shoulder. "That's alright, Meg. It happens to the best of us sometimes." Brandon, thinking that the whole commotion was about Jackson, looked at his friend with great sympathy. He missed his friend more than everyone else realized.

"Thanks," Meggie said. She looked back at him. She was grateful for such a good friend, to Jackson and to her.

191

"Hey!" Ryan shouted from the other end of the pool. "We cool?" Ryan had coped the most healthily about Jackson's passing. He really did just want to see his friends get along.

Brandon looked back at the guys. "Yeah. We cool." He looked at Meggie and nodded, then returned to the water.

Emily looked at her friend. "Still not wanting to give them any details about you and Paul?" she asked.

"They'll either pick on me because they're my friends; or they'll judge me because they were friends with Jackson." Meggie felt trapped by the situation.

Although Emily felt sympathetic, she could not ignore the fact that a zombie had visited her and told her to keep Meggie away from Paul. She also couldn't ignore that she had given said zombie her word that she would get Meggie safely to St. Joseph's Chapel at Spring Hill College. For these reasons, she could not placate her friend and her infatuation with Paul.

"Let's just not worry about that for a while," Emily said. She put her hand on the wet spot that Brandon had made on Meggie's shoulder. "I'm supposed to go back to Birmingham today. I may call my parents and tell them I'm staying for one more night, but let's just you and me hang out until I have to go."

"What about the guys?" Meggie wondered.

Emily motioned her hand toward them in disregard. "I'm sure they'll be fine. Besides, they'll all be here after I leave. You can hang out with them for the rest of the summer. Now, I'm not saying that I won't be back. I mean, Hell, I'm dating Chad now. I'm sure I'll be back. But they'll for sure be here. So, whadya say?"

Meggie thought about it for a moment. "Okay, sounds good."

Emily breathed a sigh of relief. She really didn't want to disappoint Jackson. As nice as he seemed, he was still dead to the world. He had nothing to lose. For some reason, Emily was sure that he meant what he said, and he had intentions for every facet of his plan, even if he didn't reveal it to her. "Great!" she exclaimed.

"What's great?" Jon asked.

"Oh, nothing. Meg and I are just going to have a girl's day today. Y'all can't come," Emily said. She stuck her tongue out at all of the guys.

"They're prolly just gonna talk about how hot we are," Foster said, reassuring his friends. "I understand. The ladies can only take so much of the Foster until they *have* to have a play-date to talk about it.

Chad laughed. "Yeah, I'm sure that's what it is." He looked at Emily, who winked at him.

"Don't worry, we still love y'all," Meggie said. "But sometimes, you just need some girl time." The guys almost groaned in unison.

"Whatever," Ryan said. "Time is time, and people are people. Sounds like an excuse to tell secrets to me."

"Duh!" Meggie guffawed. "Sometimes, y'all just can't understand."

"They'll never understand," Emily said. She was grateful for her gender. It gave her a valid excuse to steal Meggie away. She didn't want to have any manicures or pedicures or anything. She had secrets upon secrets, most of which she could not reveal to anyone. But the ploy had worked. She would have Meggie independent of any of Jackson's other friends, which is what Jackson, and Emily, wanted.

While the rest of the guys disregarded "girl time" and continued to splash about in the pool, Chad came to Emily. "I'm not sure what you two are plotting, but I guess I have no choice but to respect it." He was always the kind, understanding one of them.

"Thanks, babe," Emily said. "I promise we're not out to turn against y'all. Sometimes y'all are too much. We just need it."

Chad smiled. "I understand. Whatever you ladies are up to, I'm sure it's okay." He smiled at Emily. She looked up at him. Chad liked her as much as Meggie had recently liked Paul. He trusted her wholeheartedly. Emily wished that she was able to tell him about Jackson, but she knew that that was out of the question. Still, her heart longed to grant him full disclosure.

"After we're done, I'll make sure you get some time with your lady," Emily said. "okay?"

Chad smiled at her. "Okay." He leaned down and kissed her.

"Ugh! Get a room!" exclaimed Meggie. "And y'all wonder why we need to be away from y'all sometimes."

Chad shrugged his shoulders and giggled like a child. He gave Meggie a big wet kiss on her forehead before he jumped back into the pool.

Meggie wiped Chad's slobber from her forehead. "I'm *totally* okay with us having a day."

"Good," Emily said. She was glad that the guys made it easy for her to steal Meggie away from them.

17

Jackson paced on the balcony in the back of the chapel that housed the old pipe organ. He focused hard on his steps. Moving his dead body around had become gradually easier for him ever since he had returned, but as his thoughts drifted off slowly back to those he cared about, his movements became clumsy again. I'm no good to them if I can't move, he thought. He put them out of his mind again, and focused solely on mastering his movements. He had to be ready.

From this vantage point, Jackson could see everything in St. Joe's except for the front entrance, which was directly beneath him. He thought he might pace a rut up there as he awaited Emily's arrival. As he paced, Jackson leafed through the book Father Borbridge had given him.

The first story about the Lithuanian vampire in France was interesting enough. The clerical author didn't reveal anything that Jackson didn't already know. All of the Dark Ones seemed to have unnatural charisma. They all were somehow able to captivate those around them, able to make the good seem bad, and vice versa. No one even suspected these evil creatures until it was too late. They were usually seen at night, and they steered clear of holy places. As Jackson read, he thought about his own plight. How would he be able to convince anyone that Ben and his friends were bad? How could he ever protect the ones he loved from them? The biggest problem, however, was being able to accomplish all of this without revealing to his loved ones that he had come back from the dead. Jackson knew that he had no place in the living world, and that his reappearance would only complicate the lives of those he cared about. He did have to protect them; but if he could do it without them ever knowing, the better it would be.

Jackson thumbed through another story in his new book. Aside from the Order of Lazarus, and ergo leaders in the Catholic church, the Dark Ones had gone undetected from the rest of society for millennia, save one group. Gypsies, whatever that meant, were fully aware of the vampire presence in the world. Jackson wasn't even sure what a gypsy was. All he knew about them was that their women always wore long dresses, and to decline any baseless offer for a driveway repaving. He wasn't even sure how to spot one. But he did know, from reading, that they were staunchly opposed to the Dark Ones. Any ally, should he ever come across a gypsy, was better than nothing.

Tales of priests and gypsy families defending villages from vampires could only keep him occupied for so long. He soon found himself once again concerned with the situation at hand. One of his best friends knew he was alive again, and he also knew that Paul couldn't care less. Paul was friends with at least one person, that he knew, that wanted him dead; and Paul was okay with it. Whether or not he wanted to harm Meggie was unclear, but Jackson didn't want to take any chances.

Then he thought about Meggie. He was not sure if it was his zombie brain playing tricks on him or not, but he could still recall her scent. Just being near her, being able to smell her, was comforting, he remembered. It made him think about the people he had met since his return. They all had distinct smells. Father Borbridge smelled a certain way. He smelled almost sterile, like a hospital. Breann had a smell. He couldn't place it, but she smelled somehow earthy, like catching the smell of a garden in the wind as you pass it. Even Emily, whom he had just recently met, had a distinct aroma. Jackson couldn't figure out if it was more Emily or Emily's fear, but he was sure he would be able to identify her from scent alone when he met her again. Then he thought about his attacker, Ben. Jackson couldn't remember smelling anything noticeable about him. Whether his perception of the darkness Ben emanated overshadowed anything else, or he just didn't have a smell, Jackson couldn't be sure. He just knew that the foreboding feeling Jackson had around him was the prominent indicator, not his smell.

He also thought about what he had heard Ben say. "Father" had told them not to go into the chapel. Jackson knew that there were countless priests scattered around the world. It could have been anybody. But the only ones he knew that had knowledge of the undead were Father Hayes and Father Borbridge. He wasn't too concerned with it being Father Hayes. Jackson trusted him fully. Father Borbridge, however, he had just met. Jackson couldn't help but be concerned that it was he that had directed the vampires away from him and St. Joe's.

197

The alternative was just as frightening. What if there was another priest directing the Dark Ones? What if Father Borbridge knew about Jackson, and there was a whole other order of the Catholic church that were coaching the vampires? No explanation for Ben's comment could be comforting, so Jackson chose to focus on what was presently troubling him. He had to make sure Meggie was safe.

Jackson descended the set of stairs that led from the pipe organ down next to the front door. Once he was back on the ground floor on the chapel, he resumed his pacing.

The sun was beginning to set, and its angle hit the stained-glass on the church's west side directly. Jackson was beginning to worry. He had given Emily strict instructions to have Meggie there by sundown. As he watched the light of the sun wane in the colorful panes, Jackson became concerned. If they arrived after sundown, Ben, and others, would have their full strength. He wanted to get her inside before all of that.

As he continued his pacing in the direction of the altar, Jackson made out the sound of footsteps approaching the front entrance of the church. If it was Emily and Meggie, he didn't want Meggie to see him. A pair of pillars were about halfway to the altar. He ducked behind one of them and awaited the arrival of the unknown church patron.

Jackson heard the creak of the chapel's front door, followed by footsteps that made their way to the basin filled with blessed water. He couldn't make out the sound, but he recognized the homey smell. It was Breann. Knowing it was someone that knew about him, he emerged from behind the concealment of the pillar. She was as beautiful as he had remembered.

Jackson could see her brilliant green eyes even in the distance.

"Dude, what is it with you and this place?" Breann asked him. "You're always here." Her long brown hair whipped carelessly, trailing behind her as she motioned back and forth, waving her hands about the chapel.

Jackson made his way toward her. "I could ask you the same. Why are *you* here?"

She was not afraid of his presence. Her body language almost welcomed the approach that was intended to intimidate. She scoffed, almost offended at the remark. "You left me sleeping on a bench last night, making me think that this was the only safe place for me. What the Hell did you expect me to do?"

Jackson was still amazed that she had not noticed that he was a zombie. Maybe he didn't look that different. Maybe Emily had only freaked out because she knew he was dead. He thought about the night before. Breann may not have been fully aware of the dangers, but he did remember telling her enough about the situation. "Good point," he said.

"So, are you hiding from dead people too?" she asked.

"No. I'm waiting for somebody."

"Who are you waiting for?" Breann asked. "Another damsel in distress?"

Jackson thought about Meggie. And he thought about Emily. Everyone he cared about was in distress. "I guess you could say that."

Breann laughed. "Is that your angle? You get chicks to think that they're in danger, get 'em back to this church, and do your thing?"

Jackson was perturbed by her comment, but

Breann had no way of knowing the truth. He glared at her with his dead gaze. "It's not like that. Remember when you saw me walking, and I told you I was going to meet an ex?"

"Yeah."

"Well, it's the same girl," he said. "It's not an 'angle' or anything."

Breann shook her head and grinned. "Man, you gotta lighten up. I'm just messin' with you."

She always seemed to just be messing with Jackson. He wondered if she was ever serious. If there weren't people trying to kill him, he thought, he might be a little less on edge. He would have probably have joked right back with her. She didn't know the whole story, and Jackson couldn't help but know it. It was the best option. He would put up with missing her humor as long as he didn't have to tell Breann the whole truth: he was a zombie, and vampires were trying to kill him.

"Sorry," he said. "I'm just a little busy right now." Jackson's concerns increased as the light from the sun faded. It was almost completely set. What was taking Emily so long?

"Yeah," Breann said sarcastically, "it is *so* hard to just walk around and wait for somebody."

She had no idea how right she truly was. Not only did Jackson have to actively force his body to obey his commands for movements, but he also had to pace helplessly inside St. Joe's, hoping that Emily and Meggie made it in time. "Yep."

Breann sighed and walked right up next to him. She leaned against a pew. "Well, is it gonna hurt your chances with me being here?" Her tone was flirty as she looked up at him with a closed smile.

Breann was close enough that Jackson could feel her body heat on his hands and face. As he forced his lungs to fill with air for a response, he made sure to do so through his nose, so he could smell her. "Again, it's not really like that. I just have to make sure she is safe." It just couldn't be like that. As much as Jackson wanted to come back and be with Meggie like he was before, he knew that he could never interact with her in that capacity again. The best he could do was keep her safe.

Breann looked down and started carelessly traced the grain of the wooden pew with her finger. "So, what, are monsters after her too?"

"Yeah, you could say that."

Breann stopped tracing and crossed her arms. She looked back at Jackson and leaned into him with her shoulder. Just as when Emily ran into him, he didn't budge. "Man, maybe I shouldn't hang out with you. Trouble follows you, huh?"

Jackson locked eyes with her and smirked. "You have no idea."

Breann continued staring into his eyes. He watched her blink a few times, batting her long eyelashes. Then he thought how creepy he must look. As all of his Reborn movements were voluntary, he was quite certain he hadn't blinked once. Jackson forced his eyes to close and averted his gaze.

"You have pretty eyes," Breann said.

"Thanks. People always tell me that. But I didn't expect you to. Your eyes are the same as mine." Well, not exactly the same, he thought.

Breann laughed. "You're right. Maybe that's why I think they're pretty."

No more sun came through the windows.

Night had fallen without Emily and Meggie making it to the chapel. Jackson began to panic. He resumed his pacing.

Breann noticed his mood change. "What's wrong?"

"They were supposed to be here by now."

"They?" she asked. "I thought you were meeting an ex."

Jackson had inadvertently exposed more of his plan, but it was simple enough to recover. "Another friend is bringing her. She has no idea I'm here."

"Well ain't you just the little romantic?" Breann winked at him.

Just then Jackson heard the sound of a car approaching the front of the church. He could make out the familiar roar of Emily's engine. They had finally arrived. Jackson began walking to the church's front door to hear better.

Jackson heard the engine shut off and two doors open, then slam shut. Then Meggie spoke. "Paul, what are y'all doin' here? Emily. This is Ben."

Jackson's stomach turned like he was on speeding roller-coaster. How long had they been outside St. Joe's waiting? Jackson was grateful for the chapel's protection, but he was not fond of its ability to block his detection of the Dark Ones.

"You know, I'm glad you said 'it's not like that,'" Breann said from behind him. "I might have to try and make her jealous."

"Shhhh!" Jackson needed her to be quiet as he listened to what was happening outside.

"What? It was a compliment."

"Shut up, please!" Jackson whispered loudly.

Breann could sense his frustration. "Okay,

okay. I get it."

Just as he could hear what was going on outside, Jackson was sure that Ben could hear what was going on in the church. Breann was probably in danger now too. The conversation went on outside.

"Yeah, what are y'all doing here?" Emily asked.

"We go to school here," said Ben. "Aren't we allowed to walk around on our own campus?" Jackson remembered Emily's necklace. Ben wouldn't be able to just talk his way out of things with her.

"Sounds fair to me." Meggie clearly was not wearing any silver.

"Well, we're having a girls' day, Paul." Emily didn't even bother addressing Ben. "Something you would know if you would've been at Jon's today." Hearing his name made Jackson miss his burly friend.

"Girls' day brings you to Spring Hill?" Paul asked.

"Yep," Emily snapped matter-of-factly. "I like Gothic stuff, and I wanted to see this Gothic church." Jackson heard the girls walk closer to the entrance. He also felt a thud from the door. Someone had leaned back against the door.

That someone was Ben. He whispered through the crack in the door. "They're *not* gettin' in this church." The statement was directed at Jackson. He backed away from the door and tried to quickly formulate a plan. He had to create a distraction so the girls could get inside. Ben seemed to be drawn to his zombie presence like a moth to a flame. It was currently his only weapon that might get the girls to safety without him having to expose himself to Meggie.

Jackson thought about going out the side door,

but he wasn't sure just how fast Ben could get to him. Instead, he stepped quickly toward the altar. Breann noticed his urgency and followed in step behind him. "What's goin' on?" she asked.

"No time to talk," Jackson said sharply. He continued walking.

On either side of the altar there was a door. They led to an opening behind. Jackson went through. There was a staircase that led up to a door. The door opened up to the vaulted walkway that connected the chapel to the other three buildings in Spring Hill's quad. The walkway was no longer used, and the door that led to it had been painted shut. Jackson tried to open the door. It wouldn't be easily moved. On his second attempt, Jackson had more success, as he rammed his shoulder into the door. He heard some of the paint crack. The hinges were rusty and the bottom of the neglected door scraped roughly against the floor, but he got it open enough to get out.

"Whoa, cool. I didn't even know this was here." Breann was astonished that the walkway was still accessible.

Jackson turned back to her. "Stay- in- here." his panicking made his speech choppy.

"Jackson, what is goin' on?" she asked vehemently.

He tried to calm himself enough to ease her worries. "I promise I will explain when I get back inside. Just stay here, please." He did not want to endanger anyone he didn't have to.

Breann was reluctant, but she relented. "Fine."

"Thank you." Jackson stepped outside and pushed the door back closed behind him.

Almost immediately he could feel the dark

presence. This time there were two. Jackson's heart sank as the realization hit him. It was not just Ben. It was Paul too. Suddenly it didn't seem so farfetched that his old friend didn't care about him. He now had even more reason to keep Meggie away from Paul.

The two vampires were aware of his presence too. Jackson could feel them feeling him, homing in on his location. They didn't move any closer to him, though. They stood still at the front door of the church. Jackson stepped out a little on the walkway. He could see the back end of Emily's car, but the angle wasn't good enough for him to see the four people down there. He listened as their conversation continued.

"What the Hell are you talkin' about?" Emily asked.

"I'm serious, you can't go in there." Paul went on explaining. "They're repairing the floors or something in there. It's locked. No one can go in."

"Well, that sucks," Meggie said. "That's fine, Em. At least we can look at the outside."

"Yeah, the outside's really pretty, too." Ben's loud, deep voice echoed off of some the other buildings.

"Fine. I guess we'll walk around." Emily sounded equally disappointed and fearful.

Jackson felt a third presence. It wasn't on the ground, though. It was on the walkway with him. He had been so focused on Ben and Paul that he hadn't noticed a third one coming for him. Even in the dark of night, Jackson could make out a figure speeding toward him. As it rounded the far corner of the walkway, Jackson made out long brown hair whipping in the wind behind him. It was a guy. He turned the next corner and stopped. He was now on the same part of the walkway as Jackson.

"You must be Alex," Jackson said. The vampire's dark presence was overwhelming. He could barely continue to make out the location of the two others.

Alex smiled, revealing the same four tiny fangs that Ben had. "And you must be dead."

Jackson felt his jacket pocket to be sure his dagger was still there. It was. He didn't reveal it yet; he simply smiled back at the vampire. "*Un*-dead actually. But you were close."

The remark made Alex visibly angry. He stepped in close Jackson. "Well, I guess we'll have to fix that." He shoved Jackson with all of his might. Unlike the girls that had tried to move Jackson, Alex was successful. The shove knocked Jackson back, but, thanks to the closed door behind him, he was able to stay on his feet.

Jackson regained his balance and stood up straight. "Well, you're pretty strong, but you ain't got nuthin' on Ben."

Alex did not like being mocked by the zombie. While he may not have been as strong as Ben, he was definitely faster. Before Jackson could react to defend against it, Alex punched him in the face with a solid right hand. Jackson didn't feel any pain, but he heard something in his face crack.

Alex was upon him before he could even turn his head back around to face him. Jackson felt Alex's teeth sink into the flesh of his neck. He thought about the silver rosary on his neck. He was not afraid of bleeding to death, so Jackson clinched his arms around the back of the vampire's head and held him tight.

Jackson was able to squeeze tighter than he thought. Alex squirmed and pushed against Jackson trying to free himself, but the zombie's grip could not be escaped. Jackson had all but won. He could feel Alex's struggle become weaker the longer he was exposed to the silver. After about a minute of holding the vampire against the rosary, Jackson could hear and smell searing flesh. Alex released his bite and screamed muffled screams into Jackson's neck. He was in pain. After another minute, Alex's body was starting to go limp from fatigue. He still whimpered, but he was no longer fighting. The only movement Alex made was jerking from the pain. Jackson tossed his body onto the walkway.

Jackson looked at the vampire's face. Dripping from his chin was the thick, dark purple liquid he had spilled from Jackson. Perfect impressions of the rosary beads were seared diagonally down Alex's face. He lay perfectly still as Jackson knelt down, pulled out the silver dagger and showed it to him. "Did I taste like road-kill?"

"Now from the way I understand it," Jackson said as he thrust the dagger into Alex's right thigh and pulled it back out, "cutting your head off, or a stake through the heart is the only way to kill you. Now this little dagger can't cut your head off."

Alex groaned in agony as Jackson did the same thing to his left leg. "But- silver hurts you. In fact, you don't even have your quick-healing thing when it comes to silver." Jackson began stabbing Alex all over. Jackson thought about how quickly the vampires were to attack him. And he thought about them doing that to Meggie. Rage overtook him. He made sure to do it fast enough that the silver wouldn't cauterize the wounds shut. He wanted the vampire to bleed. Anywhere he didn't see red bleeding through, he stuck.

After Jackson figured the vampire was sufficiently skewered, he stopped and wiped the blade clean on Alex's shirt. A puddle of blood was beneath him. The vampire's eyes were wide open and full of fear as he looked up at Jackson. He was silent. It was almost as if he were waiting for Jackson's orders.

Jackson employed all of his focus to warn Alex. He spoke slowly and clearly. "You stay away from Meggie, and I'll stay away from you. You tell Ben and Paul to stay away from Meggie, and I'll stay away from them. Since they haven't had to face me yet- like you have- they might not choose to leave her alone. If they don't leave her alone, you had better pray to whatever god you pray to that you're not with them. Do you understand me?" Alex nodded slowly.

"Okay, good," Jackson said. "I don't wanna kill anybody, but I will. I'll get a silver saw and cut you all up before I drive a hunk of wood into y'all's hearts." Jackson surprised himself with his zealotry.

Alex looked up at him. "How can you be so cold?" he asked.

Jackson stood up and gave Alex a gentle kick with his boot. "I'm dead, remember? Comes with the territory." Then he turned around to walk back inside the chapel.

When he got to the door and tried to open it, the knob wouldn't turn. The door didn't appear to be new enough to have an automatic locking mechanism, but that was evidently the case.

Time for Plan B, he thought. Jackson pulled his hood over his head and tightened the strings, leaving barely enough open space for him to see. He stepped to the edge of the walkway and looked down over the ledge. It was at least ten feet. Knowing he would feel no pain, Jackson climbed on top of the ledge, dagger in hand, and jumped down.

While he couldn't feel pain, he still didn't want to break his legs when he landed. He still needed to be able to get around. It was a rough landing, but Jackson was able to tuck and roll well enough to redistribute the force. He didn't hear anything snap.

Back at the front of the church he heard Emily say, "What was that?" His fall had been loud enough to hear.

With his focus reestablished on the two vampires on the ground, he could feel them turning his way. "I don't know. Let's go check it out." Ben pretended to be ignorant, though he knew full well that Jackson had made the sound.

Jackson rose to his feet and began walking toward them as well. Ben was the first to come around the church and into the zombie's vision. He flashed his fanged smile at Jackson. Paul and the girls were just behind him. A look of relief was on Emily's face as she recognized the dark blue jacket.

"Hey, buddy, what's goin' on?" Ben asked. Jackson remained silent. He made sure to keep his head down. He wasn't sure if Meggie could make out his nose and mouth in the low lighting, but he didn't want to take any chances. He just kept slowly walking toward them.

Then Jackson heard Meggie screamed and start backing up. "Oh my God, y'all. He's got a knife." he knew how bad a knife-wielding hooded figure must have looked to her. He put the knife behind his back, but there was no way to hide all of Alex's blood that had splattered onto him. "Let's go." Meggie grabbed Emily by the arm and pulled her back toward the car.

Paul looked back at the girls. "Yeah, y'all get outta here. Me and Ben got this."

"Paul, are you crazy?!" Meggie said. "He'll stab you." Yep, Jackson thought.

Paul pulled Meggie in close, looked into her eyes, and began to whisper. "Don't worry, Meg. Y'all get back to your girls' night. Let the boys handle this if we have to."

Meggie, bewildered, looked up at him. "Okay."

Emily hadn't taken her eyes off Jackson. She watched him as he just stood there. It wasn't perfect, but her mission was still accomplished. Paul was *sending* Meggie away to safety. Without thinking, she nodded at the hooded figure that was Jackson. "That's fine, Meggie. Let's go."

"I'll call you later, okay?" Paul said to Meggie.

"Alright," she said. Paul kissed her. Jackson was seething with anger. He wanted to run over and stab him right there, and never stop. But he didn't. He tried his best to remain calm and focused. He needed to be his sharpest for this.

Jackson watched Meggie and Emily get into the Dodge Dart. It came to life and sped off. Jackson could still hear the muscle car's engine fading off into the distance as the two vampires began walking toward him.

Jackson removed his hood. "Your move."

18

"What are you trying to prove, Jackson?" Paul's voice was familiar, but he spoke to him as if he had done something wrong. "Why don't you just go back to your grave and stay there?"

Jackson felt the presence of the three vampires. Two were vibrant and strong, ready to attack. The force he felt behind him was incredibly weak. He could still make out the sound of Alex gurgling his own blood. Jackson wasn't concerned about that one. Nothing about Paul and Ben looked or felt weak. They were probably more than capable of handling the lone zombie.

Ben moved in closer to Jackson. "Oh, it's too late for that. If he goes back to his grave, it'll be because *I* sent him there!"

Jackson felt his dead grip tighten around the dagger's handle. "Go and drink from somebody else. Just leave Meggie alone."

The comment made Ben grin. He moved within inches of Jackson. Their noses were almost touching. In his periphery, Jackson saw Paul back Ben's play and step in closer too. Ben locked eyes with

Jackson. "See, it don't work like that, you dead bitch. We do what we want. We take what we want- when we want it. No corpse is gonna tell any of us what to do."

Jackson smiled. "Ask your boy, Alex, if he still feels that way."

Ben gritted his teeth and almost growled. He wasn't nearly as fast as Alex. Jackson saw the big vampire draw back and prepare for a punch. He ducked low and easily dodged the attack. He then parried the attack with one of his own. Jackson stuck his dagger into Ben's side.

Ben growled again and backpedaled to get the blade out of him. Jackson looked at him with satisfaction as blood began to spill from the wound.

Jackson was too busy relishing in Ben nursing his wound to prepare for Paul. He didn't see him coming. Paul charged and tackled him to the ground.

The two of them flew about ten feet. Paul finally landed on top of Jackson right next to the outside wall of the chapel. Jackson struggled, with all his undead might, to get Paul off of him.

Paul was able to overpower him because Jackson wrestled one-handed. His other hand was reserved specifically for maintaining control of the dagger. Without it, Jackson was sure he would lose the fight quickly. Because he was so concerned with keeping it, though, Paul was able to pull him to his feet and pin him up against the church.

The vampire that had once been Jackson's friend used his forearm to press against the zombie's jaw. He used his other hand to keep Jackson's right arm pinned, so he couldn't stab him, too. Jackson wasn't sure if he could have broken free from Paul's hold, because he didn't try.

He chose instead to talk to his old friend. "Don't make me kill you too, Paul."

Paul laughed. For the first time, Jackson saw his friend's fangs. Maybe it was because he had seen Paul's original smile so many times before in the past, but his looked more noticeable than Ben's or Alex's. "Do you honestly think you're winnin' this, Jax?" Paul said as he pressed harder against Jackson's jaw.

Jackson heard more bones cracking in his face. His right eye had a perfect view of the stone wall, but out of his left one, he could see Ben, still holding his side, walk over to where Paul was holding him.

Ben kicked at Jackson's legs. He could feel the vampire's shoe make contact with his shin. Ben kicked again. This time there was a crack. Ben continued kicking both of Jackson's legs until they were sufficiently smashed. He was no longer able to stand. The pressure of Paul holding him against the church was the only thing keeping him from falling down.

Next Ben went for Jackson's free arm. He tried to fight back, but Ben was too strong. It was no use. The vampire's strength was too much. Ben wrenched the arm until he heard a snap. He released it, and it flopped down to Jackson's left side.

Jackson could move his left arm at the shoulder, but that was it. Ben had broken it above the elbow, rendering it useless. Then he felt Ben's massive fists smashing into his right hand. He couldn't feel any pain, but he could feel his fingers breaking. His grip loosened on the dagger and it fell to the ground. Once the dagger was out of his hand, Paul tossed Jackson to the ground. None of his wounds were healing anywhere near fast enough to deal with this. Though its hand was mangled, Jackson used his unbroken arm to turn himself over, sit up, and face the vampires.

Paul walked over and looked down at him. "You should've stayed dead." Then he kicked his old friend across the face, knocking Jackson onto his back. He tried to get up, but Paul kicked him again. Then Ben kicked him in the side of the head. As Jackson lay on his back, having his head kicked in by the two vampires, he tried to focus all he could to heal enough to get back on his feet, if only to get away. He could feel his limbs mending, but it was not fast enough. Paul and Ben would have his brains stomped out before he could defend himself again.

Paul and Ben were completely absorbed in killing Jackson. And Jackson was fully concentrating on staying alive. None of them noticed that someone else had walked up.

"I think that's quite enough of that." Jackson immediately recognized the voice as the vampires stopped attacking him. He looked up and saw Father Borbridge glaring at the other two boys.

The giant of a priest was wearing a long black robe with silver stitching. He had a wooden stake in his right hand and a silver chain in his left hand long enough that it puddled on the ground next to him. Jackson thought he had been ready to fight the Dark Ones. *This* was how you were supposed to do it.

Without saying a single word to the priest, Paul and Ben ran away. Father Borbridge stepped closer to Jackson. Just off to his left, he heard another person walking toward him. He turned to see that it was Father Hayes, with a robe and weapons that matched Borbridge's.

The two priests were standing over him,

looking at his mangled, undead body. "Are you hurting anywhere?" Father Hayes asked.

"No, sir," Jackson said. "I just need my legs to heal so I can get up."

Borbridge placed his stake inside his robe and threw his chain over his shoulder as he leaned down and picked up the zombie.

Jackson raised his unbroken arm to point toward the church. "My knife's over there."

"Gerald, would you grab that for him?" Father Borbridge motioned with his head in the direction Jackson had pointed.

Father Hayes stepped over to the chapel wall. It was dark, so he had to fumble around for a bit until he located the dagger. He finally found it. "Got it." The old priest picked up the dagger and followed Borbridge around to the front of St. Joe's.

Father Borbridge had Jackson in his arms, so Father Hayes walked around him to open the door. "Thank you," Borbridge said.

They made it into the chapel. Though he was broken and bludgeoned- and he was pretty sure he almost died again- Jackson was safe now. Father Borbridge took him to one of the back pews and set him down.

Father Hayes handed Jackson his dagger. "Thanks," he said. The two priests continued standing over him, just looking at him. "What, do I have something on my face?"

Neither of the priests were amused. Father Hayes said, "Jackson, you could have been killed. We told you not to fight them together like that."

Jackson shrugged. "I know, but Meggie has been with them, and they've got her totally brainwashed."

"Meggie?" Father Borbridge asked.

Father Hayes remembered her, though. "His girlfriend. I mean, she was before he died."

"Oh, okay," Borbridge nodded. "That makes sense."

"I noticed your friend Paul was one of the boys kicking you while you were on the ground," Hayes stated.

"Yeah, he's definitely not my friend now. He's a vampire." Jackson was both angry and sad about the fact.

"Yes, I had hoped against that, but when I saw him and that other boy stomping you like that, I knew." Father Hayes remembered all of Jackson's friends from high school. He remembered being happy that Paul and Ryan had chosen to attend Spring Hill. Then he asked about him. "What about Ryan? Not him, too, I hope."

Jackson recalled talking to Emily about his friends. Only Paul stood out as strange. "No, sir. Ryan ain't one of them. I think there's just three of 'em. Paul, Alex, and Ben."

"Three?" Borbridge inquired. "How do you know? There were only two of them just now."

Jackson smiled a bit thinking about how he had handled Alex. "Y'all saw Paul and Ben. Alex was up on that walkway thing." Jackson pointed toward the place on the walkway where he had fought Alex. And he did it with his left hand. His arm had healed. Jackson attempted to stand, but Borbridge pushed him back down. He wanted to hear more.

"On the walkway?" he asked. "How do you know he was up there?"

216

"Well even if I hadn't been up there fighting him, I would have felt him and knew he was up there." As the sacred ground of the church blocked that undead sense of his, Jackson wondered how far Alex had crawled or limped away. The zombie felt his face form another smile.

"You fought on the walkway?" Father Hayes asked. While Borbridge was curious, wanting a recount of what had transpired, Father Hayes seemed upset that it happened at all. He did not like Jackson fighting the Dark Ones. "What were you even doing up there?"

"It's kinda hard to explain," Jackson said.

"Well give it your best shot, son." Father Borbridge *really* wanted to know what happened.

"Okay. It started when I was waiting on somebody to bring Meggie to the church so she would be safe."

"What 'somebody'?" Father Hayes asked. "How did you know someone was going to bring her here?"

"Because I told her to," Jackson said matter-of-factly.

"What?!" Father Hayes exclaimed. "Someone else knows you're back from the dead?"

Father Hayes looked disappointed and concerned. Father Borbridge only looked intrigued. He said, "Please go, on, son. Tell us everything. Gerald, try not to interrupt him. I know that you care about the boy. I do too. But he's safe now, and he can tell us things we may not know."

At that moment, Jackson trusted Father Borbridge fully again. He wasn't sure what "Father" Ben was talking about, but this one was on Team

217

Zombie.

Jackson gave the priests all the details he could about how he had spent his day. He told them about sneaking out of Father Hayes' house to go to Meggie's to warn her about Paul. He told them how he met Emily and had incorporated her into his plan. He told them how Paul and Ben tried to stop the girls from entering the chapel, and how he went out on the second-story walkway as a distraction. Then he told them what he did to Alex. Other than a shocked gasp from Father Hayes, the two priests just listened intently.

When he had gotten them up to speed, he realized he had told them everything, save excluding one person from every single detail of his story. Breann. Then he wondered where she was. As far as Jackson knew, she was still hiding somewhere in the chapel. He didn't recall hearing the church's front door opening during his fight. She had to still be in St. Joe's. But she was nowhere in sight. Jackson paused for a moment to see if he could hear any sounds that might tell him her whereabouts. Nothing. She had to be down in the basement.   "There is one more thing. But it's not that big of a deal," Jackson said.

"What's that?" Father Borbridge asked.

"There's one more person that has seen me since I came back."

"Who?" Hayes wondered.

"It's this girl, she came into the church and talked to me. But it's cool, she don't know I'm a zombie."

Always ready for more information, Father Borbridge asked, "What do you mean, she doesn't know?"

"I mean, she didn't know me before I died. And she talked to me just like a normal person. For all she knows, I'm just a kinda pale dude that was hangin' out in the church."

"So, she has no idea that you are a Reborn?" Father Hayes was concerned.

Jackson thought about the promise he made her. He told her that after he got back to St. Joe's, he would explain everything. He sort of dreaded that. It was enough to make her stay safely inside the church, though, so he would keep his promise. "No, sir." Not yet, he thought.

"That is incredible," Borbridge said. "I guess I am simply too aware that you are a Reborn, and it's all I can see when I look at you. Coming back from the dead isn't a common reason for anyone looking a certain way. I can only imagine how she must see you."

"Thanks," Jackson said sarcastically. "That makes me feel great. But I have a question for y'all. How did y'all know to come to the church, guns-a-blazin'? A little strange for y'all to just so happened to be all decked out in vampire-killing gear when I need y'all to be."

"Well it's not really that strange," Father Borbridge said. "A young girl called and tipped us off. Must have been that Emily girl you befriended today. All she said was, 'Jackson's outside the church. He's in trouble,' and hung up. We got ready as quickly as possible and came down here. Don't let Gerald make you think he hates it. We may be old, but we joined the Order of Lazarus for a reason. We live for this stuff."

Jackson smiled thinking about the two priests

suiting up to fight evil. "Well that's awesome. I wonder how she got your number." Jackson tried to remember if he had even mentioned Father Borbridge to Emily. He didn't want to look a gift horse in the mouth, so he guessed that he had to have told her at some point.

"Who knows? With the internet, nowadays," Father Hayes said, "anybody can get anybody's number."

Jackson's eyes grew wide with the possibilities. While he was very grateful for his dagger, the silver around his neck, and his old, ratty vampire hunter diary, Jackson *really* wanted to get on the internet. He could search for more information on vampires; but more specifically, he could get some information on the vampires hunting him. "I'd like to get on the internet," he said.

"For what?" Father Hayes asked. He was very concerned, and he was still being paranoid about Jackson and his every move.

"Really, Father? Does it really matter? It's *full* of knowledge, maybe some that might actually help me."

The two Jesuits looked at each other and smiled. Father Borbridge said, "The boy's got the right idea."

"Very well," Father Hayes said. "We'll get you some internet access. There are no computers in the chapel, but most of the other buildings on campus are wired for the internet, I believe."

"How ironic," Jackson said. "So, where do I need to go?"

"Your best bet at not being seen would be the old library," Father Hayes said as he pointed to the East. "Not the big, new one over there that's right next to the chapel." Then he pointed in the opposite direction. "The old one. There's internet in there, and there's no one in there, especially during the summer."

"Cool, so I'll just wait until the sun comes up, and then I'll head over there."

Father Borbridge looked amazed. "After what just happened, you're ready to go?"

Jackson placed his hands on the pew in front of him and pushed himself to his feet. His bones had healed. He wondered if he'd fall back down as he released his grip on the pew. He remained standing. "Good as new."

"You truly astonish me, Jackson," Father Borbridge said.

Father Hayes sighed. "Fine, if you believe you are healthy enough to handle it at dawn, go ahead. We'll go make sure it's unlocked so you can get in there."

"Yeah, wouldn't want me spoiling in this heat," Jackson said, followed by a slow wink. Father Hayes didn't even smile. Borbridge chuckled, at least.

"Remember: only move during the day and get to safety by sunset. And do not fight the Dark Ones in groups. If we had not shown up tonight, you would be dead again. We may not always be there."

Jackson hung his head. Father Hayes cared about him, and the priest was not afraid to scold him to keep him safe. "Yes, sir."

"Now, us living folk need to sleep," Hayes said. Father Hayes always really liked sleeping, Jackson remembered. "Take care of yourself."

"Yes, sir."

"If I don't see you at the old library tomorrow," Father Borbridge said, "I'll definitely reconvene with you back here tomorrow night. Okay?"

"Yes, sir. Now which building is the old library exactly?" Jackson asked.

"It's the tall, narrow, red-brick building with big white columns in the front that faces the soccer field. If you hit the Avenue of the Oaks, you've gone too far; but don't worry. Turn around and you should see it perfectly." Father Borbridge's directions were very descriptive. Jackson seemed to recall a long road with oak trees on either side being somewhere on Spring Hill's campus. That must have been the Avenue to which he was referring.

Jackson had a pretty good idea of the building in question. "Alright. I'm sure I can find it, no problem. But if I can't, I'll just come on back here. I'd rather not get my brains kicked in again."

"There you go, Jackson. Now you're thinking." Father Hayes was glad Jackson was ready to play it safe again.

The priests turned to exit the chapel. "Thanks for saving my second life, y'all," Jackson said as they left. Neither of them turned around, but Father Borbridge waved back at Jackson from over his shoulder. Jackson smiled as he watched them exit. Now where the Hell was Breann? He thought.

19

Emily's tires were squealing beneath her and Meggie as she went around the twists and turns in the road. More squealing ensued every time she accelerated mid-curve, fishtailing the back end of her car. She was quickly trying to put some distance between them and the undead boys they had left back at Spring Hill College.

Meggie was in the passenger seat. She was visibly shaken. She wasn't even aware of the real danger she was in, but just seeing that man in the hood had obviously scared her. Emily recalled how the blade of his knife reflected the moonlight back at her eyes so brightly, and, even though she knew it was Jackson, it gave her chills. She could only imagine how Meggie must have felt.

"Are you alright, girl?" Emily asked her friend.

Meggie had been assured by Paul when he got her to agree to get in the car with Emily and leave, but now there was no such reassurance. There was only fear. "Did you see that he had blood splattered all over him?" She was describing precisely what Emily had seen.

Emily, knowing full well that the hooded figure was Jackson, and that neither of the girls were in any real danger, hadn't even stopped to think about whose blood it might be. "Yeah, I saw. But we're cool now."

"But what about Paul? And Ben?" she asked. "What if he went after them when we left?"

Emily knew that that is *exactly* what happened. She knew that Jackson had that blade drawn prepared to kill Ben and Paul if they didn't stay away from Meggie. But she couldn't tell any of that to the girl in her passenger seat. "Dude, have you seen those guys, especially Ben? I'm sure it would take a little more than a pocket-knife to stop that fella."

Meggie took deep breaths as she tried to calm herself. She wiped the cold sweat from her face and said, "You're probably right. Paul told me he would handle it. I believe him."

Emily thought about Paul's effect on Meggie, how he could make her believe anything. But she didn't let her suspicions get in the way. Right now she just wanted to help her friend relax. "I know. I know. It'll be okay."

When the two of them made it back to Meggie's house, Emily parked the car, but kept the engine running.

"You're not coming in?" Meggie asked.

Since Emily couldn't get her safely inside the church, she had come up with a plan of her own. "Nah, I got a better idea."

"What?"

"I'm supposed to go back home tonight," Emily said. "Why don't you see if your mom will let you go with me to Birmingham?"

"Are you sure that's a good idea?" Meggie

wondered. "I mean, after what happened tonight?"

"Hell yes!" Emily exclaimed. "I think it's the best idea. What if that maniac saw my car? He might go looking around for it. The farther away we get, the better."

"Hmm. That sounds kind of smart. Okay! One sec," Meggie said as she ran into her house.

Emily breathed a sigh of relief. She might not have been able to get Meggie inside St. Joseph's Chapel, but she would be able to keep her away from Paul and Ben for a little longer. They had no idea where she lived in Birmingham. Just then, Emily heard a vibration in the passenger seat.

It was Meggie's phone. The screen illuminated, revealing that she had just received a text. The text message was from Paul.

Everything's ok. Just some loonatic. We're safe. Call me.

Emily picked up her friend's phone and deleted the text as quickly as she could. "Sorry, Paul. The dead man says 'no' to that. Plus, you can't spell, and that's not sexy."

After a few minutes, Meggie came out of her house carrying a bag on her shoulder. Her mom had said yes. Emily smile.

"Pop the trunk," Meggie said.

Emily laughed. "This is a '71, skank. You don't just 'pop' the trunk. Throw it in the backseat. It'll be fine."

"Ha. Okay." Meggie tossed her bag into the back and climbed in. She picked up her phone. Did Paul ever text back or call?"

225

Emily kept a straight face. "Nope."

Meggie sighed. "Alright. Let's go."

Emily just sat there with the car idling. As she thought about her last passenger, Jackson, she smiled and said, "Well?"

"Well, what?"

"Buckle your ass up!" she said as she gave Meggie a slight punch in the arm.

"Ugh! You're almost as bad as Jackson used to be." Meggie grabbed the seat belt and clipped it like an indignant child.

Emily couldn't help but laugh. "Whatever. Let's go."

It was about 250 miles from Meggie's house in Mobile to Emily's house. With the way Emily drove, though, it was only about a three-and-a-half hour drive. After they were out of Mobile, and on the open road, Meggie seemed to have gotten the night's happenings off her mind and started acting normal again.

"So, did you even ask your parents if I could stay?" Meggie asked. Doing seventy-five up I-65 with the windows down and the radio going, she had to speak pretty loudly.

"No, but what are they gonna do, make me drive you all the way back home when we get there?" Emily continued as she passed a slower-moving car on the road. "My parents are pretty cool. I mean, they don't let me and my friends get hammered drunk like your friends' do, but they usually don't care if somebody stays over." Not being from a Catholic family, Emily still couldn't get used to how it was just okay with Meggie's and her friends' parents if they drank.

"Don't judge us, hypocrite," Meggie said with a smile. "At least our parents wave when they see each other at the liquor store."

"Oh, I'm not sayin' it's not cool, it's just weird," Emily said. "When I was in high school, part of the fun with drinking was sneaking around."

"Well, it was more of a social thing for us. It was always there. Our parents drank in moderation in front of us, so that's what we learned to do." Meggie couldn't count how many times she had to explain to non-Catholics that not all of them were raging alcoholics.

While Emily was enjoying having her friend acting normally and cracking jokes again, her mind was elsewhere. She was thinking about the zombie she had met earlier. She really hoped that Paul and Ben just listened to him, and agreed to leave Meggie alone. For some reason, though, she knew that simply wasn't the case. If you meet a zombie, she thought, you either try to run from it, or try to kill it. Paul and Ben didn't strike Emily as runners. She worried for Jackson.

"So what do you think Jackson would have done in tonight's situation?" Emily asked. In her head, it was the perfect segue, but Meggie had not been in Emily's head for the past few minutes. She was completely bombarded.

"What? Why do you ask me that?" Meggie was a little confused.

Emily tried to connect the dots for her. "Well, I've just been thinking about it. Would you have left Jackson and any one of the other guys with a bloodied-up psycho with a knife?"

Meggie had successfully put the image out of

her mind, but Emily had brought it right back. She thought about it, then said, "Well, first of all, that would have never happened with Jackson."

"Whatcha mean?" Emily asked.

"That just wouldn't have happened. Jackson would have *never* stayed and fought; and if Jon, or any of his other friends, would've wanted to stay and fight, Jackson would've dragged them away too. He didn't like to fight at all. As much as he ran around with the guys, he probably fought with them more trying to keep them out of fights than he did with anybody else." Talking about him brought back memories. She didn't cry much anymore, but she still missed him terribly.

The Jackson that Emily knew was a little different. Undead Jackson seemed to have fire in his eyes when he talked about Ben. He had obviously pushed the zombie to his limits. As she pictured him with his hood pulled tight over his head, taking a wide stance, weapon ready to strike, Emily knew, that if what Meggie said was true about Jackson, walking away was no longer an option.

"Well, what does that say about Paul?" Emily asked. "He didn't walk away."

"It means that-" Meggie stopped suddenly. "It means he's crazy! What the Hell was he thinking? What the Hell was I thinking, leaving him with that lunatic?"

Hearing Meggie say the word made Emily think about Paul's misspelling. She laughed. "Stupid is more like it."

Meggie picked up her phone and started dialing. "I have to call him and make sure he's okay."

"Fine, just don't tell him where we're going. I

don't need those goons knowing where I live." Meggie nodded and mouthed "okay" as the phone started ringing. Emily was sorry she brought anything up at all.

"Hey. Are you okay? Is everything all right?" Paul had answered the phone. Meggie went on. "Is Ben okay too? That's good. What was up with that guy?" She became more and more entranced the longer she stayed on the phone with him.

Emily whispered, "What happened to the dude with the knife?" She wasn't concerned with Paul and Ben. She wanted to know about Jackson.

Meggie covered up the phone and whispered, "He ran away and went in the church." She resumed her conversation with Paul. "Did y'all call the cops or anything? Why not? Oh, okay. Where are y'all now? Oh, me? I'm with Em. We're on our way to Bir-"

Meggie was interrupted by Emily snatching the phone out of her hand. "The bridge. We're on our way to the bridge, so the phone might cut out." Emily made some scratchy sounds with her mouth and hung up the phone.

"What was that for?" said a perturbed Meggie.

"I *just* told you not to tell him where we were going. There's no way you forgot that fast." Emily was so frustrated with her friend, she couldn't think straight.

"I don't know. I'm sorry," Meggie said. Her phone lit up. He was calling back.

Emily shot Meggie a look. "Don't you answer that. You text him back, and you let me screen 'em before you send them. You go stupid when he talks to you. I can't trust you'll do right."

"Okay." Meggie knew her friend was right.

Whenever she heard his voice, everything melted away and she was at Paul's command. While it was happening, she was fine; but after it was over, and she thought about it, she didn't like it any better than Emily. "I'm sorry."

Emily huffed. "It's okay. So what did he say?"

"He and Ben are fine. When the guy saw that they weren't backing down he ran away. They went back to Ben's apartment. Everything's fine."

Emily raised an eyebrow. "Didn't you just tell me the dude ran into the church?"

"Yeah."

She turned down the radio to get more of Meggie's attention. "Don't you find that a little odd, Meg?"

"What are you talking about?" Meggie asked.

"When we pulled up to the church, Paul told us that it was locked, said it was closed to repair the floor or something."

"Yeah, so?" Meggie shrugged.

"How in the Hell did the crazy guy get in the church if it was locked up?" Emily saw the look on Meggie's face change from oblivious to suspicious.

"Oh, shit. He's lying about something."

Emily nodded. "Yep. There's no telling why he's lying or what else he's lying about. God only knows what happened with the psycho." Emily knew how much emphasis Jackson put on that church and how it was the only safe place. She hoped he really did make it inside. But then again, there was no way to know for sure.

Now that Meggie had caught Paul in a lie, everything she had experienced with him, and everything he had told her came into question. "You don't have to worry about me answering his phone calls- or even answering his texts. If he'll lie to me about a church, he'll lie to me about anything. Jesus! I should've listened to Jon and Ryan in the first place."

Emily smiled from satisfaction. She had finally caused a rift between Meggie and Paul. She wasn't sure if she would see Jackson again, but if she did, she would be able to tell him "mission accomplished."

The rest of the trip to Birmingham was uneventful. The girls sang along to some of their favorite songs. At one point, for laughs, Meggie stuck her head out the window and snapped at the wind like a dog. For the rest of the trip, her curly black hair was a tangled mess.

The girls finally arrived at Emily's house. Her two-story, gray and white brick house was actually located in Alabaster, a suburb just south of Birmingham. It was nearly midnight when Emily parked her car and the girls got out.

Emily's loud engine had made a few dogs about her neighborhood start barking. After a few seconds of the engine being turned off, they quieted back down. The only remaining sounds came from crickets, and from cars on the highway in the distance.

"We can just go inside. My parents are sleeping, I'm sure." Emily thumbed through her keyring until she found the one to her front door. Only using their cell phones as flashlights, they went inside and upstairs to Emily's room.

Once they were both in her bedroom, Emily closed the door and turned on her light. She spread her arms wide and said, "Home sweet home."

Meggie looked around her friend's room. Except for one accent wall, which was painted blood-red with a handful of famous quotes written in black, everything was black and white. The other three walls in Emily's room were white and trimmed in black. Her carpet was equal parts black and white, making it look a cool, gray color. She had a big, tall, fluffy bed with a white down comforter. To Meggie's surprise there were no giant posters of metal bands she had never heard of.

Aside from a computer desk, Emily had no other furniture in her room. "Where do you put your clothes?" Meggie asked.

Emily pointed to a door. "I gotta big ass closet."

"Gotcha," Meggie said. "So what now?"

"I don't know about you, but I'm going to hop my happy self in this bed and relax." She did just that.

She wasn't sure what the next step in her plan would be. Meggie was out of town and safe, but she wasn't sure for how long. She also wasn't sure about Jackson's safety. Getting Meggie safely back home would require more planning than she was willing to orchestrate at the moment.

I have no way of contacting Jackson, Emily thought. Eventually her plan would have to involve someone else. She thought about Chad and the other guys. She wished that she could just tell them all. She wished that she could let them all know that their friend was no longer buried. But that would have to wait at least one more day.

20

Wherever Breann had gotten off to, Jackson was not sure. She had definitely left the chapel, though. Jackson searched every nook and cranny of St. Joe's for the girl with no luck. All that was left to do for the zombie was to await the dawn.

While waiting for the safety of the sunrise to make his trip to Spring Hill's old library, Jackson's night consisted mostly of trying to get his clothes free of the vampire blood that had splattered on them. Jackson chose the bathroom sink to clean his clothes.

Modest even in undeath, Jackson removed one article of clothing at a time to clean. He elected to clean his shirt first. Jackson removed his jacket, which was heavy with the weight of his book and dagger, and placed it on the counter next to the sink. Then he removed his polo shirt.

Most of Alex's blood had gotten on the shirt. Jackson's jacket and pants were dark enough that what little blood had gotten on them wasn't that noticeable; but if Jackson was going to continue to wear the light-blue polo, it would have to be cleaned.

Slashes where Ben had clawed at him were still

in the shirt. Jackson stuck his fingers through them and recalled the event. Some of his blood had stained the back of the shirt. Compared to the bright-red stains caused by Alex's blood, the liquid that came from inside Jackson looked purple.

He looked at his reflection in the mirror, taking notice of the y-shaped mark from his incision. Then he turned enough to inspect his shoulder. No such marks existed from Ben's attack. "Cool! I don't scar," Jackson said aloud as he began cleaning his shirt.

The majority of the blood washed out easily, with the help of the hand soap from the dispenser attached to the mirror. It still looked like a dirty shirt, but it didn't look like crime scene evidence anymore. Jackson thought to himself. "Hmm, I wonder."

After listening through the bathroom door to confirm he was still alone in the church, Jackson exited the bathroom, with the shirt in his hand. He approached the marble basin of bubbling holy water in the back of St. Joe's and submerged his shirt in the water. When he pulled it out, the stains had vanished. Jackson held the shirt over the basin and rung out the excess water as best he could.

Once he was back in the bathroom, Jackson took the time to write something in the book Father Borbridge had given him.

Holy Water: Great for undead stains

Jackson put back on the wet shirt. He remembered just how much he disliked wearing wet clothes. Then he remembered something else. He didn't generate body heat anymore. His shirt would never get dry. He groaned and took it off again. There was a hand dryer on the wall next to the door. Jackson turned it on and held his shirt underneath it. It would take some time, but he would eventually have a dry shirt.

The loud whirring of the hand dryer reminded him of the sound made by vacuum cleaners. He remembered how it was one of his pet peeves in life. Most background noise Jackson could ignore, but vacuum cleaners, and apparently hand dryers, were just too loud to disregard. Not only did the dryer's noise make it impossible to hear anything else, it made it tougher to even remain standing next to it to dry his shirt. Jackson had to concentrate to keep the pestilent noise from overwhelming him.

As he could not hear what might be going on outside while the hand dryer was running, Jackson locked the bathroom door. He didn't want to startle anyone by having them walk in on a zombie doing his laundry.

The hand dryer had a timer, and it would shut off after about a minute, forcing Jackson to press it again to turn it back on. After countless restarts, he finally got his shirt dry. He put it back on. He could feel the last parts that he had dried still warm against his skin. Once he had put back on his jacket too, he unlocked the door and exited the bathroom.

Jackson listened to try and make out sounds of anyone else that might have entered the chapel while he was in the bathroom. He heard no movements and no breathing. He filled his lungs with air through his nostrils, almost certain he would catch Breann's scent from somewhere in St. Joe's. Nothing. He was still alone. He walked over to the basin of blessed water.

For the small amount of blood stains on his pants and jacket, Jackson simply splashed some of the holy water onto the front of his clothes. Just like it had easily removed the blood from his shirt, so too did it quickly cause the rest of the blood stains to vanish. Freshly clean, Jackson went up the set of stairs that led him to the pipe organ.

If St. Joe's has to be my hideout, he thought, this will be my spot. With nothing else to do but wait, Jackson sat on the organ's bench and pulled out the journal to read.

Jackson flipped to a random page toward the back of the journal. Since he had begun reading it, he had discovered that he liked reading entries penned by the more recent authors. There was no faded text, nor did it read like it was written by Shakespeare. The newer entries were written in more contemporary language, making them much easier to read.

A lot of the diary's entries were quite dry. It seemed that many of its authors spent more time spying on Dark Ones than they did fighting them. While there were some detailed accounts of good vampire killing, most of the entries made Jackson think about a couple of priests in a stakeout van parked outside a vampire's house.

One of the easily understandable entries caught Jackson's attention, though. It didn't take up a whole page like most of the others did. It wasn't a step-by-step recount, like other pages, either.

Of course there are other supernatural forces and beings at work besides our Heavenly Father. Our scripture tells us that our God is a "jealous god." It would be absurd for anyone, let alone our almighty Creator, to be jealous of things that do not exist. Therefore, matters of alchemy, witchcraft, and the occult should not being taken lightly.

The entry was in a handwriting unlike any other entry in the book, and it was left unsigned. It was more than enough, however, to send Jackson's imagination wandering. He already knew firsthand that zombies and vampires were real. And the priests had told him that ghosts existed. What other monsters and supernatural phenomena were out there lurking unbeknownst to the world?

Jackson put the book away for the time being. He did not want to talk himself into any unnecessary paranoia. Whatever else might be out in the world didn't matter. What mattered were the monsters, that he *did* know existed, who had their sights set on Meggie.

Daylight appeared to be breaking. The stained glass windows began to lighten up from light outside. Jackson wasn't sure if it would have been more or less torture if he had a watch. All he knew was that zombie time was different than regular time. In his life, he had been a pretty fast reader; but now, what felt like minutes of reading to him appeared to pass the time faster than anything else. The amount of concentration it took made it a time-consuming affair.

With his clothes cleaned and the sun coming out, Jackson made his way to the front door of the church. He opened it very slowly and barely stepped out with the door still ajar. He felt no dark presence. Even Alex had limped away. The zombie was free to walk about the campus.

Jackson made his way west which, according to the priests, was where he needed to go to find the old library. He could feel the balmy summer heat on his skin, and he could smell the morning dew that covered everything in a heavy mist. After passing a few buildings that didn't fit the old library's description, Jackson saw the clearing up ahead of him that was obviously the soccer field. He kept walking until he was in between a brown, brick building and another that, he was sure, was the one he was looking for. It was tall and narrow, and the side that faced the soccer field had four giant, white columns.

The columns supported an awning that covered the library's big wooden doors. Jackson grabbed the handle of one of them. Borbridge and Hayes had unlocked it for him. He stepped inside.

The interior of the building was mostly a long hallway, with doors to offices and study rooms on either side, that ran the length of the building. There were no lights on, but Jackson could see just fine from the very little bit of light that leaked in from the outside. Toward the end of the building, the hallway opened up into what appeared to be a lobby. On the right there was a door that led outside, and on the left there was a big service desk. To either side of the desk, there was a set of stairs that circled around the back of the desk and led upstairs, to the library proper.

Wooden blinds blocked out most of the sun that might have come through to illuminate the second floor. It was quite dim, but for a zombie that could see in pitch darkness, it was more than enough. Jackson made out the old bookshelves that lined the walls between the floor-to-ceiling windows that were scattered evenly throughout the library. There were several rows of bookshelves and just as many tables reserved for group projects. Jackson had his eyes set on the cluster of computers that were placed in the center of the room. He made his way to one and turned on the power.

As the machine whirred to life, tiny LED's lit up on the front of the computer's tower and monitor. After a few seconds, the computer screen came on as the machine loaded. Jackson took a seat in the chair and assumed the web-surfing position he had assumed so many times in his life.

He watched the light from the monitor reflect off the pale skin on his hands that rested on the keyboard in front of him. When the computer had finished its familiar symphony of start-up sounds, Jackson found the internet icon and opened the program.

He first searched vague terms like "zombie" and "vampire." After he drudged through the mythology of mindless brain-eating and blood-sucking, he was able to find a few morsels of truth that he could confirm with his own experiences. To the rest of the world, as well as the internet world, the undead were things of fantasy. Jackson read through the conspiracy theories with mild pleasure. He was glad that the whole world was unaware that such horrors actually existed.

His next search was for the Order of Lazarus. The search engine yielded tons of information about a charitable organization associated with the Catholic

Church that was founded in 1098. It was a chivalric order originally founded to treat leprosy during the Crusades. Whether the organization had any ties to Father Borbridge and hunting vampires, Jackson couldn't be certain. If it was, the order served as a philanthropic cover for the order's real work. After he searched "Borbridge" and "Order of Lazarus," and found no results, Jackson concluded that they were either unrelated, or the Catholic Church's elaborate cover. Either way, he didn't care. Father Hayes and Father Borbridge had saved his life. He didn't need the internet to confirm that.

It was then that he went to the website that had initially piqued his interest in the internet in the first place: FaceSpace. It was a social networking site that was so popular, that everyone he knew, young and old alike, had a profile. It was on FaceSpace that Jackson would be able to learn certain comings and goings of the people he really cared about.

His first search was for Meggie Paulez. He typed her name. His high school girlfriend was the first result to pop up. Jackson tried to click it, but when he did, the website prompted him to either log into the site, or create a profile. Knowing that logging into his old profile might spark some suspicion from any of his friends that might have been online, he chose to create a new one.

Jackson chose an inconspicuous first and last name. He filled out the online form as if his name was Mike Adams. Mike Adams was a random, upperclassman that attended Spring Hill College. He was twenty-one years old, and he loved going to parties. Jackson chose it out of convenience, and the fact that he was currently residing on said campus. An

240

element of truth snuck into the fictitious profile he had created.

Jackson chose to skip the uploading of a profile picture, and most of the profile information, and finalized the account. He had had a spare email address from over a decade ago, and accessed it to confirm the account. He was now able to search the FaceSpace.

Once his account was created, he continued to Meggie's profile. Her profile picture was some harmless photo she had posed for at a football game. He clicked it and her whole profile was revealed.

Jackson reveled in seeing the only love he had ever known. He was happy to read about her statuses that recounted her accomplishments. When he saw her relationship status, though, his zombie heart shattered. Reading the word "single" immediately put a lump in his undead throat. He knew that her moving on was inevitable, but he wanted, more than anything, to just be by her side again. When he had perused a few of her recent photos, all of which portrayed her as a happy freshman in the prime of her life, Jackson swallowed hard and decided to look elsewhere.

He went through all his friends. Jon, Chad, Ryan, Brandon, Foster- even Paul. All of his friends had new lives and new adventures. None of them included him. Aside from a couple status updates from Jon, which directly included him, the world had gone on spinning without him. That was when Jackson decided to search for himself.

Jackson reluctantly clicked his profile picture that hadn't been changed in over a year. It was a picture of the whole gang, including Meggie, having a ball down in Gulf Shores. Jackson remembered picking it because it had all of his friends in it, but also had him in the forefront. His profile was filled with messages from his loved ones. His sister, Anna, had not missed a single significant date, and she posted on his profile on every birthday and holiday that had passed since he had died. The computer screen became hard to see as the zombie's eyes filled up with tears.

Jackson was thoroughly convinced that the world could, and would, go on without him. He tried to focus on his current situation. He went to Paul's profile and browsed through his friends to attempt to identify the other vampires. His friends' list included a Ben Cooley and an Alex Stanwick. Ben was the first alphabetically, so Jackson clicked it first.

When Ben Cooley's profile picture loaded, it was definitely the vampire that Jackson had encountered. He was a big, muscly upperclassman with spiked blonde hair. In his life, he looked like the type of person Jackson would have avoided anyway. In his second life, however, his was the face of the sworn enemy. In his profile picture he bore a gleaming smile. While it may have been appealing to others, Jackson only saw the fangs, and his stomach turned in disgust.

Once he had successfully identified Ben, he clicked on Alex Stanwick, who was a mutual friend of Paul and Ben. Alex's profile picture did not seem as arrogant as Ben's, but Jackson, having encountered Alex, was fully aware of the danger he posed. Jackson had mutilated him. If his stabbings and threats did not scare him off the zombie's trail, he would probably be more of a problem than Paul and Ben combined. Then he went back to Paul.

Paul's profile picture was a recent photo of

him. Jackson could tell because of the fangs. Most people might not notice, he thought, but they were definitely there. Jackson even compared them to photos Paul had on his profile that were from high school. There was a difference.

Jackson tried to pinpoint, through the photos, when he might have turned, but he couldn't tell for sure. It was really irrelevant, though. He was turned now. He had tried to kick his head in. He was now an enemy.

After Jackson aimlessly clicked through old pictures of his friends, he decided to find a way to make FaceSpace useful. He went back to Meggie's profile to search through her friends. There were two Emily's in her friends list, but only one that mattered. Jackson clicked Emily Ross.

She was the one he wanted. After he added her as a friend, he chose to send her a direct message. She wasn't online at the time, but she would get it the next time she was.

Don't spray me in the face this time. Thank you for your help. I hope that Meggie is safe. Get silver around her neck ASAP. Contact me so we can try and fix this.
Jax

Jackson hoped it would be enough. After he sent the message, he browsed her profile a little more. All of her contact information was available. Her address, phone number, and email address were there for everyone to see. Too easy, he thought. Jackson committed the cell number to memory, if he could ever get his hands on a phone.

With no one left to search for, he typed in "Breann." he wasn't sure he spelled it right, but the second result had a picture that matched the only other person that knew he existed. He clicked it.

Unlike any of the other profiles he had browsed through, Breann Buchanon's was set to private. The only thing he could see was that she was nineteen and that she attended Spring Hill College. It was her, but he couldn't glean anything else from her profile. He added her as a friend, like he had Emily, and moved the cursor to the "x" button to close the program. Just then he heard a sound.

Emily had accepted his friend request. Not only had she accepted, but she had also responded to his message. FaceSpace did not indicate that she was online, so she must have responded from her mobile phone.

OMG please tell me what I need to do. I am almost as confused as Meggie. We are in Birmingham at my house.

Jackson was pleased that he had found an ally in Emily. He hadn't thought past killing the vampires to ensure Meggie's safety. The fact that she was miles away from Mobile comforted him some. But he wasn't really sure what to tell her. He responded, being only sure of one thing.

Keep her there as long as you can. I will contact you again as soon as I can with instructions. Both of you stay safe.

As concerned as Jackson was with Meggie, he

also wanted to let Emily know that her well-being mattered too. He did not have many friends; he had to make sure that the ones he did have were safe and sound.

ok. thanx dead man

Again, Jackson was not put off by the comment. He was pretty sure Emily was on his side. Before he was tempted to keep the conversation going, with asking about Meggie or anything else, he closed the program.

Jackson walked over to one of the big windows and split two of the wooden blinds, which splashed sunlight into the old library. Hours had passed, but daylight remained. He was still safe to walk back to the chapel. He walked back to the computer he had been using and shut it down. Once it had completely turned off, Jackson exited the old library and resumed his trek back to sacred ground.

21

As Jackson stepped outside the old library, he could see rain clouds beginning to form in the sky. It was the start of summer in Mobile, Alabama. Afternoon thunderstorms were almost a daily occurrence. They never lasted too long, hardly ever over half an hour; but they were very intense. For almost thirty minutes, nearly every day during the summer, the bottom fell out of the sky over Mobile. Jackson could feel the air pressure change. He saw the trees near him rustle as the wind blew through them. He could feel the wind blowing around him. The rain was coming soon.

Jackson began his walk back toward the chapel. He was about halfway back when big, fat rain drops began to fall. He felt one of the big drops land on top of his head, so he put on his jacket's hood. There weren't a lot of them, but the raindrops were big, and Jackson knew that they were only the prelude to the torrential downpour that followed them. He remembered this time that he didn't have any body heat. He didn't want to be stuck wearing wet clothes, so he quickened his pace.

Cottonwood flowers from nearby trees were floating on the wind around him. Some of them stuck to Jackson's clothes as he made his way to the chapel. They were pretty to watch blowing in the breeze, but the wind carried something else with it. Jackson stopped walking and took in a deep breath through his nose to make out the smell. It was the familiar earthy musk that he knew was Breann. Because of the wind, he wasn't completely sure how close she was to him, but he looked in the direction of it and tried to locate her.

The wind had carried her scent a surprisingly long distance. Jackson was amazed at how far away she was when he finally spotted her. While he had ignored any sidewalks or designated walkways, finding the straightest eastward path toward the chapel, Breann was following a sidewalk alongside a road that headed northwest.

She was wearing a purple sundress. It had a busy pattern on it that was composed of varying hues of purple. Though she didn't have a jacket or an umbrella, Breann did not look to be in any sort of hurry to get out of the incoming rain.

She hadn't spotted Jackson yet. For once, he would be able to intrude on her day instead of the other way around. Jackson commanded his lungs to fill as he prepared to shout. "Breann!" he exclaimed.

Breann turned to see who had called her name. She must have recognized him. Jackson smiled as he watched the girl run toward him. "Jackson!" she replied with equal volume and excitement.

Jackson had stopped walking toward the chapel. He didn't want to be rude, so he waited for her. She had run so hard that Breann was a little winded by the time she made it him. "What's up?" Jackson asked her. The rain didn't really bother him. He didn't want to have soggy clothes, but he wondered why she was just walking around outside during the rain.

Breann's eyes scanned Jackson. He wondered if she would be able to tell in the daylight that he was a zombie. The clouds had darkened things, but it was still much brighter outside than the church interior ever was. She gave no indication that she had noticed anything different. "Dude, what is with you and that jacket?" she asked.

Jackson didn't even bother thinking about answering her. He merely grew concerned as he looked back at her. She was paler than usual. She almost looked sick. "Are you okay? You look sick."

Breann scoffed. "You should talk! You look like you haven't seen the sun in ten years."

Just one year, Jackson thought. "I'm always pale, but you usually look better than this. Are you sick?" Breann's face looked drained. She even looked weaker somehow.

"I just didn't get a lot of sleep last night's all," she said.

Then Jackson remembered last night. After he had walked outside to fight the vampires, he had not seen Breann again. He had no idea where she had gone or what she had done. "Oh, yeah. I told you to stay in the church. Where'd you go?"

"You didn't come back for a while, and I got scared," she said. "So I snuck off back to my dorm and locked up tight."

Jackson pondered her story. He didn't remembered being gone too long; but then again, his internal clock wasn't working at 100%. Even if he had only been gone a few moments, though, her fear could have altered her concept of time as well. "Let's get out of this rain, and we can talk."

Breann reached and grabbed his hand. The rain was already beginning to make her long, brown hair stick to her as she looked up at him. "No," she begged. "Please stay with me. I love the rain."

Jackson couldn't resist her. She looked at him, with green eyes to rival his own, and he was powerless. "Alright," he said.

Breann immediately changed from her feigned helplessness she had whilst begging, and smiled big. "Yay!" she exclaimed. She had been holding her cell phone in her hand. She reached into Jackson's jacket and put it in one of his inside pockets. Luckily, it was the one with the vampire journal, not the dagger. "Make that stupid jacket useful, so my phone won't get wet."

By now, the rainfall was in full effect. It was coming down so hard that Jackson could barely make out any other sounds than the din of millions of raindrops pounding the ground. Jackson was enduring one of his biggest pet peeves, being in wet clothes, because of a pretty girl. Even though he felt dumb, he couldn't help himself. Jackson removed his hood and held his arms out wide as he smiled at Breann.

"Is this what you do for fun?" he asked her. He had to raise his voice to speak over the sound of the rain.

Breann had her arms out as she was spinning in a circle, almost dancing in the downpour. "What? You don't just love it? I *love* the rain."

Jackson remembered being alive and loving the

rain too. He recalled the many times he made Meggie go play in the rain with him. But now he didn't have any clothes to change into. The shoe was on the other foot now, because he was not going to wear his burial clothes anymore. He would be stuck with the wet ones he had on. "Yeah, I love it too."

Jackson watched her spin a few more times. She was so pretty, and she looked so happy. The zombie couldn't help but smile.

Then she stopped dancing, and turned to Jackson. Out of nowhere, she threw herself into her arms and planted a kiss on him. He was taken completely by surprised as their lips touched. She didn't open her mouth. She merely left her lips gently pressed against his for a few seconds and wrapped her arms around his neck. Her lips felt warm against his, even in the cold rain. After a few more seconds she withdrew a few inches with her arms still wrapped around him.

Jackson's eyes were wide with fear and surprise as she looked back up at him. Instead of freaking her out by telling her that she had just kissed a dead guy, he just asked. "What was that for?"

Breann smiled. "I've wanted to do that for a while now. You've got those kind of lips that just look so soft that they just beg people to kiss 'em."

Jackson had his arms around her as well. He smiled back at her. "And?"

"Very soft." Jackson began to chuckle.

Breann was grinning as she backed away from him, out of his grasp. "What's so funny?"

Jackson limited his laughter to a smile and said, "My mom always told me not to even bother with a girl that wasn't smart enough to comment on how soft my lips were." he remembered his lips being one of Meggie's favorite things about him. While he knew that there was no way he could date Breann, it was at least nice to know that his lips retained their softness even in death. "I guess you're not stupid."

"Yeah, I know I'm not," she said. "But it is a little weird that your mom kisses you enough to know that."

"Oh, shut up." The two of them shared a glance before Breann resumed her dancing in the rain.

Jackson chose to simply walk around in the rain and watch her. He wasn't much of a dancer in life, and he definitely did not have the confidence to do so as a zombie. Breann seemed just as content with him watching her, so she didn't try to coax him to do any dancing with her.

True to form, the afternoon shower stopped after a while, ending as abruptly as it had begun. "Now, wasn't that amazing?" Breann asked him.

Jackson knew she was talking about them playing in the rain, but all he could think about was the fact that she had kissed him. "Completely amazing."

The two of them were thoroughly soaked as the sun reemerged in the sky. Jackson could feel the thick, humid air beginning to heat up again, thankful that it was doing so. It would help to dry him, and it would help to warm the shivering, living girl next to him.

Jackson wondered how he would ever be able to tell Breann the whole truth now. He could only imagine her running for the hills if he told her that he was a zombie. If Breann knew what he really was, she might be scarred for life knowing that she had kissed an undead Jackson. But then he thought about the promise he made to her.

He promised Breann that he would tell her everything. It was made under the stipulation that she stay in the chapel, though. She had not, so he was not obligated by his promise to tell her *everything*. Without saying a word to her, he began walking again to St. Joe's.

"So, where are you headed today?" Breann asked him.

"Back to the chapel."

Breann gave him a confused look. "Again? Dude, it's like you live there or something."

The thought of him "living" anywhere made him smile. "It's my safe place." He continued walking.

She followed alongside him. "Safe from what?" she asked.

"Let's just get back to St. Joe's, and I'll tell you, okay?" Jackson did not want to risk being caught outside when the sun set.

"Fine," she said. "But you better be ready to tell me what's going on."

"I will."

"Good. But first, I'm going back to my dorm to change," she said. "You may be fine with wet clothes, but I'm not."

Jackson had been preoccupied with recently being kissed and thinking about how he would dance around the fact that he was a zombie. Now he was reminded about his soaking wet clothes. "That's fine. I'll be there."

"Okay," Breann said. She leaned into Jackson and kissed him again. She didn't linger as much this time, but it was certainly longer than just a peck on the cheek. "See you in a few."

252

Jackson watched her walk away, in the direction she was originally going before he had interrupted her. "Oh, boy. I'm in trouble," he said to himself. He continued to the chapel.

Once he was inside, he immediately felt safer. Even though it was still daylight, just being inside the chapel's walls gave him comfort. The vampires might not be at full strength in the sun, he thought, but they couldn't even get to him while he was in St. Joseph's chapel.

To Jackson's relief, the chapel was conveniently empty. After he had dipped his fingertips into the basin of holy water, made the sign of the cross, genuflected, and sat down, he remembered that he still had Breann's phone. She had taken off without getting it back from him. Jackson pulled out the phone and pressed a button to light it up.

She did not have any sort of lock or password on it, which was perfect for Jackson. With ease he recalled Emily's number and dialed it.

As the phone rang and Jackson anxiously awaited Emily to answer, he looked around the chapel to ensure that he was alone. After a few rings, she answered.

"Hello?" Emily sounded confused. There was no way that she would have recognized the number.

"Is Meggie where she can hear you?" he asked. He didn't want Emily to be on the phone with him while Meggie was around her.

"Hold on."

Jackson could hear sounds of movement over the phone. He heard Meggie say "what's up" in the background. Emily gave no response to her. A few seconds later, Jackson could hear a door closing. Emily had secluded herself.

"Okay, I can talk," she said.

"Cool. I'm calling you from a friend's phone." It was the best way Jackson could think of describing Breann to Emily.

"Uh- alright. So what am I supposed to do?" she asked him.

Jackson's first concerns were for Meggie. "Did you find a silver necklace, or something, to give to Meggie to wear?"

"Yeah, but what's up with that?"

Jackson hadn't fully explained things to Emily. "It protects you. Look, Ben, Alex, *and* Paul are vampires, so-"

Emily cut him off. "Wait, what! What the Hell is goin' on?"

"It might sound crazy, but it's true. They are vampires, and if you wear a silver necklace, they can't charm you. I think it's kind of like brainwashing, or something." The other end of the line was silent for a moment. "Are you still there?" Jackson asked.

"No, I'm here. That actually makes a lot of sense. I gave her a silver necklace. She didn't really think it worked with her complexion, but I guilted her into keeping it on."

Jackson felt relief. He wasn't sure if the vampires would get violent with Meggie, but at least now he knew that they couldn't brainwash her. "So, you're not freaked out about them being vampires?"

Jackson heard Emily laugh. "Why should I be? Hell, I'm talking to a zombie right now, ain't I?"

"Good point."

Emily went on. "The question now is: what are we supposed to do about it?"

Jackson heard a noise from the front door of the church. Someone was coming. He figured it was Breann. "I'll let you know real soon, okay? Until I contact you again, just keep Meggie up there, alright."

"So you just tell me there are vampires and-" Jackson didn't wait around for the rest of what Emily had to say. Someone had opened the door to the church, and Jackson ended the call and put the phone back into his jacket pocket.

When he turned around, he saw Breann walking toward him. She changed into a tank top and cut-off jeans. They exchanged a smile, and she sat down beside him.

"Alright, start talking."

"What do you want to know?" Jackson replied innocently.

"I want to know everything, dude."

Jackson chose his words wisely. "Well, you know how I told you that there were dead people after me?"

"Yeah, you said some crazy shit, like zombies were after you or something."

"Well, they aren't exactly zombies."

"What the Hell are they?" she asked.

Jackson paused for a moment to prepare himself for telling Breann. "They are vampires. There are three of them, and they are trying to kill me."

Breann laughed. "Oh, so they're vampires now, huh? Dude, you are off your rocker."

"No I'm not!" Jackson became defensive. His mind was one thing that worked perfectly in his second life. "That's why I stay in the chapel. They can't come here."

Breann raised an eyebrow and looked at

Jackson suspiciously. "Why do you think these vampires are just out for you?"

Jackson thought about how to answer. The real reason was that he was a zombie. For some reason, his undead presence threw the Dark Ones into a homicidal rage. He didn't want to tell her that, though. "Because one of them used to be my friend."

"I think having a vampire for a friend would be awesome. Why does he want to kill you though?"

"It's not awesome," he said. "And he's not my friend. For some reason, he wants me dead. Him *and* his vampire friends."

Breann was deep in thought for moment. "So, that's what was chasing you, and that's what you made me stay in the church for?"

"Yes."

"How am I supposed to believe you?" she asked.

Jackson pulled out the old leather-bound journal. Breann's cell phone fell out of his pocket as well. "Oh yeah, you left this with me." he handed her the phone.

Breann took the phone from him without ever averting her gaze from the book. "What is that?"

Jackson handed her the book. "It is a journal of different vampire hunters through the years."

Breann held the book in her hands. Her eyes were wide as she examined the outside intently. "Really?"

"Yes. Really. It has some cool stuff in it about how to deal with them."

Breann didn't respond. Jackson wasn't even sure that she had heard him. She wasn't paying attention to him anymore. She flipped through the book and scanned the pages. "Where did you get this?" she asked.

Jackson did not want to expose Father Borbridge or the Order of Lazarus. As he remembered that parts of the book explicitly stated the order's name, he took it back from Breann. "I got it from another person that knows about the vampires."

Breann looked disappointed as Jackson snatched the journal from her hands. "So, what are you? A vampire hunter?"

Jackson thought about it. "They hunt me. I'll just kill them if they get too close." Jackson felt a sense of pride as he said the words. He was more capable that anyone else to protect the people he cared about.

"You're gonna have to give me more, dude." Breann remained unconvinced.

Jackson shook his head. "Fine. After the sun goes down, I'll walk outside and you can see them come out and get me. They can't help themselves."

"Well that's not for a few more hours," she said. "I got shit to do, but I will gladly come back and you can show me."

"Fine."

"Fine," she snapped back, mocking him. Then she smiled.

Jackson did not want to endanger her, but he also wanted her to be informed. She seemed to like him, and she needed to know that the vampires hunting him had no intentions of stopping until he was dead again.

"Alright," Breann said. "Well I'll be back later and you can show me these vampires, okay."

"Okay."

She kissed him again. Jackson really liked the

attention and affections of the pretty girl, but he didn't want her to make it a habit. He was a zombie. "Sorry, I just like doing that," Breann said.

She exited the church, leaving Jackson alone with his thoughts.

22

It had been three whole days since Emily had heard anything from Jackson. Her instructions were to keep Meggie in Birmingham until he contacted her again, but she couldn't help but wonder that something was wrong. She hadn't received any new FaceSpace messages, nor had Jackson called her again from that strange number. She sat at her dining room table with a laptop in front of her.

For the past two days, when Meggie was not right beside her, Emily had been surfing the web. She had searched for anything about zombies and vampires she could find. All she could really find were a bunch of websites dedicated to movies and TV shows. She couldn't find anything about how someone might come back from the dead and have vampire college kids trying to kill him.

Emily wished that she had had longer to talk to Jackson when he called. She had so many questions. Although she could have asked one of several hundred questions about this whole new supernatural world to which she had been introduced, her biggest concern was about the phone. Was it Jackson's? If not, whose was it? Emily wondered about who else might know of his undead existence.

She was not allowed much time to wonder about it, though, because Meggie came downstairs to distract her. Her big, curly black hair was a mess around her face as she asked, "What's with the early-bird routine, skank? You used to love sleeping in at the dorms."

Emily couldn't tell her friend the real reasons why she had not been getting much sleep. "You've been snoring," she lied to her friend. Meggie did snore sometimes, but it had nothing to do with anything presently.

"Oh my God! Really?" Meggie said as she put both of her hands over her face. "I must be stressed out or something. I usually only do it when I'm drunk or really tired. That's so embarrassing."

She had totally believed Emily. "It's okay. Maybe we can get you some of those sexy strips that go on your nose."

Meggie gave her a look of disgust. "Ugh! Negative. Sorry, you'll just have to deal with it."

Emily laughed. "Nah, it's cool. I can just come down here and sleep on the couch or something."

"Cool. So what's for breakfast?" Meggie asked as she walked past Emily at the table and made her way to the kitchen.

"There's some cereal on top of the fridge," she said, but Meggie had already begun reaching for it. She tiptoed to grab the box she wanted.

"Do you want some too?" Meggie asked.

"No, thank you. I already ate."

After she grabbed the gallon of milk from the refrigerator, Meggie opened and closed a few of the kitchen cabinets until she found the one that contained bowls. After doing the same thing with drawers, looking for a spoon, she came into the dining room and sat down, with her breakfast ready to assemble, across from Emily.

Emily was amazed by her friend. She was always able to eat. When she had stayed with the Paulez family, she felt like she ate five meals a day. Somehow, though, they all stayed thin. She was both impressed and envious. "I should've known better. You're gonna eat me out of house and home."

"Whatever," Meggie said. She finished pouring the cereal and milk into her bowl. "You invited me. Deal with it."

Emily laughed. She would much rather be low on groceries than have her friend be in danger. "I knew the risk, I suppose."

After a few bites, Meggie took a break from devouring the cereal to breathe. When she finished chewing she asked, "Where are your mom and dad?"

"They've *been* gone to work," Emily said. "It's almost noon. You really should be having lunch instead of breakfast."

Meggie held up an index finger while she finished chewing again and swallowed. "Good idea. I'll finish this and maybe I can cook us up something for lunch."

Emily laughed. "Fine by me."

Other than sounds of the cereal crunching as Meggie consumed it, the girls were silent as she finished the cereal in her bowl.

As Meggie turned up her bowl to drink the milk that was left over, Emily asked her, "So, have you heard anymore from Paul."

To Emily's surprise, Meggie said, "Yep. He woke me up this morning. I haven't been answering his calls, but I was half-asleep this morning, and I wasn't paying attention. I just wanted the damned noise to stop."

"Well what did he say?" Emily was anxious to learn how differently her friend interacted with Paul now that she had on the silver necklace, which Jackson said would keep her from being "charmed."

"He said he just wanted to make sure I was okay," Meggie said. "And he knows I'm up here with you."

"What!" Emily exclaimed. "I told you not to tell him."

"Relax. I didn't. Mom did." Meggie stood up and took her empty bowl, along with the cereal and milk, and took them into the kitchen. "After I stopped responding to him, he went over to my house. Mom told him where I was."

"Oh," Emily said. She hadn't even thought about that. "Well, what else did he say?" She still wasn't convinced on the silver necklace theory.

"He asked how to get to your house, 'cause he wanted to come up here."

Emily wasn't sure she wanted to know Meggie's answer, but she reluctantly asked, "What did you tell him?" She winced as she awaited Meggie's response.

"I told him to get his story straight about that man with the knife, then maybe we could talk." Meggie's response to Paul had been greater than Emily ever expected.

Emily was trying to contain her satisfaction. She never really saw Paul's appeal, and had hated his affect on Meggie. Now she knew that silver was the factor that separated their opinions of him that night at the bowling alley; she wasn't so confused about how Meggie had become so quickly enamored with Paul. Emily was just glad she had tried to get Chad's attention that night with the extra jewelry. "Then what did he have to say?" she asked.

"He told me that he couldn't tell me over the phone. He said he wanted to tell me in person. Then he tried *again* to get me to tell him where you lived so he could 'come tell me.' Stupid boy." The air quotes Meggie made as she said "come tell me" made Emily snort with laughter. Spunky attitude and all, Meggie was back to her old self again.

"You didn't tell him then, did you?" Emily didn't need anymore convincing about the necklaces' effectiveness; now she was simply being entertained by Meggie's storytelling.

"Hell no!" she proclaimed. "I told him when I got back down there, *I* would contact *him* if I wanted to talk. He was just trying to smooth-talk me into telling him how to get up here. I don't know why he wants to come up here so bad. It's kinda creepy."

Emily knew that Meggie had no idea how creepy it was. If Jackson's claim was true, which from all indications, it was, then it could get a lot creepier. "I'm just glad you didn't cave and tell him how to get here."

"Nah, you don't have that to worry about," Meggie said. "I don't know, but after you caught him in a lie, and you pointed it out to me, I don't just blindly believe whatever he tells me anymore."

Emily knew that it wasn't because she had caught Paul in a lie. She knew that it was because of that necklace around her friend's neck that Meggie could once again think clearly. "Uh oh, Paul's done."

"Maybe not. But he better be straight with me from now on if he *ever* wants to be anything with me."

"Good for you, girl," Emily said.

"Yeah. Good for me." Meggie seemed to be glad to be thinking clearly again. "Now, about this lunch, is there anything in particular you want?"

Emily laughed at her friend. "I don't really care. Whatever you want." Every time she had eaten anything that Meggie had cooked, it was delicious. Emily had complete faith in her friend in the kitchen.

"Works for me," Meggie said.

As her friend started rummaging through the kitchen in search of utensils and ingredients, Emily picked up her laptop and said, "Let me know if you need help with anything. I'm gonna be in the living room."

Meggie loved to cook. She didn't stop her rummaging to even look back at her friend. "That's fine."

Emily sat down on her sofa and opened the laptop again. From where she was sitting, her back was toward the kitchen. Periodically, she would turn around to see if Meggie was peaking over her shoulder. Once she heard sufficient banging of pots, pans, and wooden spoons, Emily reopened her web browser.

She felt like she was running out of things to search for. She had searched for links between the undead and the Catholic Church. Emily even searched for "zombies in St. Joseph's Chapel Spring Hill." Nothing. The internet had apparently not gotten wind of the zombies and vampires that lived in Mobile yet.

As Meggie prepared lunch for her and Emily, pleasant smells filled the air. Whatever she was cooking was bound to be delicious. Emily could smell the different spices Meggie was using, and it made her laugh. She could smell the garlic that her friend was using. Emily wondered if Paul would want to be at her house now. "Smells delicious!" she yelled at Meggie in the kitchen.

Meggie yelled back. "Thank you!" Emily went back to searching.

After a few more searches that turned up nothing useful, Emily decided to log into her FaceSpace. Once she was logged in, she immediately went to her friends' list and typed in "Mike Adams," whom she knew to be Jackson. She clicked the name and his profile came up. It was mostly blank. Emily figured that Jackson had filled out only the necessary fields and left everything else unanswered. But she knew who it was.

Waiting on him to get back to her was beginning to try on her patience. Especially since vampires had been thrown into the mix along with the zombie, Emily wanted answers now more than ever. Emily decided that she would contact him.

Just as she was about to click the button to send Jackson a message, Emily heard from over her shoulder, "Who's Mike Adams?"

Meggie's voice startled Emily. Her whole body jerked reflexively, and her laptop fell out of her lap. Emily grabbed it just in time, before it hit the floor. She slammed it closed and said, "What?"

Meggie pointed at the closed laptop with a spatula, "Mike Adams. I just saw you looking at his profile on there. Who's that?"

Emily knew that Jackson hadn't put anything on the profile that might lead anyone to think it was him, but she still didn't really know what to say. "Just some random guy on here. We had some of the same mutual friends and I was just checking it out."

Meggie looked at her suspiciously. "Hmm, awful jumpy. Anything I need to know about? Or Chad? You guys are still together right?"

"No it's nothing. You just scared me. You were supposed to be in the kitchen."

"Sexist pig," Meggie said as she walked back toward the kitchen. "Lunch'll be ready in just a little bit, sneaky."

"Okay."

Meggie's comment about Chad made Emily think about him, something she had not done a lot of since she had joined forces with the zombie. Aside from a few texts messages here and there, she hadn't really talked to Chad since she left Mobile. Emily hadn't even told him goodbye. She started to feel a little guilty. She decided to send him a text.

Hey there. Sorry I been too busy to talk to you the past couple days. I feel like a bad girlfriend :(

In less than a minute, Chad had already responded.

No worries. Just you using the word girlfriend is enough. I forgive you hows you and meggie time goin?

Emily continued her text conversation with Chad. She was grateful that he was such a nice guy.

266

She brought him up to date with everything she could, while making sure to leave out silver necklaces and undead folks.

As Emily's thumbs typed out the carefully filtered version of the past few days to Chad, she walked into the kitchen. "Is it ready yet, skank?" she asked Meggie.

Meggie turned around to reveal two matching plates, each with equal servings of grilled chicken, steamed vegetables, and rice. "Ready enough for you?"

Emily laughed. "Quite," she said as she took one of the plates from Meggie and sat down at the dining room table. "How do you do this? It all looks awesome."

Meggie smirked at her friend. "Presentation is everything." she handed Emily some silverware, then set her own plate and silverware in the spot across from her. She walked back into the kitchen. "You want something to drink?"

"Water is fine," Emily said.

After about a minute Meggie returned with two glasses of ice-water, and sat down. "Enjoy."

"Damn. I could get used to this," Emily said.

Meggie had already started eating. She swallowed her first bite of food, then said, "It was nothing." she started eating again.

"Jeez, Meg. Where do you put all the food you eat?" Emily asked her friend. "Do you have a hollow leg or something?"

Meggie scoffed. "Don't be ridiculous. Hollow leg. Whoever heard of such?" She paused to get a couple more bites of food. "It's a hollow arm, dumb ass." Both of the girls had to cover their mouths, for fear that they might spew food on the other due to laughter.

The rest of the meal went without incident. Meggie and Emily both finished their plates, then Meggie asked, "Do you want any more?"

Emily rubbed her belly. "Nah, I think that's all for me. I can't eat anymore." She stood up, took her dishes and took them to the sink.

Meggie came into the kitchen with her dishes and did the same. Then she gestured to the remaining food that was on the stove. "I made some extra in case you wanted some more."

She had indeed made extra. "We can just put it in the fridge and eat it later if we want to," Emily said. "I'm good for now."

"Sounds like a plan." Meggie began transferring the food from the pots and pans and placed them into three different plastic containers to put in the refrigerator.

"I'll get the dishes," Emily told Meggie.

"Cool. Well I'm gonna go upstairs, get dressed, and try and do something with this rat's nest," Meggie said as she pointed to her hair.

"Alright, you do that." Meggie headed upstairs.

Emily chose to wash the dishes by hand. There were only a few of them, and her mom liked big pots and pans. They didn't really fit into their dishwasher very well. Emily knew that the three Meggie had used to cook would never fit in the dishwasher together. She grabbed the liquid soap and a sponge from atop the sink and got to work.

Emily washed the little things first. Once the plates, silverware, glasses, and Meggie's cereal bowl were clean, she now had room in the sink for the pots and pans. As she began scrubbing them she felt her phone vibrate in her pocket. She had soap and water up to her elbows, so her conversation with Chad would have to wait.

After about twenty minutes, she had all of the dishes washed. They wouldn't all fit in the dish drainer to dry, so Emily got a dish towel out of one of the kitchen drawers and started drying them off. One by one, as she dried them, she put each dish away. Except for the lingering smells of Meggie's cooking, there was no way to tell that anyone had even been in the kitchen.

Emily finished drying her hands off with the dish towel as she walked back into the living room. Once her hands were dry, she threw the towel over her shoulder and pulled out her cell phone to resume texting Chad. While she did have a text from Chad, Emily had something even more important. While she had been washing dishes, she had received a text from the number Jackson had called her from three days ago.

She was excited to read the next step in her new zombie friend's plan, but she was also afraid. Whatever the text said, she was pretty sure it involved leaving the safety of being miles away from everything. She opened the text from the strange number, and it revealed a very different plan of action than she was expecting.

Chapel. Tonight. Bring EVERYONE.

Emily was shocked. What had changed in the past three days that would make Jackson want to reveal himself to everyone? She was scared and confused. Was he going to use all of his friends as some sort of bait to draw out Paul and the others? She wasn't sure exactly what Jackson had planned, but he appeared to be competent so far, so she had to trust him.

The scared little goth girl just sat on her couch in silence, unsure of what to do. She had noticed that Jackson's main goal thus far was to remain hidden from Meggie. Now it was totally different. Maybe Jackson had weighed his options, and had decided that exposing himself would be less traumatic to everybody than risking them being the victims of vampires. As Emily tried to wrap her mind around the fact that vampires might actually be a reality, she heard Meggie come downstairs.

She had tamed her hair, and she had changed out of her pajamas and into regular clothes. "There. Now I feel like me again."

Emily didn't say anything back to Meggie. She only looked at her with consternation. It must have been apparent to Meggie. She rushed over and sat down next to Emily.

"What's wrong, Em? You look upset."

She knew that whatever came next, would not be easy. Emily put one arm around her friend and said, "You're probably not gonna believe a single word of it, but I gotta tell you."

"I'm your friend," Meggie said. "You can tell me anything."

Emily sighed, then took another deep breath as she prepared to fill Meggie in on what she knew. She hoped that by the time she got Emily back to Mobile, she would have everything explained to her.

23

After Breann had not returned after sunset three days ago, Jackson wondered if he would ever see her again. Perhaps the things he told her were just too much for her to take. He had not seen her since he told her about the Dark Ones and showed her the journal given to him by the Order of Lazarus. Jackson found himself missing her.

Over the past three days, Jackson had resided mostly in his "spot," the second-floor balcony that housed the church's pipe organ. But he was currently seated in one of the many aluminum folding chairs located next to the piano up front near the altar. Jackson figured the chairs were reserved for choir members during services. He was seated backwards in one, with his legs straddling the back of the folding chair. He crossed his arms and propped them on the chair back. The zombie rested his head on his hands as he contemplated.

Other than one visit from Father Borbridge, Jackson had been completely alone in the chapel. For the past three nights, he stepped outside the chapel after sunset. He even walked around some outside, though he was always cautious not to get too far away from St. Joe's, lest one of the vampires suddenly show up.

They never did, though. As a matter of fact, Jackson had not felt the presence of any of the vampires since the night they almost smashed in his head. While it was comforting to know that they were far away from him, it made him worry for the others he cared about. For some reason or another, the Dark Ones loathed the mere existence of a Reborn. He did not believe they would simply stop harassing him. His imagination was running wild with hypothetical scenarios in which his friends and family might be used as leverage against him.

It was incredibly inconvenient that Paul knew Jackson's true identity. If he was just some random zombie, the vampires would only have one target. But Paul knew Jackson, and he knew who Jackson loved. They were all in danger. Jackson could see no other way out of it. Either he had to die, or he had to kill the vampires. Neither the zombie nor any of the zombie's loved ones would be safe until one of those conditions were met. While he had never been one to rush to violence, or even confrontation, he did not plan on going back to the grave without a fight.

While he had been pondering the different possible situations, Jackson could feel his grip tighten on the chair. The fact that people he cared about were in danger- and because of him- made him furious. And the anger he felt toward the Dark Ones was almost overwhelming. All of a sudden there was a large popping sound that sounded as if it had come from the chair. Jackson looked down at his hands. He moved them to reveal two zombie-hand sized dents in the back of the chair in which he was sitting. Jackson stood up and backpedaled in awe.

Such strength had to be an undead development. He recalled being alive and sometimes having to use both hands on the spring grippers in McGill's weight room; and yet now, he looked down at the damage he had caused to the aluminum chair. It looked like it had been put in a vice. While it would certainly spark some speculations from the choir on Sunday morning, Jackson couldn't help but relish in his feat of strength. The zombie smiled his crooked smile.

Jackson decided to redirect his emotions. He took a seat on the grand piano's bench and pulled it in close to the keys. In life, he had taken piano lessons to try and impress Meggie, before they ever started dating. He got good enough that he could play some classical pieces from memory, but he found it far more effective at making Meggie smile when he could play little snippets of pop songs with piano parts in them.

Even when he was alive, he was nothing special at piano. He was fearful to think about how bad he might sound as a zombie pianist. The dexterity required for piano was not something Jackson felt confident that he had in his second life. Nevertheless, it was less destructive than crushing chairs with his hands. He decided he would try and play.

Just as he suspected, his dead fingers were difficult to command. He sounded more like a toddler banging on a keyboard than someone who knew anything about music. Jackson laughed at his sloppy playing, but tried to focus more. With all his concentration, he was able to control his fingers enough to make it sound at least like he knew how to play. "This is what a drunk piano player sounds like," he said to himself. "when both of his hands are asleep."

He was playing a piece by Mozart, but he imagined that only he and Mozart himself might be able to discern it. But he kept playing. A piano-playing zombie might not be useful, he thought, but it is good practice.

And it was. The longer Jackson played the song, the better he could concentrate, and the clearer his keystrokes became. By the end of the song, Jackson thought that it may have sounded as good as any time he had played it in his days with the living.

Reverberations of the last notes he played were still bouncing around the chapel as Jackson stood up. The amount of concentration required to make his hands and fingers obey would be useful when he had to face the vampires. He would have to be as nimble as possible if he was going to defeat two, perhaps three, vampires at once.

Having to fight them all at once is what had kept Jackson from springing to action sooner. He had experienced first-hand what they were capable of together. One on one, he was confident that he could take any of the three. He could overpower Alex. He was faster than Ben. And, though it made Jackson feel a bit arrogant, he had always been better at things than Paul. Jackson was always a little stronger, a little faster, and a little smarter than his friend. He figured he had to be better at being undead, too.

Then Jackson thought about it. Had Paul been jealous of Jackson all his life? Jackson had gotten the position Paul wanted on the soccer team back at McGill. He had gotten the athletic scholarship to

Alabama that might have been Paul's had he beaten Jackson out for the striker spot. Jackson even got the girl Paul wanted. Though Paul never made any kind of move on Meggie, he always had feelings for her. Paul was the only one of the rest of the guys that didn't see her as a little sister.

Was Paul's envy the reason he became a vampire- and ultimately targeted Meggie? Jackson and Paul never fought before he came back as a zombie; but was that because he and Paul never really talked about anything that may have been bothering him? Jackson felt guilty all over again for getting his friends caught up in the middle of a battle between vampires and a zombie.

Then he thought about his family. What if Paul and his friends targeted Jackson's mom and dad next? Or his sister, Anna? He refused to let that happen. He might die trying. But he was fed up with waiting. He was tired of being hunted and stalked by the vampires. Jackson would go after them first this time.

The sun had long set. It was completely dark outside. Jackson had been outside earlier to try and feel for their presence. He recalled storm clouds blocking out even the light from the moon and the stars. Jackson had heard thunder rolling all throughout the night. A fight to the death in the rain sounded better than sitting in a church all night worrying about his family and friends.

Jackson started walking from the altar to the front door of the chapel. The front door began to open. Jackson stopped in the center aisle and awaited the mysterious arrival. Though he knew that the Dark Ones wouldn't step inside the church, he still drew his dagger.

To Jackson's relief, it was only Father Borbridge. He wasn't ready for battle anymore. He was back to his oversized shirts with too many pockets, his socks, and his sandals. "Jackson, what are you doing?" The priest was concerned and rushed over to him.

Jackson was seething with anger, and he kept his teeth clenched as he spoke. "I'm going to get 'em, Father. I'm gonna end this."

"If you go after them, they'll kill you, son." Father Borbridge was hopelessly saddened by the thought. "Jackson, it's suicide."

"I'm dead, Father!" Jackson exclaimed. "It doesn't matter about me. What does matter is my family. My friends. They matter. As long as I'm alive, they're all in danger. The vampires will use them to get to me."

The old priest asked, "So, that's your plan? To just die?"

Jackson thought about dying again, especially at the hands of the vampires, and curled his lip in disgust. "No, sir. I'm gonna kill them first."

It was clear to Borbridge that the boy wasn't going to be talked out of it. "I see. They want you dead. Either you die, or they die."

"Exactly," Jackson said. "But you are right. They are tough in numbers. I'm gonna need some help."

The old priest tried to keep a straight face, but it eventually turned up into a grin. "I thought you'd never ask."

Jackson smiled back at him. "Let's do this." the zombie extended his hand for Father Borbridge to shake. The priest obliged.

"Now," the priest cleared his throat and

276

adjusted his glasses before he continued. "I'll need to head back to my place and get changed. After I do, I'll meet you back here, okay? Then we'll get started."

"Alright," Jackson nodded. "What about Father Hayes?"

Borbridge shook his head. "He does not approve of you fighting the Dark Ones, but I will let him know what is going on."

Jackson replied, "Yes, sir," but the priest did not wait for his response. His back was already turned, and he was headed out the door.

As he heard the door close behind Father Borbridge, Jackson couldn't help but notice that he felt the way he did before a big game. But there was no adrenaline and the burning sensation it gave to every nerve in his body like it did when he was alive. This time he was driven by raw emotion. He was calm and focused. He was ready.

Jackson could hear everything clearly. He could hear cars driving around outside. He heard the thunder rolling slowly. He could even hear the resistance from the dimmer-switches in the church as electricity flowed through the wiring. Then he heard a familiar sound he did not expect to hear. He walked to the front door of the church and pressed his ear against it to confirm it.

He heard it loud and clear. It was the rumble of Emily's engine. What was she doing here? He had not contacted her. She was supposed to be safe with Meggie in Birmingham. When he heard her car shut off, he heard *another* vehicle shut off right behind it. What was going on?

One after the other, Jackson heard several car doors being opened and closed as he heard people step out of the two vehicles. Meggie's voice was the first that Jackson heard.

"This better not be some sick joke," she said.

"I'm just following orders." Jackson heard Emily trying to reassure Meggie.

"I sure hope you got a good explanation for this, Emily." It was Foster! Jackson had to know what was going on outside, but he still didn't want his friends to see him.

"I promise y'all I'm not crazy. Jackson told me to come here." Emily had told them about him. Even worse, Emily thought it was Jackson that had told her to do so. All Jackson could think was that the vampires had gotten to her while she wasn't under the safety of a silver necklace. "What are y'all doing here?" he heard Emily say. His friends were in danger. He had to act quickly. Emily had apparently told them that he was back as a zombie. With that out of the way, he had to protect them. Jackson opened the door and stepped outside.

Almost immediately he could sense Ben and Paul. Over by Emily's muscle car and Foster's SUV, he saw all of his friends. All of the guys were there. Jon, Chad, Foster, Ryan, and Brandon had shown up. Meggie was standing next to Emily. Even Breann was there. The dark presences of Ben and Paul also came from that direction. Jackson was confused, but he knew that he had to get the vampires away from his friends. Ben and Paul emerged from shadows in the distance. Jackson made his way toward everyone.

"Oh my God, Jackson, is that really you?" Meggie couldn't clear make him out in the darkness, but she had clearly been debriefed.

Jackson drew in a breath to respond. He knew

that Meggie would hurt whether he answered or not. "Yes."

A collective gasp came from his friends. No one could believe it. As Jackson stepped closer to his friends, all of their eyes were on him. His eyes were on Ben and Paul, who were closing in from the other direction.

"How did this happen man? I saw you in your coffin. You were dead." Jon had tears in his eyes as he looked upon his best friend.

Paul interrupted any reunion that might have taken place. "He's not Jackson. He's not even human. He's an abomination. He's some demonic spirit that has come here disguised as our old friend to trick us." Paul spoke with confidence and conviction. "We need to kill him, and send him back to Hell, where he came from."

Even in the darkness, Jackson saw Foster raise one of his eyebrows in disbelief. "Paul, what the Hell are you talking about?"

"Yeah, dude," Ryan reiterated. "You sound nuts."

Such responses were clearly not what Paul expected from the humans. He scanned all of his friends for an answer.

It was Emily who offered one. "Silver necklaces, dick. All around. None of your vampire brainwashing is gonna work on us." Her words discouraged Paul.

Ben, however, was undeterred. He charged toward Jackson, who was still concerned with what might have brought all of these people here, was taken off guard. Before Jackson could defend against it, Ben had seized the zombie. He had one hand on Jackson's wrist, protecting himself from another knife attack, and one hand around Jackson's throat.

Ben lifted Jackson into the air effortlessly. Jackson could hear all of the girls shrieking as he was hoisted above the vampire's head. Before he was sent flying, Jackson could see Jon and Brandon running toward Ben to stop him. He saw Paul standing in front of the other three guys, blocking them from assisting the zombie. Before Jon or Brandon could get his hands on Ben, he tossed Jackson like a rag doll. He had been thrown so hard, that he sailed too quickly through the air for Jackson to brace himself.

A loud, echoing crack boomed across the campus as Jackson's skull struck the side of St. Joseph's Chapel. It sounded almost like a gunshot. The zombie landed next to the church, lifeless. A dark, bloody spot remained on the off-white stone wall where Jackson's head smashed against it. The last things Jackson saw were bits of his own brains falling down off the side of the chapel's wall, landing on his face. Then everything went black. As he lay there, at first, he could hear the screams and shouts from his friends. But then that went away too. Everything faded away until there was nothing.

***

If Brandon and Jon had been a little faster, they might have been able to stop Ben. But even if they had gotten to him, Emily thought, it might have done no good. Jackson smacked into the church like he had been shot out of a cannon. The two boys grabbed hold of the vampire as soon as Jackson hit the ground, but he slung each one of them off of him as easily as an old coat. As Brandon and Jon got back to their feet, Ben took a few steps back, ready to defend against another attack.

Emily looked at Meggie. She was in tears. Just moments before she was convinced that Emily had lost her mind. Now that she had seen Jackson walking and talking again, the feeling of losing him showed all over her again. "What the Hell is all of this?"

Paul was the first to attempt to explain. "We told you," he pointed back to where Jackson's lifeless body lay, "that's not Jackson."

"Oh, shut up." Breann had had enough of the lies and twisted stories. "That *was* Jackson. And they *are* vampires."

Emily had never seen the girl before in her life. "Who the Hell are you anyway?"

"I'm the one that sent one of y'all a text to bring everybody here." Breann laughed. "He might have come back from the dead, but, honestly, he was as easy to play as any living guy I've ever met."

Emily was burning with rage. "That someone was me." Emily couldn't believe that she was so gullible. Of course Jackson hadn't sent the message. He didn't want anyone to know he was back, and he *certainly* wouldn't have said to come at night. She had played right into the enemy's hands.

Meggie controlled her sobbing long enough to speak. She pointed at Breann. "You're that girl that was kissing up on Ben the night I first met them."

Ben walked over to Breann and kissed her. "One in the same," he said.

Emily wasn't shaking with rage as she spoke. "So, what? Are you a vampire too, bitch?" If Breann was a vampire, Emily would probably regret calling her names. But she didn't care. Where, the other people who had witnessed Jackson's head bursting against the stone wall had fear, Emily had unadulterated fury.

"No," Breann said with an innocent smile. "I'm human, and I'm pretty. That's why I was perfect for getting that silly little dead boy to do exactly what we wanted him to do."

Speaking so derisively about Jackson caused all of his friends to widen their stances and look defensively. "That's cute," Paul said. "But it won't do any good. You can't hurt us. And besides, Jackson died, he needed to stay dead. We just did everybody a favor."

Foster was as tense as anyone else present, even if he was a little slow on the uptake. "Wait, so y'all are tellin' me that y'all are *really* vampires?"

Ben laughed, walked over to Foster, and got in his face. He flashed his fangs and asked, "What do you think?"

When Foster saw the fangs, he gathered that it was real, but he didn't want to show fear. "I think your breath smells like gorilla shit."

The remark infuriated Ben, and he punched Foster in the face, knocking him to the ground.

Chad tried to diffuse the situation. "Let's all calm down. I'm not sure what just happened, but we're all a little stressed right now. Let's all just go our separate ways and get out of here, alright?"

Ben guffawed. "Do you honestly think I'm going to let that happen?" he approached Chad. "You're not getting out of this alive, but don't you at least want to fight? Pussy!"

Faster than anyone could react, Ben lunged at

Chad and sank his teeth into his neck. Chad screamed in pain as the vampire suckled. All off Jackson's friends rushed to his aid and tried to peel the muscly vampire off of Chad. It was no use, but after a few seconds, Ben relinquished his bite voluntarily. The silver chain had seared his face. As soon as the vampire released him, Chad collapsed onto the ground, convulsing from shock due to blood loss.

Ben wiped his lips and chin, leaving behind a pink spot were Chad's blood had dripped. He smiled and said, "Who's next?"

24

Once again Jackson found himself in total darkness. He saw nothing. He couldn't hear or smell the outside anymore. The last thing that he remembered feeling were the gooey insides of his skull dripping down and splattering on him from the church wall. He could remember his own brains landing on him. And then everything went away. Now there was nothing.

As all of his senses failed him, he could recall his ability to sense the Dark Ones wane as well. Everything that let him know that he had rejoined the living world had once again gone away.

Jackson assumed that he had finally met his end. He tried to visualize what crossing over to Heaven or Hell might feel like, how it might look. He couldn't even do that. He was alone in the darkness with his formless, thoughts.

He assumed that wherever he currently was, he was certainly not in his body anymore. He couldn't feel the vampires stomping on him, which he assumed they were doing back on Earth. He didn't hear the sounds of his bones crunching beneath their feet.

Where the screams of Meggie and his friends had been, there was now only silence. Jackson wondered how long dying again would actually take.

Along with losing all of his senses, he had also completely lost his concept of time. Jackson had no idea how much time had passed since he had been hurled into the side of St. Joe's. It could have been seconds. It could have been days. Jackson was just as lost as he was the first time he regained consciousness back in his coffin in the crypt.

Just as he was beginning to get used to the idea of being a zombie, just when he was beginning to master his undead body, Jackson was forced back into the darkness.

He wasn't in any pain, nor was he very concerned with the people that had just seen his head smashed against a stone wall. There was absolutely nothing. As Jackson awaited oblivion to overtake him fully, so he could be truly dead, he heard a familiar-albeit bothersome- voice.

"You aren't seriously doing this to us again, are you?" Jackson recognized it immediately. It was his damned logical self again.

"Haven't heard from you in a while," Jackson said, mocking his inner monologue's absence. "Doing what, exactly?"

"Dying. And the reason I haven't been shouting at you since I went away is because you haven't been half-bad."

"What do you mean?" he asked.

"You haven't needed me," said his logical voice. "You've fully accepted what you are and what you can do with it, which is why I am back now. What are you doing?" The logical Jackson was getting annoyed with him.

"I don't know," Jackson said. "I think I'm dying."

"Ugh!" his rational side was definitely getting fed up. "And *that's* why you're dying. How can you not see that?"

Jackson knew full well that the conversation he was a part of was simply two halves of himself. But the split had occurred for a reason. For some reason Jackson needed a logical voice in his head to try and make sense of his new supernatural life.

"The last time I cracked my head open, I stayed awake," Jackson said. "The last time, I could still see. I could still hear everything."

"Maybe that's because the last time you cracked your stupid head open, that shit you call brains didn't get busted out of your skull."

"So the vampires won. They destroyed my brain, the main thing that brought me back."

The logical voice laughed. "The fact that I know the term 'cellular death' means that *you* know it, too. Your brain is as dead as the rest of you. It ain't what brought you back. How can you not figure it out?"

In the current void, Jackson had lost all regard for himself. "I'm gone now. The vampires won't mess with my friends or family anymore. That's all I really wanted."

The voice scoffed. "You can't possibly be that naive. If that's the case, then why are you still here?"

"Because you won't let me die!"

"You're damn right, I won't let you die!" Logical Jackson was shouting. "I'm not just gonna let you kill us that easily."

"What do you want me to do, huh?" Jackson asked the voice. "I can't just get up and go fight them. I can't see. I can't hear. No touch, taste, or smell. I can't do anything!"

"Maybe that's because you're wearing the parts of your brain that control all of that."

"So, what are you saying?" Jackson asked. "I can just grow those parts back, and I'm good to go?"

"I mean, that Ben really did knock a lot out of your old noggin. It would take some regrowing."

"So, I can just heal back?" he asked.

"Think about it Jackson," the logical voice said. "If you just think about it, you won't need me at all."

Jackson tried to think about it. He *had* grown the organs back that had been taken out of him when he was embalmed. And the vampires had not torched his body. Except for a chunk of his brain missing, he was still pretty well intact.

"As long as there's something left of me, and I'm still willing to live, they can't kill me," Jackson said.

Jackson heard the logical voice sigh in relief. "That's the ticket. Now get up and do what you came to do."

Jackson was skeptical. "But how do I do that?"

"How did you do it when you were in a coffin for a year?" Jackson's logical self asked.

"Them," he said.

"Bingo."

Jackson focused with everything he had left. He thought about his friends and his family. He thought about Meggie. The vampires may have wanted him dead, but the book that Father Borbridge had given him had described the Dark Ones' nature. As long as they were around, and Jackson wasn't willing to stand up and fight them back, everyone they met would be in danger. That everyone included the people Jackson cared about. He refused to let that happen.

With his fervor restored, Jackson concentrated on healing his wounds, so he could rise again and defend his loved ones.

Nothing was happening. His vision wasn't returning. He didn't start picking up faint sounds to indicate that his hearing was coming back. He began to get discouraged. He tried to stay focused on healing, but the lack of evidence was making him feel like it was in vain.

"I'm not your coach," the logical Jackson said. "I'm not going to cheer you on or give you words of encouragement. You know what you have to do."

Somehow Jackson knew that those were the only words he was going to get from his logical side to boost his confidence. But it was enough. Without any signs of his improvement, Jackson continued to concentrate on healing.

His thoughts returned to his friends. While he lay lifeless on the ground next to the chapel, they were in grave danger. The only thing that had kept him going this long was them. It would have to be enough still.

Just then, Jackson began to hear a faint sound. It was a strange slurping sound. He wasn't sure what it was, but it was something. Whatever it was, it strengthened his resolve to stay focused and get back to protect his friends. The wet, slushy sound became more prominent. Then he was able to pinpoint its origin.

It was his head. His brain was healing and regenerating. Jackson was washed with a wave of joy as he heard the gurgling continue. There was more than hope now. He was going to come back.

Soon he was able to make out other sounds farther away. He could hear the voices of his friends and the vampires talking. He couldn't make them out over the sloshing sounds in his head as his brain reformed.

Slowly his vision returned. His eyes had been closed, but he could make out the light from one of the campus' nearby street lamps. Jackson forced his eyes to open.

At first everything was blurry. Only being able to discern light from dark, he could barely make out shapes. That too, though, slowly sharpened. After a few seconds, his vision had improved enough that he could see the wall of the chapel on his right. He was on his back, looking up. He moved his eyes around to see exactly where he was.

Then his sense of the Dark Ones returned. They were near his friends. They were stronger than ever, but they still hadn't noticed him. From what Jackson could hear, they were too consumed with whatever ruckus was going on with his friends.

Tiny drops of rain began to fall as Jackson rose to his feet. He stumbled at first, but then he regained his balance. He was standing firm. He had not been defeated. Jackson looked up at the chapel wall where he had hit. Pieces of his skull and brains were still stuck to the stone. Then he looked down at his chest. Brain matter riddled the front of his blood-soaked jacket. It was his blood, that dark, almost purple, zombie blood. Jackson wiped away the parts he could.

Most of it just smeared into his jacket.

Then he felt the side of his head that had smacked into the chapel. It was wet with his blood, but he could feel the cracks beginning to close. Jackson wiped his face as best he could with his jacket sleeve. He was going to be a gruesome sight to his friends.

Jackson drew his dagger from the pocket inside his jacket and faced his evil attackers. He could hear Ben threatening his friends. Lightning flashed, followed quickly by the loud sound of thunder. The lightning had illuminated everything for an instant, and it formed almost a photograph in Jackson's mind of the scene. Chad lay on the ground, bleeding from his neck, and Ben was taunting the rest of his friends, not allowing them to get near him to check on him. They still had not noticed him. Jackson began walking toward all of them.

Ben had his back to Jackson. He was much too preoccupied with frightening his friends to notice Jackson's presence. But Paul looked over. Paul had sensed him, and now he had seen Jackson.

"Ben," Paul called out to his fellow vampire, never turning away from Jackson. Jackson never blinked as he locked eyes with his old friend. Jackson could see fear and rage in them. "Ben," he called again.

"What!" Ben shouted as he looked at Paul, who slowly raised a finger to point at Jackson. He turned around to stare at him too.

"That," Paul said.

Ben looked a little confused, but flashed his fangs at Jackson. "What the Hell *are* you?" he asked.

Jackson's mouth formed his usual crooked smile. "I'm a zombie. And I'm your worst fuckin' nightmare."

25

Before the last syllable even passed his undead lips, Jackson had hurled the dagger at Ben with every bit of zombie strength he could muster. He was at least thirty feet from Ben, but he hoped that it would find its mark. If it didn't stick, he would be left defenseless against the vampires. It was his only chance. Luckily, his aim was perfect.

Ben, the slowest of the vampires Jackson had encountered, turned to run; but he wasn't fast enough. The silver dagger landed square in Ben's back between his shoulder blades.

The musclebound vampire growled as Jackson marched toward him. "Leave it in!" He screamed to his friends. They obeyed him. Jackson remembered how exposure to silver had affected Alex. He wanted his dagger to remain stuck in Ben's back for as long as possible.

Jackson saw Breann start walking toward Ben. She was interrupted when Emily stepped in her path and said, "Don't even think about it, bitch." Breann backed up.

Ben was groaning in pain as he struggled to pull the dagger from his back. The muscles in his arms were too bulky, though. He couldn't reach the spot on his back where the dagger was. Paul could have helped him pull it out, but he was already running toward Jackson.

Paul came at Jackson with a fist drawn back. He swung it at the zombie's face, but Jackson was ready. He stopped the strike by grabbing Paul by the wrist. Jackson clamped down on Paul's wrist with the same force with which he had gripped the aluminum chair inside the church. He could hear the cracking of bones, but this time the sound wasn't coming from him. He was crushing Paul's wrist!

His old friend screamed. "Oh, you can feel that?" Jackson asked mockingly. "That's gotta suck." Jackson kept his grip and twisted Paul's arm, steering the rest of his body. While Jackson tried to drag him by one arm, Paul swung his other arm at the zombie. Jackson deflected most of the punches with his free hand. Paul became frustrated and began to growl and snap at Jackson like a rabid dog. In his dodging of Paul's attempt to bite him, Jackson stumbled, and the fight went to the ground. Paul landed on top of of him. Jackson didn't want to be pinned beneath him, and he struggled to push him off or roll him over.

As the two grappled, Jackson never released his death grip he had on Paul's wrist. Paul began focusing his efforts on freeing his arm from Jackson's grasp. Paul tried desperately to bend his fingers back and slide his arm free, Jackson was determined to tear off anything on the vampire's arm that was below his hand.

Exposure to the silver dagger had begun to take its toll on Ben while Jackson wrestled with Paul. He had given up trying to remove it. He was simply on all fours trying to crawl away. The guys were not about to let that happen. Emily kept Breann from helping him while Jon and Brandon each took a leg to hold. Foster planted a knee in Ben's back, and the vampire fell onto his stomach.

As Meggie and Ryan were tending to Chad, who was still convulsing on the ground, Jackson heard Breann start screaming to the top of her lungs. The noise echoed all over the campus. Jackson didn't want to attract the attention of anyone else for all of this. The shout distracted him enough for Paul to wriggle free of his grip, as he was looking over at Breann.

Jackson saw Breann. She was just standing in place, just screaming. It was almost like she was screaming for help. She maintained a steady shriek until it was instantly silenced when Emily punched her square in the nose. "Shut the fuck up," Emily spat to Breann, whom she had just punched to the ground. Just then Jackson felt a fist on his face as well. Breann's scream was so distracting, Jackson almost forgot he was in a fight as well. After being violently reminded, he concentrated all his efforts on his fight with Paul.

Jackson moved his head from side to side to dodge a few of Paul's punches, but he swung so hard and so fast that he couldn't dodge them all. Paul had managed to straddle Jackson, with his knees pressed in Jackson's biceps. He couldn't raise his hands to defend his head.

Paul continued to pummel Jackson's head. He arched his back and tried to buck him off, but it was no use. He wasn't in pain. He knew that Paul wouldn't be able to kill him this way, but he knew that him going unconscious again was inevitable if Paul continued punching him in the head.

Jackson could hear the cold smacking of Paul's fists on his face, and on the ground when he was lucky enough to dodge a strike. In addition to the rain falling on his face, he could feel blood dripping from his nose. He could see that the viscous, purplish liquid had stained Paul's knuckles as they came crashing down on his face.

All of a sudden, the punches stopped. Jackson looked up and saw Paul grasping at something around his neck. He sounded like he was choking when Jackson looked up at him. It was a silver chain. Jackson felt Paul's body weight being slowly pulled off of him. When he was completely free, he got to his feet. Jackson followed the faint, silver line off into the distance. At the end of it was Father Borbridge, who had apparently thrown the chain like a lasso from several feet away to trap Paul. Father Borbridge approached the vampire, who was writhing in pain from the chain's touch. He gathered up the excess of the chain and dropped it on Paul's chest. "I've got this one under control, Jackson," he said. "Go deal with the other."

Jackson was afraid to go "deal with the other." He was not afraid of Ben. Ben was barely conscious at this point. The silver had hurt and weakened him to the point that he wasn't even struggling against Jackson's friends anymore. He was just laying there suffering. It was not the Dark One that Jackson feared.

It was his friends that the zombie feared. All eyes were on him as he approached them. His face was broken in several places, and he was covered in his own zombie blood from the top of his head, all the way down the front of his clothes. Jackson could only imagine the horror his friends were experiencing.

Meggie had that little, quivering wrinkle between her eyes that, Jackson knew, meant she was uncontrollably upset. Emily's gaze went back and forth quickly between him, and Breann, who was nursing a bloody nose on the ground at Emily's feet. The right side of Foster's face had already swollen so much from where Ben had hit him, that he only had one eye to look at Jackson.

Ryan looked lost, totally confused as he tried to keep pressure on the wound on Chad's neck. Brandon had an almost blank stare as he looked at Jackson. He looked battle-ready, and much more concerned with keeping Ben in place than worrying about why his friend was back from the dead. Then there was Jon. Jon's cheeks were wet with tears. He was overjoyed to see his best friend again, regardless of any circumstances.

It seemed as though everyone was awaiting his command. Other than waste any time with any niceties of hugs and kisses, Jackson immediately went to Chad. He walked past where his three friends were holding the vampire in place and knelt down beside his wounded friend.

Jackson picked up one of Chad's hands and held it between his two. His body temperature had dropped from blood loss. He looked at at the mark on Chad's neck. He had been bitten. Jackson was still unsure about the details of becoming a vampire.

He turned his head and spoke to Ben. "Is he going to turn?"

Ben grunted, but he did not respond. Jon released the vampire's foot he had been holding and walked around to his head. With his burly, hairy hand, Jon grabbed a handful of blond spikes and wrenched Ben's head and forced him to look at Jackson. "Answer my friend's question, damn it!"

Ben looked exhausted as he took ragged breaths. Jackson could see blood on his chin. "No," Ben said.

Jackson didn't fully trust the vampire. He stood up and looked over at Father Borbridge and motioned for him to come over. Instead of leaving Paul unattended, Father Borbridge grabbed the silver chain and dragged the vampire behind him as he made his way over to everyone else. "What is it, son?" the old priest asked.

"Ben bit my friend," Jackson said. "I need to know if he's just hurt, or if he's gonna turn into one of them."

"He's gotta drink from one of us to turn." Paul's voice was scratchy and weak as he offered the explanation Jackson wanted.

"He's quite right, Jackson," Borbridge said. "Dark Ones' feeding is irrelevant. A person has to-

"That's all I need to know, Father. Thank you." Jackson knew that the priest couldn't help himself when it came to sharing knowledge, but now was not the time. He returned his attention to Chad.

"J- J- Jackson?" Chad struggled to form words. "Is th- that really you?"

Jackson grabbed his friend's hand again. "Yeah, buddy it's me."

Chad seemed to be choking between every word. He looked at Jackson with weary eyes and gave a weak smile. "You- look- like- sh- shit."

Jackson had started to cry. As he laughed it

knocked a couple tears from his cheeks, and they fell on Chad's chest. "It's just a bad hair day, man." He tried his best to make a joke with his injured friend.

Beneath Chad was a massive puddle of blood. It was too late to save him. The only way he could survive would be to drink from either Paul or Ben. And Jackson didn't want that for Chad. He had lost too much blood. Chad wasn't going to make it.

"Jackson?" Chad asked. His eyes no longer indicated that he saw anymore. They were just open as they blankly stared at nothing.

"Yeah, dude?" Jackson wiped the tears from his eyes so he could see his friend.

"I- Is this real? Are y- you back f- f- from the dead? And did a v- vampire just bite me?" All of the color had faded from Chad's face. He was as pale as Jackson.

"Yes. It really happened."

"Okay," Chad said. He was gasping slowly for air, and his voice became weaker. "W- well will you m- make sure my f- family don't see me l- like this? They don't need to know that m- m- monsters ex- x- ist."

"Yeah, Chad. I promise." Jackson felt the same lump in his throat that he had felt when he was alive.

"Thanks, man," Chad said. He took a few more breaths, then stopped. The last bit of air rattled out of his body. Chad was dead.

Jackson collapsed on Chad's chest and sobbed. He picked his friend up in his arms and rocked back and forth as he wept. Though his own cries were loud in his ears, Jackson could hear the rest of his friends crying too.

After a few minutes of mourning, Jackson's sadness slowly transformed into rage. He placed

Chad's body back on the ground, stood up, and stomped over to Ben. He didn't even look up at Foster as he pushed him out of the way. His eyes remained fixed upon the dagger. Jackson dropped to his knees beside Ben. The vampire flinched when Jackson pulled the dagger out of his back. But his relief would be short-lived.

Jackson began stabbing Ben wildly. For every time I stabbed Alex, he thought, I'll stab Ben five times. Ben was crying in pain as the stabbings continued. When Jackson couldn't see a spot without blood on Ben's back, he rolled him over and started stabbing his front. Jackson stabbed his arms, his legs, his crotch. Nothing was off limits. Ben was crying and Jackson was screaming through clenched teeth as he kept stabbing.

"Please, stop," Breann said. She was still on the ground, where Emily's punch had put her. She was crying too.

Jackson stopped, mid-stab, and asked, "What?" as he drove the dagger into Ben and walked over to Breann.

"Please," she said again, "Just stop."

"Why!" Jackson exclaimed. "That bastard just killed my friend. Hell, he's not even human."

"She already knows that," Emily said.

"Huh?" Jackson was confused. He saw Breann stand up.

She looked like she was about to try and run, but Foster grabbed her by the arm. "Oh, no, little lady," he said. "You just stay riiight here." Ryan walked over to her other side and held her by the other arm.

Breann had fear in her eyes as Jackson

approached her. "What is she talking about?" he asked as he moved in close and placed a hand around her waist. She winced in pain. Jackson was intrigued, but he removed his hand.

Before Breann could say anything, Emily filled Jackson in. "She's the reason we're here. You must have used her phone the other day when you called me, 'cause I got a text from that number today telling me to meet you tonight and to bring everybody."

"And that didn't seem weird to you?" Jackson asked.

Emily shrugged her shoulders and waved her arms in the air. "I don't know dude. I hadn't heard from you in three days. I just panicked. I told all your friends everything I knew and got them all here- like I thought you asked."

Jackson looked around at his friends. Someone they barely knew had told them some unbelievable story about their friend being a zombie, and they all came. It warmed his heart to know that his friends cared about him that much. But as he saw Chad lying dead on the ground, he was saddened again. His friends were, too. It was clear on their faces. Chad is dead because of me, Jackson thought. But if Emily's story about Breann was true, it was *actually* Breann's fault. "Good thinkin' with the silver necklaces, Em," he said.

"Thanks," she said.

As he turned back to look into Breann's eyes, he found that they didn't reveal anything. She was clearly afraid, but her intentions were as well-hidden as they had ever been. "Does anybody know anything else about Breann?"

Foster responded first. "Yeah, she's kind of a

bitch, and she kissed Ben."

Jackson was shocked. "What!"

While his friends nodded in agreement, Meggie finally spoke to Jackson. "I saw her with Ben the first night I met him." Just hearing her voice made him weak in the knees. All of his friends knew what he now was, but more importantly, Meggie knew. And they were still here.

Jackson looked at Breann and pointed at Meggie. "That girl was the love of my life. I tend to trust her."

Breann just looked at him. "Believe whatever you want to believe, Jackson." She was either offended at the accusation, or deflecting. Even though he was a zombie, he didn't think that all of his friends would lie about her.

Once again, Jackson moved into to her waist; but instead of putting his hand around it, he lifted up her shirt enough to reveal her stomach.

All over her stomach were hickeys with fang marks in them. Jackson tried not to think about her being intimate with any of the vampires while she allowed them to drink her blood.

Suddenly it was clear. The reason Breann always conveniently showed up was because she had been working with the vampires. Vampires didn't have a smell, so he never smelled them on her when she came to visit him in the chapel. Jackson thought about the night that he had to pick her up and run with her to get back to the safety of the chapel. Even then she was trying to keep him outside so they could kill him. She had locked him out on the second-floor walkway. "You knew what I was the whole time, didn't you?" he asked her.

Breann looked up and away. "Yeah. So? When did you plan on telling *me* that you were dead? You were being sneaky too."

Jackson thought about the danger she had put him in. she had tried to get him killed. She *had* gotten Chad killed. "Just shut up!" he shouted at her. He then walked back to Ben.

Ben was lying where Jackson had left him. When he stood over him, the vampire looked up at him like a child that knew he did wrong and was about to be punished.

Paul's voice was weak, but Jackson heard it. "What are you going to do now?"

Just hearing the sound of his voice infuriated Jackson. "What do you think, Paul? Y'all killed Chad, and you tried to kill me! I told Alex to warn y'all, but it looks like he's the only one with any sense, 'cause he stayed gone."

"Are you gonna kill us?" Paul asked.

Jackson thought about everything that he had seen and done. He thought about everything he had heard since his return from the grave. Jackson reached into his pants pocket and pulled out the little pencil he had taken from the pew. He remembered Paul's own words, looked at him and smiled. "Y'all are already dead, Paul. You're just walkin' around for some reason."

Jackson watched Paul's eyes grow wide as he plunged the tiny wooden pencil into Ben's chest, in the location of his heart. Unlike the dagger, stabbing Ben with the wood did not just cause a bit of blood to splatter. As soon as the miniature stake was in his chest, Ben began to stiffen all over. Then he began to glow like the embers of a fire. Jackson wasn't sure what kind of fire it was, or if it could even harm him. He wasn't taking any chances though. He had cheated death enough times for a while. He took a few steps back from the vampire body that resembled burning coals.

After a few seconds, Ben's body stopped glowing, and all that was left were ashes. They were in the shape of Ben, but they quickly collapsed and fell apart as the rain spattered on them. The ashes that had been the vampire's chest caved in under the weight of Jackson's dagger that was stuck in him. The zombie sifted through the ashes and retrieved his dagger. He put it back in his jacket's inside pocket. Paul was next. The rain had started falling a little harder. It was already washing Ben's ashes away as he walked over to his old friend.

He looked down at Paul. He wasn't sure of vampire physiology, but he was pretty sure Paul was in a cold sweat. Jackson could smell the fear on him. "Please, don't kill me, Jackson."

Jackson tried to calm down. He tried to think rationally. Ben had killed Chad. Ben had terrorized his friends. Paul had only attacked him. While Paul was trying to kill him, the only other thing he could be blamed for was trying to date his girl. Jackson really couldn't blame him for that. "I've already seen one of my friends die tonight, I don't want to see another one."

Paul's look changed from fear to surprise. "Friend?"

Jackson had to control his anger. Paul had tried to kick his brains out one time, and he had tried to punch them out another time. His gut reaction was to torture him until he begged for death. But Jackson stifled those urges. "We were friends once. Good friends. And now we're not. Shit happens. Things change. Hell, people die. We don't have to be friends, but we don't have to be enemies either."

The relieved look on the vampire's face was one of almost ecstasy. "So, are you gonna let me go?" he asked.

"Why not?" Jackson said. "I do have some very serious rules for you, though."

Paul blinked as he looked up at Jackson. "Yeah?"

Jackson leaned down and pulled the silver chain wrapped around Paul's neck until it brought Paul to within inches of his face. "You stay the Hell away from me and mine. You don't touch them. You don't contact them. If you think about them too hard, you better find me so you can apologize. And if one drop of blood from anybody I care about ever touches your lips, I swear to God, I'll make sure you spend the rest of that thing you call a life in a silver box. Do you understand me, Paul?"

The vampire nodded.

Father Borbridge was the only person close enough to them to hear everything Jackson had said to Paul. To everyone else, Jackson appeared to just be whispering to Paul. "Are you sure about this, Jackson?" Father Borbridge asked.

"I know it's selfish to turn a vampire loose on the world. But if he doesn't mess with my friends and family, that's enough." Jackson just wanted them to be safe. "*They're* the reason I came back, right? Not the rest of the world."

Father Borbridge shook his head. "You know that it is not in their nature to keep promises *or* follow orders, right?"

Jackson looked up at the giant of a priest and smiled. "Oh, I *dare* him to cross me again."

"Very well," Father Borbridge said with a sigh as he bent down to remove the silver chain from Paul's neck. "Catch and release, I suppose."

Jackson looked over at Ryan and Foster. "Let her go." He looked back at Paul as he pointed to Breann. "Make sure you take your whore with you."

As Breann walked over to Paul, she stopped at Jackson. "Jackson, I-"

Jackson stuck a zombie finger to her lips, indicating her to stop talking. "Just. Go. Away."

After a few minutes, Paul was able, with Breann's help, to get back to his feet. She threw his arm over her shoulder to help him balance. Paul nodded at Jackson as the two of them walked away. Jackson nodded back. Then he turned to face his friends again.

He took in a deep breath as he prepared to address them. "I know y'all got a lot of questions for me, but they're gonna have to wait. We have to get Chad to the cemetery."

"Jackson, what are you talking about?" Emily asked him.

"Chad made me promise that his family wouldn't see him like he is."

"Dude, that's *crazy*," Foster said. "We gotta tell his family."

Jackson looked at Father Borbridge as he spoke. He hoped the priest would back him up. "Are you telling me that y'all don't want to respect a man's dying wishes?"

A few of them mumbled, but Father Borbridge

spoke. "Jackson's right. It would be disrespectful not to."

With the priest on his side, he knew that he would eventually win them over, but he chose to offer a rhetorical question for them. "Besides, what are you gonna tell his family, that he died in a turf war between vampires and zombies?"

When Jackson had everyone in agreement, he told them to wait a few minutes. He went back inside the chapel and down into the basement. He remembered all the extra robes the he and Breann had used as pillows and blankets. Jackson grabbed what he thought was enough to wrap Chad and made his way outside.

Everyone was gathered around while Father Borbridge was praying over Chad's body when Jackson arrived with the robes. "Jon, will you help me?" Jackson asked his friend.

"Sure, Jax."

Once Jon had helped him wrap Chad up in the robes, he then helped Jackson get their friend into Emily's trunk. Jackson tried to make sure Chad's body wouldn't roll around too much during the ride.

"Where am I taking him?" Emily asked.

"To my coffin. I'm not using it," Jackson said. "And nobody will look there."

"Okay," Emily said.

"Jon and Meggie, y'all come with me and Emily. The rest of y'all head to Callaghan's. We'll meet y'all there." Jackson watched all of his friends nod as they seemed to listen to him without question. Whether his being a zombie commanded fear or respect from him, he didn't care. It was effective.

As the teenagers piled into their respective

cars, Father Borbridge pulled Jackson to his side. "I will stay here and clean up."

Jackson looked up at him with a solemn smile. "Thanks, Father."

"I also need to make sure that no one saw any of that; and, if they did, I need to convince them that's not what they saw. Father Hayes has been patrolling the area all night, so it's probably all clear. We need to be sure, though."

"Yes, sir." Jackson thought about Ben's comment that had made him doubt Father Borbridge earlier. "Father, I heard on of the vampires say that a priest told them not to go into the church. What's that about?"

Father Borbridge tried to think for a second. "I have no idea. That requires some investigation. I suppose it's a good thing that you left one of them alive then."

"Yeah," Jackson grumbled. He had actually let two of them go, and he still wasn't sure how smart it was to let Paul go.

"Let us worry about that for now," Borbridge said. "You need to deal with this."

"Yes, sir."

Borbridge put his hand on Jackson's back and gave him a nudge. "Now go, son." Jackson climbed into Emily's backseat, next to Meggie. Jon got in the front seat and they drove away, headed to the cemetery.

26

The ride to the cemetery was awkward. The three breathing people in the car were still in shock from witnessing Chad's death, that they didn't even seem too concerned with the fact that they had a zombie riding with them. Meggie had even grabbed his hand and held it. Jackson knew all about old habits dying hard. Whether it was an old habit or not, his undead stomach filled with butterflies when she touched his hand.

"Alright, bro. What the actual fuck just happened?" Jon sounded almost delirious, as if he wasn't sure what he had just experienced. He turned around and started touching Jackson's face and squeezing his shoulders.

Jackson squirmed and batted his furry hands away. "Dude, back up. It's me, okay? I know it's totally crazy, but, yes, I came back from the dead. I am a zombie."

Emily kept one hand on the steering wheel, but threw the other into the air. "I told y'all."

"How long have you been back?" Meggie asked.

308

"I'm not really sure," Jackson said. "'cause I'm not really sure how long I was awake just laying in my coffin."

"Oh my God, baby, that had to be Hell." Hearing Meggie say that word to him again felt right. It didn't feel forced or anything. Jackson could tell that she still loved him.

As Jackson retold his story of how he came back from the grave- pausing periodically to tell Emily where to turn- he decided that he would have to remain in touch with them. While he was a zombie, and he had no real place in the world, *they* were the reason he had his second existence. He wondered if he could move somewhere far away, somewhere people didn't know him in his life. If he lived there, then his friends could come visit me.

"Okay, here it is," Jackson said. "Why did Foster follow us here? I told him not to."

"Oh, yeah, I remember this place," Emily said. "The Hughes family crypt is awesome."

"Thanks, I guess."

Emily drove as close as she could to the crypt and shut off her car, and Foster did the same. With their headlights turned off, they were in pitch darkness.

"Okay, this is super creepy," Jon whispered. He jumped a little when he heard Foster's doors open and slam shut. When they had made their way to Emily's car, Foster knocked on her window. Jon jumped again. "Alright, Jax, now what?"

"Let me out," he told his friend. Jon got out of the car and pulled the seat forward for Jackson to exit. The rain was still falling over Mobile.

Once Jackson was outside, he scanned the

graveyard with his heightened, undead senses. He was searching for any signs of other people around. There were none. They were safe.

"Okay, we're good," he said. Then he turned to the other guys. "Why did y'all come here?"

"Come on, Jackson," Ryan said. "We're burying a friend. You had to know we'd come."

Emily unlocked her trunk and the boys carried their friend to the crypt. As they carried Chad to what was supposed to be Jackson's final resting place, Jackson couldn't help but think of his own funeral. It must have been a lot like this. Now that Chad and he had switched places, tears began to well in his eyes.

The girls opened the double-doors to the crypt, and the boys came in. Meggie and Emily closed the doors behind them. Once they were inside, they placed Chad on the crypt floor.

"Which one?" Jon asked.

Jackson didn't bother to respond. He had already pushed the stone slab aside and opened his coffin.

"Jackson, what are you doing? How can you even see?" Meggie whispered as she lit up the crypt by pressing a button on her cell phone. "And how did how did you move that by yourself?"

When the others could see what Jackson had done, the boys proceeded to place Chad in the coffin. He was about the same height as Jackson. He fit fine. Jackson closed the lid and replaced the slab. When he stood up, he said, "Let's have a moment of silence."

Everyone bowed their head and was silent. Several minutes passed without a sound. It was finally broken when crypt echoed with Emily's sobs.

Jackson had noticed that, when Chad got

attacked, Emily was almost emotionless outside the chapel. While the others were crying at Chad's death, she was more concerned with keeping Breann on the ground. Now that the battle was over, though, Emily was crying into the zombie's chest. Jackson put his arms around her and consoled her. The rest of the teenagers gathered around her and made a big group hug, just like they had done for Meggie when Jackson died.

After a few moments, they separated, and Emily began wiping her eyes. "I'm sorry y'all. I thought I was okay. But I'm not."

Meggie lit up her phone again, so Emily could see. "Look at us." Emily noticed that everyone, even Jackson, was crying. "It's okay." Meggie gave her friend another hug.

Everyone was silent while Meggie and Emily hugged in the middle of the crypt until Foster whispered, "So are we still goin' to Callaghan's?"

A few of his friends laughed. "It's what we did after Jackson's funeral," Jon said. "It's only fitting."

The teenagers got back into their vehicles and rode to Callaghan's. This time, in addition to holding his hand, Meggie leaned on his shoulder. It couldn't last, he thought, but it was amazing to him now.

Callaghan's was always open late, and it was usually packed. Emily and Foster had to park their cars several blocks away.

As they were walking to the pub, Foster turned to Jackson. Everyone was quiet, and their sadness was apparent. Foster tried to lighten the mood as he said, "So, Jackson, what are you gonna order when we get there? I don't think they have brains on the menu."

Everyone laughed. "I don't eat brains. I don't

eat anything. I'm just here for the good company."

"I just had to know," Foster said. "I wouldn't want to let my guard down and you be trying to bite my head."

"Relax, Foster, if I had to live off your brains, I'd starve to death." Jackson's friends laughed at his comment as he continued. "And I'm already dead. You can't starve a dead man to death *again*."

As they got closer to the front of Callaghan's the green lights that illuminated the porch spilled into the street. As the group walked through them, it gave them all a greenish-looking appearance. "Hey, look at our faces," Emily said. "Now we all look like Jackson."

Jackson laughed, but as he looked down at himself. He was covered in vampire blood. While he may have been doing the world a service by killing Ben, he would look like and ax-murderer to everyone outside the group. "Um, guys," he said. "I can't go."

"What?" Jon asked.

Jackson pointed to all of his clothes, they were stained red and purple.

"Oh, damn, dude," said Foster. "Yeah, you can't go anywhere like that."

What was Jackson doing there anyway? Callaghan's was a place where people went to drink beer and eat great food. It wasn't a place where a zombie could go and pretend he was alive again. Jackson took his bloody clothes as a sign to step back. "It's fine. You guys go on without me."

"What are you gonna do?" Jon asked. "Where are you gonna go?"

"I'll be okay. I'm pretty decent at not being seen. I'll get back to the chapel and hide out like I have been, I guess." Jackson wasn't really sure what he was going to do. "I'll stay in touch, though."

"You better," Jon said as he grabbed Jackson and pulled him in for an embrace.

"Easy, big guy. Don't get this stuff on your clothes too." Jon released him.

Ryan was the next to say good-bye to Jackson. "Dude, I was super sad when you died, but then I dealt with it. And now you're *back*? You better take care of yourself."

"I will," Jackson said.

Then there was Brandon. "I leave for Iraq in a week. I think what I saw tonight will mess with my head more than anything I might deal with over there."

"I'm not sure about the psychological stuff," Jackson said, "but you just stay safe. I really don't know how this coming back from the dead thing works, so be careful."

"Will do," Brandon said.

"Take it easy, man. See ya later." Foster was not really good at farewells.

Jackson smiled. "No need for smalltalk, Foster."

Jackson looked at Meggie. She put her arms around him and pulled him in close. She didn't care about ruining her clothes. "I thought I lost you, Jackson. I thought you were gone forever. And now you're back. Where does that leave us?"

Jackson thought about professing his undying love for her. He thought about telling her how she was the main reason he had come back from the dead. She would have probably loved it. She would have fallen in love with him all over again, and she would never leave his zombie side. But that wouldn't have been fair to her. "I died over a year ago. You moved on. I'm not mad. It's what you were supposed to do. If you had stopped living your life, it would have been my fault."

"So what about us?" she asked again.

"We were great," he said. "We were perfect and we were madly in love. But that's over. I'm *this* now. I'm still Jackson, but I'm zombie Jackson."

"I love zombie Jackson too," she said as tears began to well up in her eyes.

Jackson put a cold hand on her cheek, "And I'll always love you." Jackson leaned down and kissed her forehead. "Take care, baby."

"Well, damn, how am I gonna top that?" Emily asked. "My good-bye better be awesome."

Jackson laughed as he began walking away from his friends. "Oh, don't worry, Em. Mike Adams will be in touch with you soon."

"Ha! He better be, dead man. Take care." Emily waved.

"*That's* Mike Adams?" Meggie exclaimed. "You *are* a skank, Emily."

Jackson watched his friends make their way into Callaghan's. When they got a table, Jackson heard, with his impeccable zombie ears, the waitress ask, "Jesus, what the Hell happened to your face?"

Then he heard Foster respond, "You should've seen the other guy."

Jackson smiled his crooked smile as he resumed walking, with the sounds of his friends' laughter in his ears.

About the Author

DustOn Dueitt was born in Mobile, Alabama. After graduating high school in Greene County, Mississippi, he came back to go to Spring Hill College. Though his adventures have taken him all over the world since then, Mobile has been, and will always be, his home and inspiration.

Made in the USA
Lexington, KY
28 July 2012